AF364256

Mothers
Daughters
Liars

'Las penas y las olas nunca llegan solas'

'Sorrows and waves never arrive alone'

Patricia Román

First published in March 2024 by Txto Editorial.
Second publication July 2024 Patricia Roman Books
Cover background image copyright digital artist © Lynn Amass Hardy

Cover design: PTB Design in collaboration with Jesús Bordera of Txto Editorial

ISBN: 978-84-09-63550-4

Depósito Legal: V-0000-2024 · Spain

Contents

Acknowledgements

Thanks go to Lynn Amass Hardy for her beautiful image on the cover. To Lorraine Mace for her sharp insight and developmental editing skills, to Julie Hoyle for her excellent dotting and crossing and wheedling out of anything that shouldn't be there and to Jesus Bordera of Txto Editorial for his formatting and publishing skills. Huge gratitude also goes to the beta reading team at The History Quill for their insights and encouragement, and to Clive for his unswerving support for my writing life.

Trigger warning: Mothers Daughters Liars contains some sexual violence.

Mothers Daughters Liars is a story from yesterday, reflecting the #metoo movement of today. It is dedicated to all those souls affected by gossip and lies.

Mothers Daughters Liars was shortlisted for the Flash 500 International novel competition 2023.

Part One – Mariangeles and Tia

1. Mariangeles

Mariangeles stood on the quay, legs braced against the sudden gusts that rushed through the harbour. High above, a girl leapt across huge boulders towards a castle, raising her arms to claim dominion.

'Look, Ma. I'm queen of the ocean!' she yelled over the spray.

'Be careful, you might slip,' Mariangeles called back, but the girl ignored her, so she tried again. 'Come down. It's dangerous.' Still no response. This time she shouted, and her words came out sharper than intended, propelled by the five quick syllables of her daughter's name. 'Seb-ast-i-a-na, get down here now!' The girl leapt to the ground and approached her mother, sulking as the wind whipped the sea into froth. Mariangeles sighed. Even the squawking gulls seemed to sense the disconnection between them. Perhaps this constant discord was something to do with their surroundings. Living on the edge of the land and the beginning of the ocean was like living in limbo - a narrow space at the water's edge, with disconcerting winds and no place for troubled dust to settle.

The gulls flew off. Mariangeles grabbed Sebastiana's hand and hurried back through the square as the town clock struck five. She was late. But then she stopped. Towards the outskirts, down by the river, a fine line of dark grey smoke was curling up over the rise. For the second time this week they were burning bodies.

Crossing herself, she marched down Main Street stumbling over the cobbles towards the shop. 'Should have opened five minutes ago,' she muttered, quickening her pace. Halfway along, she stopped, leaning against a neighbour's wall to catch her breath. Perhaps having a child so late in life had been a mistake. This girl sapped her energy and Bartolome was no help either. After years of cajoling, she'd finally persuaded him to have a baby and she'd looked forward to holding Sebastiana in her arms and making the child a reflection of herself. But it hadn't turned out like that. The baby had cried throughout the night and taken badly to her breast. And at forty-two, Mariangeles had been too proud to ask for help from the younger mothers in her neighbourhood. So she'd struggled on alone and miserable until it was too late. Even now she had no idea how to handle a petulant eleven-year-old dragging her feet while she was trying to make up time. She looked up, as if appealing for help from the heavens, and there it was again - smoke gathering overhead, white this time, with that cloying certainty of death. It must have blown in from the river. 'Those poor creatures,' she muttered.

The shop was at the far end of Main Street, in a square next to the boarded-up church of San Francisco. No one practised religion anymore and the carved doors had huge metal chains and a padlock the size of Mariangeles' hand. The building sat there decaying like an empty carcass and the only sound coming from its interior was the buzzing of bluebottles at the stained-glass windows. Every Sunday rich people - cotton-growers, bull-breeders, and stud-farmers - huddled in groups outside the church, assembling as if Mass was about to start and muttering about how good life used to be before the Republic. They didn't agree with the new regime and Bartolome didn't either. But Mariangeles wasn't sure. Surely life better when everyone had an equal share? Besides, she'd been raised to be humble, to accept her lot, not ambitious like her husband.

She opened the shop, looked in the till and sighed, knowing that the wine cellar would be full, and the till would be empty. She tidied her hair to make herself presentable to customers and saw within the mirror, a ghost of the woman she used to be; eyelashes gone, and lips, once so receptive to passion, withered into two thin strips that arched downwards towards fleshy jowls. She let out a deliberate sigh so that Bartolome could hear it from his workshop. Why should she have to put up with all this on her own - running out of money, losing her looks, a problem child, and now white smoke billowing over the town? There was so much to worry about, but what could she do? How could she hold back fate? She remembered her mother's saying; *Las penas y las olas nunca llegan solas – sorrows and waves never arrive alone*. What if that's true? she asked herself. What if those waves never stop coming? What if disaster keeps occurring over and over, just like it did for my mother and her grandmother and all the mothers before her? Then what will happen to Sebastiana and *her* daughters and *her* girls after that? What if the sorrows of our mothers are the future disasters of our daughters? How can I hold back the tide? How can I break us all free?

'Yes,' she said, repeating the words as she had many times before, until they had acquired their own little rhythm in her head. *Sorrows and waves never arrive alone.* The impertinent little phrase gave her something solid to grasp hold of, a mantra to live by, a legacy of her mother and all those that came before her. But now she felt these words were taking over, controlling her mind, like those waves, always coming, never stopping, on and on, forever moving, relentlessly advancing and she was beginning to reach the edge.

2. Tia

I hated Ma for spoiling my fun. I wasn't stupid. I knew exactly where the waves missed the rocks so I could land safely, and where stagnant waters created a green-black slime that would make me slip. I hated my name too - so long-winded and old-fashioned especially when she shouted it across the harbour for everyone to hear. 'Call me Tia,' I asked her once, but she shook her head. 'Don't be so ungrateful,' she said. 'It's your grandmother's name - the poor, tortured soul - so be more respectful.' Then she crossed herself as if getting rid of some imaginary demons, but I didn't ask her to explain nor did I ask her to call me Tia again. Ma always had the last word so what was the point?

And why was she so miserable, standing down there on the quay with her arms on her hips as if she was mad? Perhaps because she couldn't see what I could see up there on those rocks. A harbour full of comings and goings, of sailing boats tacking and slipstreaming across the horizon - of waves coming in and steamships moving out, and hulls listing to and fro on loud clanking chains and, further off, folding sand dunes meeting the sea. I loved that harbour and our town too, with all those strangers talking funny languages and wandering the streets as if they owned them. There was a spit of land jutting into the Atlantic, like a finger pointing towards Africa, and the town sat on it, as bright as a diamond, sparkling on the very edge of the world. So when I reached Ma, I tried to cheer her up by stamping hard on the cobbles and saying, 'Look, Ma. I'm going to flip the whole of Spain on its head so it falls into the sea!' but she turned away, head down, in a hurry, as if the whole world was about to stop turning.

We marched along Main Street when all I wanted to do was take my time. This was my playground - me and the children of the rich people. On Sundays I was allowed to play with them all dressed up in their Sunday best and we'd charge down Main Street making such a racket! Once we found a gap in the church doors where a panel had shrunk in the sun. We peeped in and as our eyes adjusted to the gloom, we saw figures in gold and purple and deepest blue. 'Ghosts, ghosts!' we screamed and ran down the street, away from that dark old church with plaster angels sealed up inside, towards the deafening rush of the sea. The long, narrow street had overhanging balconies filled with bright-red geraniums and tiny front doors where neighbours would sit to feel the breeze and watch us play. Sometimes it was tug-of-war with old ropes, hauling ourselves up and down like maniacs. 'Pull! Pull!' we shouted over the ocean. At other times it was the canes from the marshes. We'd point them over their heads, screeching 'Charge! Charge!' and run at full speed down the street; above our heads a bright blue ribbon of sky. We were warriors rushing to fight the sea dragon.

Ma opened the shop and she was in such a bad mood that I went upstairs to my room. Then, all of a sudden, church bells began to toll. I hadn't heard them before and when that horrible deep sound rolled over the town I imagined a magician sweeping a big dark cloak over us to conceal his trick.

'Why are they ringing the bells?' I asked Ma but she wouldn't answer and a few days later I overheard my parents talking by the well, where Pa had just drawn water.

16

3. Mariangeles

'Don't drink that!' Mariangeles screeched, grabbing the cup.

Bartolome snorted. 'Why in god's name not?'

'It's contaminated, Bartolome. We'll get sick like the others.'

'Rubbish. I've been drinking this all my life,' he said.

Mariangeles sighed, smoothed down her apron and patted his arm.

'People are dying, Bartolome. I beg you, listen.' But still he shrugged her off.

'It's in the air, woman, not the water,' he scoffed. 'Anyway it's that rough lot in shacks by the river getting sick, not well-off people living up here like us.'

'You're a fool, Bartolome. Let's get out before it is too late.'

'Don't be ridiculous, woman.'

'But think of Sebastiana and the danger she's in.'

'Think of my clients too. The finest families of Andalucía come to my shop. Why should I give up selling my bridles to rich farmers and suede shoes to their pretty little wives? Why should we leave this place when my goods are in such demand?' Mariangeles sighed. What her husband really meant was that he was too busy enjoying his drinking bouts with his customers. How many times had she sent Sebastiana down to the cellar to collect the empty bottles of manzanilla he shared? She couldn't bear to fetch them herself, nor count the money they were losing.

'You and your boozy friends!' she said, before wandering off to rest her swollen ankles and get some peace.

What a horror that cholera was! People vomiting and shitting a bloody death. Over the next week Mariangeles saw bodies wrapped in makeshift shrouds being carried across fields. Families would drop the muck-ridden remains of a mother or brother right there before scurrying away, leaving those poor men, desperate for a duro or two, burning the cadavers all night. The sickly sweet stench drifted across the town in gusts of white smoke and people covered their heads for protection. But Mariangeles was right. She knew she was right. It wasn't air that carried that dreadful disease. It was water. 'At last they've seen sense,' she muttered to herself, as she watched them dredge the arroyos and douse everything in lime. Bit by bit, death spread from the 'barrio del rio' where the poor people lived, all the way up to their neighbourhood until it was too late to save the town. The sixteenth of July was a day she would never forget. People were running about in the streets, others hiding behind their doors, too scared to come out.

'Lord, help us. The mayor is dead. The mayor is dead!' someone shouted

A notice was pinned on the church doors announcing that the council had been disbanded and that they'd cancelled the Romeria. This meant that no one ordered Bartolome's riding boots, no one bought his embossed bridles for their horses, and no women dared order Mariangeles's delicately embroidered lambskin shoes. It would have provoked a rebellion. So profits didn't materialise and when Mariangeles heard her husband crying in his workshop she knew they were destitute.

Las penas y las olas nunca llegan solas,' she wailed, justifying her mantra as though disaster was always meant to be. They would have to leave. They would have to abandon this life or else they would all be dead.

4. Tia

Just like that, we moved. I lost my friends and I lost my happiness. We dismissed our weeping maid, loaded our belongings onto a crude, open cart, and paid our last savings to Pepe, the carter. It wasn't enough to cover his costs, but the dear man took us anyway, into the countryside to my uncle's tiny house in a little village latched onto the side of a mountain. I hated it. A roaring wind swooped between the houses, forcing me to wear a shawl as I walked the grubby, tilted streets looking for someone to talk to. But the villagers were horrible to us. Perhaps they thought we'd brought that sickness from town. They trudged, heads down, in those dingy, unlit streets, looking sideways with granite stares, and shoulders hunched in grey-washed rags. In my childish way I imagined they were old fossils chipped from the mountain itself.

Our comfortable life by the sea had transformed to one of squalor. My uncle's house had a leaking roof and an old outhouse in which to relieve ourselves. Our waste dropped down a gulley that ran alongside the road, and ended in a stinking lake at the bottom of the hill. With no one to play with I became withdrawn and still. Pa and Ma did too. We sat motionless at the threshold of our new home waiting for someone – anyone - to pass by and call out a greeting, or we stared out of broken windows at the cold grey landscape hoping for some colour that never emerged from the gloom. Ma, Pa and I were lost, with no idea how to be, especially Ma. I heard her chanting everyday *Las penas y las olas nunca llegan solas* and I thought she was going insane.

Pa sent me to work at the tannery.

'You have to, Tia. How else can we eat?'

It was housed in low buildings at the bottom of the hill, sitting on the crossroads of the main highway from Seville to Gibraltar. People said travellers mistook the place for a tavern until they got up close and the stench hit them. Every Sunday evening Pepe swung his cart into the yard and men sauntered out to unload his cargo, hauling great layers of hides onto their shoulders and grunting as they slapped them down onto the benches with such a thud that the sickly smell wafted up and made me retch.

'You'll get used to it,' Pepe said, but I never did. My job was to scrape away the flesh still clinging to the insides of the skins and to carry the overflowing buckets outside. I often slipped as I emptied the slimy mess into a sluice. And no sooner had I finished but another batch of hides would arrive and I'd have to start all over again.

Pepe explained. 'Every Saturday from every town, them creatures is dragged from the bull rings - all clamour and gusto - to the slaughterhouse - all quiet and calm. Seen it myself - disembowelling, sawing 'n scraping.' I nodded because my life too, had been one of removal; of things taken away. A life disconnected, skinned, gutted and reduced. It made me feel wretched, and poor Pepe, even though he made his living from these dead creatures, I think he disliked it as much as I.

After a while I was given a different job, learning how to make a tanning solution by grinding tree bark in a pestle and mortar to make a fine powder. This was better, but the smell worsened as the hides lay soaking. This was the odour that lingered most. The slow corrosive perfume crept into my clothes and settled in my hair, and it wouldn't leave me, even when walking back up the hill in that raging wind. I think the manager sensed my distaste and took pity on me, because I was transferred to the polishing area. Here, I placed freshly soaked hides on my bench, smoothing my hands across the surface so that the animal's outline re-emerged, flattened yet somehow whole. For a moment, it felt as though I had brought it back to life and when I pressed coloured oils into its surface, I leaned forward and whispered across its nourished skin, 'There. Look at you. See how you shine,' as if the creature could hear me from within. My sentimentality kept me going, but in truth, I felt powerless in the face of the brutality of the *corrida*. Those poor bulls didn't stand a chance.

As for my parents, Ma cried through the night, wailing her usual refrain and perhaps she was right because Pa's clients had deserted him and he was forced to repair harnesses for a pittance.

Every day he would ask, 'Why me?'

And Mama's exhausted reply, 'You didn't listen, did you?'

I heard her turning over in their bed, muttering about the booze and calling him an old fool, but that made things worse. Now poor Pa retreated into himself, sewing with his memories under the light from a small window, his shoulders hunched and the bones in his fingers suffering painfully from the cold. Then one day he turned to me,

'You don't like it down at the tannery, do you child? How would you like to work with me instead?'

'But Pa,' I said. 'There isn't enough work for both of us.'

'We'll manage, Tia. Please, won't you come?'

It was lovely to hear my nickname on his lips, and I studied his drawn face and his blinking eyes as he waited for my reply. Poor lonely Pa, he looked so desperate. Besides I hated the tannery.

What a place his workshop was! Converted from my uncle's animal corral, with a rusty tin roof and old stone walls, it had taken on a new life of Pa's creation. His old templates hung from the rafters like bats in a cave, and wooden lasts, carrying the names of his old customers, were huddled in a corner like old friends. On the bench sat all sorts of redundant hand tools waiting to be of service. Jars of wax stood to attention on the windowsill. They smelt divine, like ointments made for the gods, and their perfume was so entrancing that I soon forgot the misfortune of those poor animals. I learned to avoid their scars and position the templates with respect for their imperfections. I became expert at tracing the knife around the contours of the wooden block and pulling each part away with a clean incision.

'Here, Pa,' I said proudly, handing him my first bundle of perfectly cut pieces. We started planning how to develop the business. Pa said we'd mend the roof first so the hides wouldn't get damp and then start making day shoes for gentlemen. We planned and plotted together, laughing at our errors and praising each other for our good ideas. We didn't notice that Ma was listening, and didn't remember that she, too, was a skilled craftsperson who used to embroider Pa's little suede shoes for the ladies. Now all she did was tend the house and I don't think she liked it because I heard her muttering under her breath as if she was going mad. But for me things were getting better. One day Pa put his arm around me. 'It's so good to have you with me,' he said, and I felt as happy as any good daughter should.

Over the year Pa and I improved the family fortunes. I spent hours in his workshop, and when I wasn't with him, I was lurking in the shadows, listening to Ma and her new friends chatting in the kitchen. Most of it was tittle-tattle – all 'this and that!', and 'ooh and aah!' and 'did you know?' but Ma seemed to tolerate it and I hoped that the madness I'd seen when we had first arrived would eventually fade, now that she had company.

Nothing in their usual conversations seemed of importance until one day I overheard something that made me realise that words can be as dangerous as a tiger and as sharp as its teeth. It was the day our neighbour dropped by.

5. Mariangeles

'You in there, Mari?'

Mariangeles winced as she opened the door, hating the way Incarna changed her name to the shorter Mari as if reducing it made conquest easier. Mariangeles sighed.

'Where else would I be? Come in I suppose.'

'Ooh, they smell good.'

'Hands off! They're just out of the oven. Anyway why are you back? Did you forget something this morning?'

Incarna seemed pleased with herself. She leaned forward to smell the still-warm madalenas.

'Actually yes … forgot to tell you about old Juan.'

'Incarna, please. I don't want to know about that man's perversity. And leave those cakes alone. They're not for you.' Mariangeles moved them onto a dresser to cool. 'Is that why you came all the way back up that hill? To remind me of that man?'

'No, not really,' Incarna said, settling her huge body into the old wicker chair. 'Is something bothering you, Mari? Only, you hardly spoke this morning. You know you can always talk to me, don't you?'

'Yes, and in half an hour it'll be all round the village.'

'No, not between us. Not between friends. So what is it?'

'It's nothing.'

'Alright, if you say so.'

'Shouldn't you be getting back home, Incarna?'

'Those do smell good.'

'No, Incarna. They're for Bartolome.'

'How is he? You know how men of his age can be.'

'Incarna, please!'

'And that girl of yours? Saw her in the shop. Hardly recognised her...'

'Incarna, I don't want to be rude, but it's none of your business.'

'Breasts nearly falling out of her bodice, they were.'

'Incarna, it's getting late...'

'Far cry from that ragged little thing she used to be, wandering the streets looking for a playmate.'

'She's growing up, that's all. Learning to be a woman.'

'You need to get her some new clothes before people get the wrong idea.'

Mariangeles clenched her teeth. How dare this woman interfere in her business? 'Have you seen the time?' she said.

'And Bartolo? How's he taking it with his little daughter blossoming before his very eyes?'

'Incarna, please!'

'Well you never knows how they'll take it, do you, Mari?'

'Would you like a madalena, Incarna? I'm sure a couple won't be noticed and you can eat them as you go back down the hill.'

When Mariangeles closed the door, she shook her head trying to release her neighbour's words from her already agitated mind.

Her world was decelerating, grinding to a halt, yet her heart was racing and she couldn't think herself back to normality. *'Blossoming before his very eyes?'* Incarna had said, and she nodded as if this was confirmation of her already-formed fears.

6. Tia

It started with the smell of fresh dough floating through the windows. Ma was in the kitchen and I was in the workshop with my head down listening to birds arguing in the bushes. After years of misery, that gorgeous smell of baking and the pretty sound of chirping birds were making me smile. I finished my bundle, wrapping the twine carefully around it, before passing it up to Pa. But instead of seeing pride in his eyes, as I had many times before, I saw that his forehead was creased into a frown and his mouth was stretched into a strange grimace he was struggling to control.

'What is it Pa?' I said, but he didn't answer. He turned away. And that hurt me because Incarna was right. I *was* changing. My hair had thickened and my eyes were deep set and dark. My bodice hardly fitted and my hips moved awkwardly under my skirts. So, when Pa looked at me in that strange way, I thought he didn't like this new ungainly me.

Next day I was preparing pieces for a pair of riding boots. They had to be cut from the strongest part, so I reached across the workbench to the centre of the hide. I remember turning the knife, piercing the surface and twisting it around the contours to get a clean cut. I heard a cough and looked up. Pa was staring down. His face was grey but when I straightened, it turned bright red.

'What's the matter, Pa?' I asked, but he lowered his head and wouldn't speak. The same happened the next day and the day after that, and when I smiled to make him feel better, he became restless, and the more troubled he seemed, the more I thought I'd done something wrong.

One night I couldn't sleep so I went downstairs for water, stopping at the door of the kitchen, because there he was by the sink. My father was not a religious man - he'd been pleased when the churches closed - but there he was, on his knees, hands pressed together in prayer and his chin resting on his fingertips, looking like someone in an old religious painting. His speech was slurred as though he'd been drinking and he spoke in short whispers, like a man undone.

'Oh Lord, how can I be this person?' And after that, 'My own dear daughter!' He shook his head, his hair more ragged than I'd seen it before. 'Her beauty is my passion and her innocence is my shame. Oh my angel child, she bursts into my dreams and I cannot block her out. I beg you, Lord, rid me of this evil urge. I am cold yet hot. I am hollowed out yet filled with desire. Oh Lord, what should I do?'

I took a step back, letting the shadows catch my fall, then retreated upstairs and lay on my bed. What was the matter with Pa, talking about me like that? Perhaps he was lonely, perhaps he was in pain. Perhaps it was just a nightmare and tomorrow he would be fine. But next day Pa seemed to shrivel like an old tortoise hiding in his shell, peeping out only to check if danger had passed, and he ordered me to stay away from the workshop. To make matters worse, Ma saw all this and became watchful and stern.

Ma and I were collecting sloe berries from the hedgerows. They had a sprinkling of pale dew and I wanted to say 'Ma! Look how pretty they are', but I knew she wouldn't respond. She'd been horrible all morning. Back in the kitchen, Pa's goat skins hung on the rack above us, making the room dark and grim. We were boiling the berries to make a dye, as we often did, and I enjoyed this time together, me and Ma talking about this and that. Today, though, her jaw was clenched and her lips pinched. She fetched an old newspaper from the drawer and the only sound was her flattening it onto the surface of the table. I stirred the fruit round and round, wondering what was wrong. She continued smoothing the paper over and over until the palms of her hands looked black.

'Ma,' I said. 'Are you all right?' But she ignored me, and in that thunderous silence, I didn't know what to do. The simmering berries were beginning to stick to the pan so I agitated them, trying to release their hold. They were so hot that a red mist rose into the space between us, making me sweat so much that my hair became stuck to my forehead. I used my arm to push it back as Ma leaned across to remove the pan.

'Get your hair fixed, Sebastiana,' she snapped, and her cheeks were taut and pale. She strained the berries through a sieve and I watched through watery eyes as the untamed liquid ran steaming into the bowl. Why was she being so horrible when I'd done nothing wrong? I snatched the pan from her and rinsed it under the tap and when I'd finished I wiped my hands down the front of my apron where a stain appeared, smeared scarlet against the bright white cotton. Ma stared at it then snarled in a low, threatening voice.

'You're overripe, my girl.' Then, grabbing a goatskin from the rack, she plunged it into the bubbling dye. I saw her jaw twitch as the colour surged up the skin, turning it from pale cream to a vivid red. To me it looked beautiful but it seemed to make Ma madder still. She turned on me, holding her wet hands above the still-bubbling bowl. Finally she seemed ready to speak. 'Sebastiana, you know nothing of men but I will tell you how it is.' Her eyes were narrowed, her face contorted as if she was crazy. 'A man's touch can be heaven or hell…' Then her words tailed off as if she'd finished and I frowned. What had this to do with berries? She lifted the skin from the bowl. Red liquid dripped into the silence. She stabbed the air with a stained finger. 'I will tell you how it is. Your father is a dull, weak man, and you come to his workshop - you, with your soft young body and your bright ideas. You march in and set him afire.'

'No, Ma. That's not true,' I wailed. How could she say such a thing? But she carried on, shaking her head, wagging her finger. Spittle appeared at the side of her mouth.

'He's besotted, can't you see?'

'No, Ma, you've got it wrong.' I wanted to tell her that I hated my body and what it had become, but she was still talking.

'Oh those wonderful nights before coming here to this terrible place.' She twisted the skin causing dye to splash over the floor, but she didn't seem to care. 'Now he comes to our bed, looks at me with leaden eyes, and jabs at my breasts as if I'm not there.' She moved closer, holding the dripping skin against her apron. I could feel her breath hot on my already burning cheek and I knew to remain silent because she was wild with it all and I stood there, perfectly still as terrible words came bursting from her mouth. 'He reaches down and forces me open, then he closes his eyes to seal your face within his view and enters me like a thief in the night, stealing my soul, sealing me in. How could you do this? How could you do this to your own poor mother?'

I felt sick at her words. I wanted to close them down, to cool her fury with my love. But I couldn't. I couldn't protest my innocence, nor reassure my frantic mother that she'd got it wrong. The heat drained from my cheeks as I took in what she was saying. Surely she shouldn't speak of such intimacies to her only child? But I could see that she was sick with jealousy, and her words burst from her mouth like daggers, and the force of her outburst made me lower my head.

'Ma, please!' I said, but there was no response. She'd already walked out leaving me to clean up the remnants of our work. Ma's madness was getting worse.

Like spiders lurking in the corners where no one cared to clean, we didn't mention the problems between Ma, Pa and I, but they were ever-present in our sighs and in the dislodged gazing of our eyes. I couldn't be that sweet daughter anymore because Ma's anger had shamed me and provoked my own. I had to get away.

So, one morning I climbed to the top of the village where goats were grazing on the mountain plateau. Standing feet apart in the prickly gorse, balanced against the ferocious wind, I looked down on the village with its jumble of terracotta-roofed houses, animal corrals, and our abandoned church. I felt safe up there on that ridge where no jury of gossips could deliver its verdict and no judge would point his finger and look at me with scorn. I was still innocent and free to speak without restriction and I wanted to tell the world that they'd got it wrong – that it wasn't my fault that Pa felt that way and that Ma was so jealous. I opened my mouth to speak but wild wind snatched at my protest and threw it into the cold air. I wrapped my shawl about me and watched silently as a gust of leaves shot up from the ground. A crosswind had caught them and now they were leaping, as if on strings, travelling haphazardly down the slope towards the village. I let my eyes follow their trail, over chimneys belching out pale wood-smoke and between the white painted houses and over the lichen-covered walls. A few leaves hovered above the newly repaired roof of my father's workshop, reminding me – asking me - would I ever escape? I was desperate for answers and foolish enough to think I could find them up there on that mountain. I looked down at the church. If it had been open, I might have asked a priest for advice, but what would he have known about such desires? So I looked out towards the distant sea, at the vast waves raging at the shoreline then crashing on the dunes. Sunlight was bouncing off the rocks, as if flashing coded messages just for me. Perhaps they contained the answers I needed. I clapped my hands as if to catch them, but then snorted at my childishness. I looked south instead where the morning sun had already lit up my lovely old town with its mass of roof turrets sending out warm air into the cold blue sky. I thought of the street where we children used to play, narrow and dim, but buzzing with a lightning rod of excitement whenever we rushed along it. The town was thriving again but our family couldn't go back there - we'd lost too much to recuperate. Even the shop had been repossessed to pay off Pa's debts. I looked down towards the quay where ships - some with masts, others with huge funnels - stood unmoving in a gleam of light, as if frozen in ice. But as still as they were, I knew that by tomorrow they'd all be on the move again, sailing somewhere – anywhere. I thought about stowing aboard, going wherever a ship would take me, but how could I do something as brave as that?

Beyond the quay I could just make out the grey outline of North Africa with the lighthouse on Cape Spartel. Was it winking? Was it telling me what to do? I imagined working in Tangiers, perhaps in a rich household for a good family. Maybe they would be from France or Germany and I'd have to learn their language. But how could a girl like me do such a thing? So I turned towards the west, to the bull-breeding farms and cotton fields and beyond that to Seville. They called the city the jewel of Andalucía and for a moment I wondered if I could go there instead. Perhaps join the girls on the benches in the Royal Tobacco Factory of Seville. Incarna had told us they only employed women there, that the men had been useless, constantly on strike and taking to the streets to demand more money. She'd laughed her head off sitting in our kitchen with her fat behind overlapping our rickety old chair, and Ma and I did too, when she told us how much money the women were making. 'Doin' a lot better than them men - lazy buggers.' I pictured myself in Seville, in that fabulous building with its ornate façade, where the whispers of women were guarded in shady courtyards and where no man could trouble me. But then I shook my head. How could a simple girl like me, work in a place like that? Fancy giving in to such hope, standing there all puffed up with expectation on that windy ridge. So I abandoned my search into the distance and turned to the vast chunk of rock where I stood. It was a fearful thing, full of shiny granite protrusions and darkened hollows, casting chilly shadows over the village until midday, when the sun would appear around its jagged edge, blasting the streets with sudden sunshine. But it wouldn't come round for ages yet, so I shivered in my shawl, feeling the chill of my fears and kicking the stones at my feet. What could I do? I was an awkward child, growing out of my clothes, growing out of my old life, searching for something new. But I'd found no answers up there on that hill, and in the end I turned around and walked back to the house, dragging my feet at every step.

As usual, Incarna was sitting in the kitchen and when I entered, she leaned back and stared. It was obvious they'd been talking about me because her eyes were filled with scorn. No longer did she see the leatherman's simple, innocent girl. She seemed to be weighing up the possibility that I was a harlot, as my mother had surely suggested, and thanks to Incarna, word would soon be on the streets. *My* wrongdoing would be on the end of our neighbour's tongues - not my father's wrongdoing - not him for his yearnings.

'Sebastiana, you're getting to be quite a woman now,' she said.

'I'm only thirteen,' I said hoping that would finish the matter but I became bewitched by Incarna's words, and over the next few days her unspoken meaning became a kind of truth - a probability that I was overripe for my age like Ma had said. I knew that this was bad and her words grew inside my mind as if they were true, incubating until I *was* that wicked girl. I was becoming who they thought I would turn out to be.

7. Mariangeles

Mariangeles paced the kitchen, shaking her head at her foolishness. What had she been thinking of, raging at Sebastiana, revealing her feelings about Bartolome's lovemaking? What kind of mother did that? And what's more, in her rage, she had told Incarna - the village gossip - all about it. How stupid was that? She shook her head trying to release the regret from her mind, but it was too late. She had allowed those lascivious words to slide from her mouth as if they were honey. And words were dangerous. Words couldn't be unsaid, and now the relationship with her daughter was worse than before and Incarna had juicy tit-bits to tell. Soon, the whole village would know about it. She sighed deeply at the depth of her foolishness and her continuous maternal failure, then slumped down into a seat by the window and reached for her embroidery. Sewing was her only escape. With a thimble on one hand and a needle in the other, her stitchery was quick and accurate. She hardly looked down at the graceful shapes being formed under her skilful fingers, because sewing didn't require thinking. Sewing was at the other end of the spectrum to anxiety. She imagined a fancy silk cord running the length of her mind; at one end the burdensome troubles of Sebastiana, and at the other, the soothing weightlessness of a beautifully formed stitch. Was she going mad?

Gradually she allowed her thoughts to stray to *Incarna's* words. They were damaging but only because they were true. Sebastiana *was* growing up too quickly, and she could do nothing to control it. And what were the neighbours to make of her overripe girl? They were always quick to talk and make judgements. She shook her head, weary at the continual exchange of gossip in this uncultured village. Set back on the long road from Gibraltar to Seville, the villagers knew little of the world beyond their boundary. It was from carters like Pepe, carrying skins and other goods, that they learned news from afar. Travelling the same route as the smugglers who brought Cuban cigars to the interior and Caribbean rum onto the sideboards of the rich, he seemed to delight in the life of strangers. She, too, had the same curiosity. She had learned so much about the world, living in a harbour town so rich in different cultures. She used to approach the sailors and their companions to ask where they were from and what their lives were like back home and how they compared to hers. She had been curious and hungry for knowledge beyond her tiny world. She sighed again. In another life she would have been much more than this. A school teacher, perhaps, or an administrator mingling with open-minded people and then she wouldn't have had to put up with shallow-minded gossip infiltrating itself west to east and east to west. Just like cholera, she mused. Just like that dreaded disease, gossip ran through the stream of life, carried along by eager mouths and contaminated by pure conjecture, bloated with spite, until, puked into willing ears, opinion became fact, lies became truths which became secrets traded for an extra drink in the bar or whispered into a prostitute's ear. Mariangeles tied off a thread and sat back, pleased with herself. She liked the comparison between life and disease. It sat well in her mind-set because life was like that - hers anyway - filled with the prospect that, any minute now, something bad was going to happen, just like when that terrible cholera had come to town and ripped her hopes and dreams apart.

40

Incarna was sitting in the kitchen clutching a cup of steaming camomile, making her face glow like an unintended angel. It was obvious from the woman's smile that she'd come with something to tell. Incarna lived at the bottom of the village and it was she who carried the gossip, like a laden donkey, panting up the hill, into Mariangeles's house where she would tell her stories like a revelation, leaning into her task with the air of someone who has the edge.

'You know what they done to old Juan, Mari?' she asked, not waiting for a response. 'Chucked him down the ravine, they did. Serves 'im right the old pervert.' Incarna swivelled in her chair to face Sebastiana, fixing her eyes on her like a beacon issuing a warning. 'Still, that niece of his started it, the hussy.' Sebastiana stared out of the window unable to maintain Incarna's stare whilst Mariangeles imagined the villagers throwing old man Juan down the rock face onto the boulders below. She saw his broken body, his neck snapped and legs flung into unnatural rest. She imagined their bitter, vengeful faces turning smug with satisfaction as they wiped their hands clean and walked away. Surely they wouldn't do that to her Bartolome? He may be a fool but he was her fool and she would not let that happen. Incarna wriggled herself further into the chair, ready to peddle more poison. 'Been thinking, Mari, You heard of a man called The Fixer?' She paused for a moment. Less for an answer, more for effect, Mariangeles observed. 'No, course you haven't, Mari. Manolito they called him. Ten years old he was when his ma sent him to the seminary. Said it was to protect him from all the wickedness of the world. But word was he was born illegitimate so that's a bit rich comin' from her!' She shivered as if in mock disapproval and Mariangeles shifted uncomfortably.

'Incarna, why are you telling me about a man I don't know?' But her neighbour wasn't ready to disclose her motive... yet. Instead, she lowered her voice so that Mariangeles had to move closer.

'Still, we knows what happened to religion don't we, Mari? Liberals closing down them monasteries, churches, shrines, the lot.' The wicker chair creaked as she teased out her words, unravelling her information at just the right pace to keep Mariangeles interested. 'And that religious lot – the Jesuits, Franciscans, and Dominicans – the whole lot of 'em thrown out onto the streets! When little Manolito came out, he was a grown man. Tall he was, gave himself the title *Don* Manuel even though he was only twenty.' Mariangeles looked interested now.

'So, what did he do?'

'Went back home to his ma. Sharp as a knife, she was. Got him a position at the University of Seville, teaching Theology.' Mariangeles nodded, impressed by the idea of a University and something called Theology. 'They say his ma had been especially friendly with one of them profs so you can imagine how Manolito got that job!' Incarna smirked as if with satisfaction at her clever insinuation. 'Started wearing a long black cape like those gents wear, to make him look more intellectual, but it didn't work. Made him look a fool 'cos he kept tripping over it. They reckon he was carrying too much sin under that mantle. Still you can't believe everything people say can you?' Mariangeles sniggered at Incarna's hypocrisy but her neighbour hadn't noticed. She was too busy rubbing her hands together. 'Well you'll never guess what happened next. His hands started to shake, and his legs, all spindly and long, struck out as if he were doing a pagan dance. People made jokes about seeing a devil in a black cloak, prancing in the cloisters. S'pose he couldn't help it, had some kind of disease or something, but women wouldn't go near 'im. They laughed at 'im, made jokes about his tall frame and his tiny you-know-what. He got so mad that he tried to kiss one of 'em in the cloisters. Turned out she was the wife of the bursar and she kicked him in the knackers in self-defence. So 'e was chucked out. They said it was the last drop in a full cup.'

Mariangeles sighed. 'What's this got to do with me?'

'We're getting there, Mari. Hear me out. It's important you knows about him so you can decide.'

'Decide what?'

Incarna ignored the question and carried on as if she'd memorised this bit just for the drama. 'So, his ma got him another job, this time in the department of Health and Hygiene and he started looking into the plight of fallen women – even wrote about it. You know, one of them document things. What was it called now?' Mariangeles smirked, certain that Incarna knew exactly what it was called. 'Oh yes. A thesis. "Hygiene Amongst the Ranks of Lowly Women" he called it, and juicy stuff it was too, writing about the deviant bodies of prostitutes who was diseased and in need of the continual vigilance of the police. Reckon women hated him so much for his affliction that he started hating them back, cos he made no mention of the men wot paid for their services. Just the women, saying they was a threat to the social order, the bastard.' Her words echoed around the kitchen, her love of gossip momentarily replaced by her hatred of men. 'In the end though, them profs weren't having none of it. Seemed nothing in that thesis could be backed up with facts, just his steaming hatred of us women, so they chucked him out again!'

Mariangeles was wide-eyed by now. As usual, she'd been befuddled by Incarna's breathless spin. 'So, what did he do this time?'

'Well, third time round his poor ma refused to help, so he had to find his own way. Took his full name - Manuel Jiménez Torres - and began doin' *enchufe*. Know what that means don't you, Mari? Networking with the old families of Seville, chatting over a manzanilla and rubbing shoulders with them gents that was setting up factories in the city. They call him The Fixer now, and that's where you come in.'

She sat back with her message laid bare, like a cat offering up its prey at Mariangeles's feet. Mariangeles looked shocked.

'Me?'

'Yes, Mari. You.' Incarna's voice changed to a louder, more urgent pitch. 'I got to thinkin' see, after what you told me about… you know who.' She glanced furtively around as if to check that Sebastiana wasn't listening but the girl had already left and was indeed listening from the salon. 'He's got this thing going. Finds work in the new factories for young women. All respectable and above board like. Finds them somewhere to live too. That's why they calls him The Fixer see?' She folded her arms as if closing her argument to scrutiny. 'He's a bit odd, mind, wot with his affliction, but good with country families who can't afford to feed their daughters or perhaps them that wants them out the way for some reason.' She'd lowered her voice again. 'And, Mari, you never knows what that girl will get up to next.'

Mariangeles hesitated. Perhaps she should contradict Incarna, tell her that her daughter was a good girl, to prevent any further gossip from seeping into the village. But no. Instead, she adjusted her apron to give herself time to think. Then she looked Incarna straight in the eye.

'I'll give the girl one more chance,' she said. But from beneath her words surfaced a different thought. Here was a solution to her problem. Here was a way to soothe the struggles of her agitated mind. Suddenly the waves had cleared and she had seen the light. She smiled at Incarna and winked.

8. Tia

I saw it. Even watching from the salon I saw that quick flash of movement against my mother's cheek, her eyelid squashed up tight, so sudden, so powerful. It hurt as much as if she'd swiped me across my face with the back of her hand. How could she? My mother, my ma. How could she consider sending me off with some stranger with only a moment's hesitation? But maybe I wasn't surprised. There was something about Ma that frightened me. She'd begun talking to herself, repeating her mantra about waves and sorrows over and over and giving me long hard stares that could have been anger but which might have been a mixed-up kind of love. I couldn't tell. At night, too, I heard her whisper sweetly to Pa, but in the morning she became sour, like milk that had suddenly curdled and all the while she was watching every move between Pa and me, and it felt like some kind of loss. My mother had faded. My mother had gone. And *I* had changed too, becoming petulant and sullen. If I was to be the harlot of the house then she would know it. I began to strut and puff and raise my chin, flash my eyes and swing my hips, and even though underneath it all I was desperately frightened, I carried off the charade to perfection. A rebel is meant to roar like a lion, but behind my bravado I was broken, like a porcelain cup. If you'd held me to the light you'd have seen right through me and if you'd thrown me to the ground I'd have shattered into a thousand pieces. Betrayal is what I felt, and I couldn't forgive that wink. That treacherous assent.

The following week Ma dragged me down the hill to the cross-roads where we caught a landau headed for our old town. A wind was up, darting like a genie in and out of the narrow streets, and whistling through the latticed archways until they seemed to bend like lace. People claimed they went mad on days like these. When we arrived, she instructed me to stand by a statue in the square while she walked off towards the castle. A gust roared in and Ma strode forward on her thick legs like a woman on a mission. It was me who saw The Fixer first, silhouetted against the castle walls. He was tall, thin, and struggling to control his black cloak flapping wildly in the wind. An extra gust came charging up from the sea and he lost his balance, leaning on the castle wall for support. What a pathetic sight, and my mother must have thought so too because she stopped for a moment, elbows out, her hands on her hips as she always did when she found something amusing. We watched the man struggle with his cape, his thin spiky limbs jerking out like a spider caught in a hurricane. We'd heard from Incarna that The Fixer was more used to the sophistication of Seville with its tree-lined promenades and gentle breezes over the Guadalquivir River, than here, where the wind was robbing him of his dignity. Yet the blast vanished as quickly as it had come, and soon he was smoothing out the folds of his black cloak and mincing towards Ma with the precision of a hunter inching towards its prey. He stooped down to her level, took her hand and kissed it with an exaggerated flourish. I listened from a distance.

'Hello, Father, 'Ma said. 'Should I address you as Father?'

'Manuel Jimenez Torres at your service, señora. But Don Manuel will suffice. Now, in what way may I be of assistance?' The wind started up again, making it impossible for me to hear more, so I walked towards them and as I approached, Ma's words got caught in her throat as if she'd been strangled by her own shame.

'Away from home,' she said then stopped when she saw me.

There was a smell of spearmint as Manuel Jimenez Torres opened his mouth to acknowledge my presence, but he didn't address me directly.

'Madam, in Seville I have the perfect employment for your daughter and I can assure you of my utmost vigilance and protection against certain elements.' His voice trailed off and I wondered what he meant. Then it rose higher and I could hear the sarcasm in it as he added 'Madam, I'm sure that your concern for your daughter's welfare supersedes all other considerations.' I saw Ma blush and the man seemed to be smiling as if he recognised the advantage he had over his soon-to-be client. There was a long pause while Ma considered his proposal and I waited for her to answer. What would she say? Surely she wouldn't send me away? How could she even contemplate such a thing? I was only thirteen and knew nothing of the world. Surely my mother really *was* going insane? But then I imagined what she was thinking. With her daughter gone, there would be no more cruel comparisons with her worn-out body. *I will suffice. I'll help him in the workshop by day, and fulfil his desires by night.* I watched her bite her lip as Don Manuel or Jimenez Torres or The Fixer - whatever he was called - stood there inscrutable. Not a twitch passed over his face as he waited for my mother's answer. And when she did, her words escaped like an over-dark cloud that could no longer contain its load.

'This is just an enquiry, mind; a precaution just in case.' The man bowed deeply and leaned in to catch her hand again. As his lips brushed the back of it, he remained for a few seconds, hunched in a low stance as if he was pretending to grovel.

'Madam, I will be in town for the next few days. If you decide to go ahead with my offer you won't regret it.' Then he raised himself up tall and proud and took his leave, striding hurriedly across the square, his black cloak flapping in the wind like a bat rushing back to the darkness of its cave.

My mother was not a stupid woman, but having to raise her gaze to this tall condescending man had made her flustered. On the way home she kept muttering, 'How dare he presume to know me,' and 'Why is a man of the cloth doing this anyway?' I wasn't stupid either. I realised that her mutterings were simply a way to conceal her guilt and when I caught her eye she warned me, 'One more chance, girl.' Then she turned and stared out of the window, cancelling any further discussion on the long and tortuous journey home.

9. Mariangeles

Several times Mariangeles stirred the pot on the stove dragging the coagulated lumps of meat into the centre and pushing them round and round. She raised her elbows, digging into the task until she had created a meaty vortex that seemed to have no end. Her head was spinning; her shoulders felt heavy, and she could hardly breathe. She retreated into the salon and grabbed her embroidery again. Anything to calm her mind. Collapsing on a chair she began to weep. What a fool she had been letting Incarna into her life, disclosing her worries to that gossip-monger, telling her about Bartolome's obsession with his daughter. If the villagers dragged her husband away, it would be her fault, her foolishness that made it happen, and then if they killed him, there would be no income, so how would she live? And now that Incarna had introduced her to The Fixer, she had another dilemma. Which option should she choose? Relinquish her daughter into the hands of a stranger? Or try to make peace with her? But surely life would be so much easier without this rebellious girl around the place, without the constant comparison with her worn-out body and her worn-out mind. And in her heart she knew that the second chance she had offered her daughter was as fine as the thread she held between her fingers and oh how easily she could make it snap. She shook her head. Where did it all go wrong? The baby she thought would bring her such happiness had grown into a strong, independent character and the love Mariangeles had hoped to give to her daughter, was – dare she say it? - slowly turning into hate.

She returned to the kitchen, placed the meat stew into two bowls and carried them down to Bartolome's new wine cellar. It was fiesta week and he'd been busy making shoes for the villagers. Now though, he was relaxing with his new client, Don Francisco, who ran the '*La Veloza*' stagecoaches that passed along the main road from Seville to Gibraltar. Don Francisco was lounging on an old settee and Bartolome was sitting forward listening to every word his new client spoke.

'My carriages are the best in Andalucía,' she heard him say, as he waved a cigar in the air. She raised an eyebrow at the man's boastfulness, but they didn't notice her reaction. Why would they?

Bartolome nodded. 'Yes, indeed, Don Francisco. Everyone admires them. They truly are the best.'

Don Francisco grabbed the bowl from Mariangeles and plunged the spoon into the hot liquid. She studied his round face and tiny eyes, reddened from too much booze, and was unimpressed. Then she looked on the table where Bartolome had already opened a second bottle of wine. Here we go again, she thought, remembering the many empty bottles retrieved from their cellar in the old town.

'Best horses, too,' Don Francisco added. 'They go twice as long as my competitors without stopping to rest.' Then he gulped down his wine as if it were water.

As Mariangeles was leaving, Don Francisco slapped Bartolome on his back and she heard him say, 'You're one of us now, my friend. I invite you and your family to the *feria* as my guests.' She saw Bartolome's eyes light up at the thought of being included in Don Francisco's social circle and next day he strutted around the house like a man restored. He called on his nephew, Guillermo, to represent the family in the *'paseo de caballos'* – the horsemanship competition held every year in a clearing high up in the cork forests. 'I will make us all new boots and you can make the flamenco dresses for Tia and Guillermo's fiancée, Curra,' he declared. Mariangeles smiled. Her husband seemed happy again, so perhaps things would work out after all. She spent hours making beautiful garments, including one that took in the remaining curves of her aging body and a simple shift dress with ruffles at the hem for Sebastiana.

On the morning of the Romeria, Mariangeles cornered her daughter in the kitchen.

'Keep yourself decent, Sebastiana. We don't want you showing off like a hussy.'

Tia looked at her with resentment but said nothing, so Mariangeles let it drop. Perhaps the girl would respect her wishes after all.

10. Tia

I wasn't a hussy and she knew it. For days I'd been on my best behaviour, avoiding Pa and helping Ma with the housework whilst she was sewing. That way she wouldn't get mad and send me to The Fixer. But when I heard those words spilling off her tongue, I realised that nothing I did would make it better, so why should I even try? I pulled my new dress off the rack and stomped into the bedroom where I altered the side seams so that it clung more closely to my body and ruched the neckline to reveal more cleavage. The newly-altered dress was as blue as summer and dropped over my hips before falling into a cascade of white frills like waves on a turbulent sea. Then I draped an embroidered shawl over my shoulders. There was only a small mirror perched on a shelf but I could see that the fringe fell in delicate strands onto my chest. Most girls tied their hair into elaborate confections but I let mine drop down my back. I knew it was wrong, this brazen immodesty but it was my only weapon against Ma. She had let me down and wound me up. I flounced out of the house and into the sunlight where Don Francisco was waiting by his horse. He lurched towards me smelling of booze, took my hand and winked.

'Bartolome, where have you been hiding this lovely creature?' he cried and I lowered my eyes at the compliment. Then he offered his arm and we walked off with the rest of the villagers, followed by Ma, Pa, Guillermo and Curra. I heard my mother tut when Don Francisco leaned in to ask if I would be his sponsor in the *paseo*, but this didn't stop me grinning with pleasure at the attentions of such an important man.

11. Mariangeles

No one noticed Mariangeles as they made their way to the parade ground. No one remarked on her beautifully made flamenco dress or on the way she had skilfully twisted her hair into an elaborate bun, nor did anyone look into her eyes, lined in kohl with lashings of mascara. From her ears hung dazzling paste earrings, so long and intricate that they framed her face making it sparkle, but no one noticed her efforts and therefore, it seemed, nobody cared. Bartolome, who had smoothed down his hair with oil and close-shaved his face with a cut-throat razor, had not noticed his wife's efforts either. He was constantly pulling his fob watch from his waistcoat pocket, more anxious to get to the parade ground and mix with Don Francisco's friends than take time to compliment his wife.

They progressed in silence, Mariangeles simmering with anger at her husband's neglect and Bartolome desperate to make eye contact with anyone who might look his way. On they travelled to the sound of drums, up the long track, through the cork forest to a plateau surrounded by trees where the festivities were about to begin.

12. Tia

At every step, the ruffles of my skirt moved to the rhythm of the band and with every movement, I felt my hips swaying inside my dress. Everything felt so nice. We walked for an hour, landowners and farm workers, villagers and visitors, all progressing upwards together in a spirit of comradery. Step by step the weight of my troubles eased and my stride became longer and more relaxed. Pa was grinning with pride. I overheard someone say, 'Isn't that the daughter of the man who's made these fine bridles?' and I wondered what they would think if they knew about Pa's desires and Ma's raging jealousy. Then someone added, 'So, that's Mariangeles' girl. What a beauty.' I turned to study Ma's face, but she had already looked the other way. When we reached the plateau I took no heed of my parents who sat under the broad canopy of a mulberry tree – Ma upright with her mouth firmly closed like a watchful frog whose tongue was about to leap out to catch a passing fly and Pa leaning against the trunk with his back to Ma, taking in the scene like a king on his throne.

When the *paseo* started, I studied Curra's actions so that I'd know what to do. She stepped into the arena and took an elaborate bow. Then, above her head, she raised a metal ring covered in colourful ribbons that blew erratically in the wind, colliding together like an escaped rainbow. I noticed that Curra was standing at a slight angle in case the horse came too close and knocked her over. Guillermo mounted his animal and wedged a long wooden baton under his arm. Then he pulled his knees in tightly and charged, gathering speed until he was close enough to stab the pole into the ring, whisking it out of Curra's hand, and carrying it off to the end of the field in victory. They did it three times out of four and everyone clapped, making me dizzy with pleasure, and I saw Pa grinning with satisfaction for our family honour. Then Don Francisco invited *me* into the arena. I was a little scared when I took his arm, but I raised my head good and proud to conceal my fears and took a bow, waiting for the same applause that had been given to Curra. There were a few handclaps, splintered by someone saying, 'Look at her strutting about as if she owns the place.' And someone else replying 'And with a man twice her age.' Then another person said, 'No wonder there's trouble in that house.'

Their words crashed around me like debris from an earthquake. They knew about Pa and they knew about me. Suddenly my dress was too revealing, my cleavage too low, and my waist too slim. Oh how I wished I'd pinned up my hair. How I wished I wasn't there. But what could I do? I couldn't run away, not now, not with everyone watching Don Francisco and the hussy he had on his arm. I stood shaking with fear and copied Curra's angled stance, pushing the ring high into the air just like she had. Don Francisco mounted his horse, lurching into the saddle, grabbing at the pole and throwing the animal off balance. For a second it seemed Don Francisco might topple, but then he waved enthusiastically to the crowd and they cheered back. It was obvious that no one cared if he was drunk. Everyone knew that Don Francisco was a master horseman. He yanked at the reins, forcing the hard iron bit against the animal's soft mouth. The creature pawed the ground in resistance. Don Francisco dug his spurs into its flesh - still wobbling, still smiling - as the untamed ribbons flew wildly above my head. We began. Don Francisco and his horse came charging towards me and as the sound got louder and the horse grew larger, I saw the panic in its eyes and it seemed to see the same in mine. I stood firm but the poor thing was distressed. It tossed its head and veered off. Don Francisco missed the ring and the wayward ribbons continued to flutter, not on the pole as they should have, but above my head showing the world that we'd got it wrong. Don Francisco thundered away down the track, yanked his horse around and rode back.

As he came near he whispered, 'Stupid girl.'

That wasn't fair. I'd copied Curra's actions and stood as firmly as I could. Besides I'd never done this before. But Don Francisco didn't make allowances. I supposed his pride had been damaged and his reputation too. He repositioned for another try, digging his spurs into the animal's side as he made his next charge. But now I was so nervous that the ring wavered in my hands. Condemnation had made me falter and for a second time the pole missed the ring. This time Don Francisco came back slowly and I saw that his knuckles were white, as if he wanted to punch me. We tried twice more but his next attempts were no better than the first, and many in the crowd were laughing because I was a nobody – an upstart girl - a hussy who'd shown herself up and let Don Francisco down. Pa was devastated.

I heard him say 'Don Francisco I am so sorry. The girl is young. She is inexperienced at these things.' But Don Francisco scoffed and walked away. I saw Pa run after him. Not only was his family honour in doubt but losing the order for so many saddles and bridles for his stables would be a severe blow. So to make amends he invited Don Francisco back to our wine cellar and they must have downed their manzanillas in grumpy silence because I heard nothing until four in the morning when Pa came up the stairs to bed, and I heard Don Francisco snoring on an old couch in Pa's cellar, where he often stayed to sleep off the booze.

13. Mariangeles

It was four in the morning when Mariangeles woke abruptly from her sleep. Bartolome was snoring beside her, but someone was stumbling around downstairs, banging into furniture and mumbling words she couldn't make out. It must be that old drunk Don Francisco, she thought, causing a nuisance as usual. So she turned over trying to get back to sleep, but she couldn't. Yesterday had been a disaster; the *paseo* had embarrassed the family and made Bartolome mad. Oh, those ribbons, those terrible ribbons, mocking their family in front of the crowd. And Sebastiana in that dress. How could she have done such a thing? It's true, she thought to herself. My mother's mantra was right - waves and sorrows never arrive alone. Then she raised her head and whispered it into the ancient rafters, as if speaking to all the generations of women in her family so that they could hear it too.

'Waves and sorrows never arrive alone,' she said. Mariangeles clenched her teeth. Her mind was spinning, and her head felt thick. Was she really going to send her daughter off with The Fixer? The moment for an answer was getting close. It would have to be yes or no, not maybe or perhaps anymore. But she was in turmoil, as if an impetuous monkey had landed in her hair, scratching at her scalp, tangling her mind, scaling her thoughts until she was a ragged mess. Was she really going to do that thing? She shivered under the blanket, longing for her husband to turn over and cuddle her - anything to have him close and warm against her skin and distract her from the tortures of her mind. She remembered the time, just after giving birth, when Sebastiana would not take to the breast, and Bartolome had consoled her, first with cuddles then with greater urgency as he found her breast and suckled upon it with such delight that she did not stop him. It seemed to give him such pleasure that every night she allowed him to roll over and hold her breast gently in his fingers as he drew her milk into his mouth, purring like a kitten, and she felt the draw, long and deep and satisfying. Afterwards he had surrendered into her arms like the baby she had so desperately wanted to enjoy. Those were times of exquisite contentment despite Sebastiana crying in the adjacent room.

14. Tia

I thought I was dreaming. Something was moving on my chest. I opened my eyes and, through the thin curtains, the dazzling light from a harvest moon was pouring in, creating an odd blue glow across my room. Then, close up, I saw his face, big and round and red. Don Francisco had pulled back the blanket making my skin glow like a ghost.

'You were waiting, Sebastiana,' he mumbled, his boozy breath settling on my cheek. Before I could rouse myself from slumber, his hand had reached into my nightgown. It slithered across my stomach. I flinched, but only for a second because now I was wide awake and roped down by fear. He brought his hand to my breast and my nipple stiffened - a new sensation I couldn't control. With his other hand, he reached down to open his breeches, grunting as saliva gathered at the sides of his mouth. His shoulders rose and fell. His eyes rolled backwards like the devil. I shuddered and tried to move, but he leaned in further and his bulk obscured the moon, casting a shadow that enveloped me like a magician's cloak. I lay rigid under his spell whilst he squeezed my breast, once, twice, three times, over and over, as if kneading dough. Then suddenly it stopped. A long brutal sound came from his half-open mouth.

Don Francisco stood up, leaned unsteadily against the wall and re-buttoned his breeches. He didn't look down or speak, just left my room without a word.

What happened? What did he do? I lay there for the rest of the night as dead as stone with that big cold moon hanging over me. I tried to sleep - to block it out - but I had been weakened, flattened against the bed by that horrible man. Why didn't I resist? Why didn't I scream? My breast was sore and my mind undone, as if a rabid dog had rushed through me, scratching at my most secret parts, before burying me in the cold dark earth. Then, falling asleep, I dreamt of those hides in the tannery, those poor empty skins smoothed out and lifeless on my workbench, just like me pinned against my bed, and I felt the creatures' powerlessness in the face of man.

In the morning I woke with his words remembered from the night before. *'Sebastiana, you were waiting,'* and I persuaded myself that Incarna was right about me. That it had all been my fault. Don Francisco must have seen me dressed like a common girl, quivering in the centre of that ring with a vulnerability that assured him of my consent. Then back at our house he must have imagined I was lying there in the darkness, waiting for him. He'd even used my full name – Sebastiana - just like my mother did, and it had sounded like a profanity, a confirmation of my very certain guilt. I was a hussy – my mother had called me that - and I became convinced that she was right.

He came again the following night when the moon was still up. Oh, that moon. This time I blocked him completely, closing my eyes tightly until it was over. I smelt his rancid breath and heard his grunts of desire as he pumped my breasts to his unnatural rhythms, but I didn't call out nor protest because speech would have rendered it more real and the more I disconnected, the more it hadn't happened. I told no one. There was no point. Don

Francisco was my father's special client and I was too ashamed to tell Ma, for fear that she would judge me yet again.

The third night he launched at me so violently that I let my body go limp, shrinking into the bed, submerged in a well of disconnection. But my passive resistance must have offended him because he slapped me hard across the cheek before plunging his tongue down my throat so I could hardly breathe. And when he withdrew it, I let out a gasp and it sounded like that rabid dog again with its lip curled and saliva dripping from its teeth. Then I heard the latch lift on my bedroom door.

Pa was staring at the hunched spine of Don Francisco and I watched in horror as his hand came up, as if in slow motion, to cover his mouth in disbelief. Don Francisco sniggered then rolled off me, stuffed his shirt back into his breeches and swaggered past Pa and out. He didn't care about me and he didn't care about Pa either.

Pa turned away.

'Wait, please,' I called but he'd already gone. I dashed down the stairs and found him in the kitchen leaning over the sink, about to be sick, so I retreated into the darkness, listening to him retching, hearing his crying. It was so loud he must have woken the street.

15. Mariangeles

In the middle of the night Mariangeles heard the outer door slam. Someone had just left the house. Bartolome wasn't in their bed so she got up and rushed past Sebastiana who was standing on the stairs in her nightgown. Her husband was leaning over the sink, sobbing.

'What's going on?' she asked.

'Oh Mariangeles. What horror!'

'What do you mean?'

'Why him, Mariangeles? Why not m...' Bartolome stopped just in time, but Mariangeles had already worked it out - the door that slammed - those noises tonight and the two nights before that...Don Francisco had done something to the girl and here was her husband lamenting that it wasn't him. She wanted to be angry. She wanted to feel fury at Don Francisco for abusing her girl and at Bartolome for his tearful confession. But for the first time in years her husband had called her by her name, her *real* name – Mariangeles – the name that hardly ever passed his lips, and it sounded so fresh and reassuring that suddenly she felt safe. Bartolome raised his arms in supplication as if he wanted to be held, pleading with his eyes, asking for help. She should have refused. She should have left him there, shaking in his nightshirt. She should have walked away and supported her girl. But she wanted to hold him, to comfort him and tell him everything would be all right. I am his wife, she thought, and as soon as she opened her arms, he fell into them and rested his head against her chest sobbing violently into her nightgown. His body felt warm and soft like the child she had always wanted, the infant she longed to pacify with her arms. She held him firmly and waited until his sobs came to a halt then, slowly, she spoke. The long-awaited decision had just been made. 'Don't worry husband. I'll deal with her,' she said.

16. Tia

I put my hand to my cheek and carefully touched the part where Don Francisco had struck me. It was beginning to swell. Then I turned and climbed the stairs back to my room. There was no more sleep to be had. In that dreadful moonlight I walked to and fro across my room, as if movement itself could erase what had just happened. But it *had* happened. Don Francisco had assaulted me and now Ma and Pa were embracing downstairs as if it had all been my fault. And perhaps it was. I sunk to my knees. Why hadn't I told Ma? Why hadn't I explained about that man's visits in the middle of the night? Instead, I'd kept Don Francisco's grubby little secret and now I was complicit - as guilty as he. And each night the rabid dog had gnawed inside me, weakening my spirit, raising something that I didn't recognise nor want to feel. 'I must be evil,' I reasoned. A line had been crossed and there was no way back to the safety of my once innocent self.

The walls of our little house were paper thin and perhaps my parents' whispers were louder than they thought or maybe the neighbours saw Don Francisco stride away from our house at dawn. But whatever was true, the day must have been thick with conjecture as news of my downfall spread through the village. I stayed hidden in my room, and when Incarna came knocking to declare that she had some gossip to tell, I dived under the blankets and sobbed myself to sleep.

At dawn a cock crowed. Dogs barked and an unfamiliar sound rolled over the village. I went to the window and felt the panes rattling with vibrations as disused bells pealed out in the air. I saw villagers rushing up the hill to our locked-up church, and someone was releasing the padlock from the door. And all the time the bells were thundering across the village so loudly I could hardly think. I shivered with the memory of cholera and death the last time I'd heard them, and when I opened the window, the sound poured in like an overzealous tide. The melody was different now... more triumphant, more uplifting. A man was shouting, 'Glory be to God. They're opening our church.' And now I heard the message of those brass bells as clear as the bright morning sky. *'We're back, we're back,'* they seemed to say. And then I thought I heard them saying, *'They're coming, they're coming, they're coming for you'*, and although part of my mind told me I had done nothing wrong, the other part was overcome with defeat. The bells tolled and my heart pounded, as if in unison with their recriminating rhythm.

Incarna came by in the afternoon and told us that across Spain, priests were returning to their pulpits and people were flocking to their pews. I wondered if perhaps the faithful had never gone away. Perhaps they'd been storing their religious fervour like blankets packed in summer trunks waiting for winter to come, because now the village was transformed. I saw people shuffling about with shoulders even more drooped than before, as if weighed down by long-forgotten sins. I knew nothing of religion but imagined priests like fishermen, hauling in their catch of reluctant sinners and turning them into dead-eyed flapping fish. And I was one of them. I was a sinner too. It's us and them. Some of us are bad and some of us are good, I thought, as I retraced my memory of Don Francisco and that terrible moon. Until now I'd been in limbo, neither a good girl nor bad, but now the whole of my world was being divided into black and white, east and west, depraved or devout. I shook my head.

'It's too late for me now,' I said.

17. Mariangeles

The Fixer visited daily to confirm arrangements for Sebastiana's departure and Mariangeles was beginning to realise that Incarna was right. Manuel Jimenez Torres was indeed odd. But she held no sympathy for the man and his affliction because beneath that cloak she sensed he was cruel and his behaviour was so changeable that she decided he wasn't 'The Fixer' he was a 'Chameleon' altering his demeanour to suit his situation. On Monday he came flushed with drink. On Tuesday he was as pale as a worm, writhing with flattery. On Wednesday he was a bloated toad, splattering his venomous words loosely across the room. On Thursday he came to talk to Sebastiana, with his unkempt hair and his thin lips quivering at the manzanilla glass Bartolome had provided. Then, as he spoke, his head jolted as if struck by lightning, a leg shot out and his arms waved wildly above his head as if conducting an exorcism. No wonder women found him unappealing. On Friday he rested his hands on the kitchen table like a salamander poised on a whitewashed wall, waiting for its prey. She imagined a long tongue flicking out from his mouth, devouring her words in a blink. On one visit he had twitched so weirdly that she and Sebastiana had sniggered in unison, and in that temporary, joyous moment Mariangeles almost regretted her decision to send her daughter away. But these playful thoughts were solitary rainbows, moist and bright in their otherwise dried-up house where she couldn't wait to release herself of her problem. It was all too late. Her mind was set. There was no way back. The girl's presence was stealing any hopes still lurking in her heart, that their family mantra wasn't true; stealing the hope that those waves and sorrows could somehow be controlled. Sebastiana had to go, Mariangeles decided, and the sooner the better, or else she would truly go insane.

The Fixer must have sensed her mood. 'Have patience, Doña Mariangeles. These things take time. Your daughter needs an introduction. There are protocols. People need to be encouraged. The list is long. Furthermore your daughter will need protection from those who offer placements in return for…favours. Sorry, I do not wish to offend. But you know what I mean Doña Mariangeles. Was I not a priest? Do I not know something of the sins of man as told to me in the confessional? And she will need somewhere to live. I know a place not too expensive in the old quarter.' Mariangeles sighed at the man's verbose manner and the way he seemed to spin things out. Surely it didn't take that long to make these arrangements?

After two more weeks visiting daily, drinking their manzanilla and eating their food, The Fixer finally announced it was done. 'Madam,' he said. 'Early on Monday morning your daughter will travel down to the main road where I will collect her. It will take us two days and three nights so she will need money for wayside lodgings before I personally escort her to the new bridge in Triana where there is a girls' hostel overlooking the great river Guadalquivir. You see, madam, everything is arranged and at considerable cost.' He pushed his bill across the kitchen table and it sat there between them on the bleach-white tablecloth as if he'd offered her a present. Mariangeles studied it, but she didn't put her hand in her purse. The Chameleon was very clever with words although never once did Mariangeles consider them sincere.

'You will get it later,' she said. 'When the girl is delivered.'

18. Tia

Ma's hands were shaking as she folded my blouse, bending the back over the front, smoothing it down and placing it in the suitcase. My skirt came next, folded then rolled and pressed into place. Underwear, a nightgown, hairbrush and a pair of house shoes followed, until no space remained. I sighed. She was squeezing me in, making me small, making me disappear. I scoffed at her attempts to make the process seem acceptable.

'Don Manuel will look after you,' she kept saying as if her repetitions would make everything all right. So, how could I now disclose that each evening before he left, The Fixer, the Chameleon, Manuel Jimenez Torres - whoever he was - placed his excitable body close to mine, forcing me back against our white-washed walls and pinning me there so that I was unable to think? But there was one moment when he seemed to fall under my spell. I must have looked at him a little haughtily because he blushed. If only I'd appreciated then, the power I had at my fingertips – the power only women understand. If only I had been able to use it to my advantage. But that power was as nothing when set against the realisation that I was as worthless as a rat in a sewer, and in any case he quickly recovered his composure to become The Fixer again. Perhaps I should have protested at my life being rearranged without consultation, but I had no defence. I'd enticed Pa, dallied with Don Francisco and brought disgrace on the household. It all seemed to make sense. My parents were right. I had to go.

On Sunday evening it became real. My parents shook his hand. The Fixer looked over at me with a smile as smug as a frog, and winked as if we were sharing a secret.

'We will meet at dawn tomorrow at the crossroads, Sebastiana.' Then he took my hand and kissed it lightly as he had done with Ma. Then, after my parents waved goodbye and closed the door behind him, they embraced and slapped each other on the back at a job well done. I heard their sighs of relief as, ignoring me completely, they retreated arm in arm, into the salon without another word. The final act had been played out. The curtains had closed. I had been abandoned and there was nothing I could do, so I took myself to bed.

The realisation came just after midnight. I would not go with that horrible man. Instinct told me he was a liar and a fraud. For a moment I wondered if my escape might put Pa in danger, but I doubted it. As for Don Francisco, they'd probably raise a glass to his lechery because he was the master and I was a silly harlot who'd fled rather than stay to defend my honour. Besides, Incarna would surely have dirtied the remains of my reputation by now. So, with my suitcase of tightly packed possessions and money stolen from my parent's strongbox, I slipped out of the house as quietly as I could.

The cold air hit me as I stumbled down the hill, letting the momentum of my anger carry me on. I ran through streets full of sleeping villagers, until I reached the cesspit at the bottom of the hill where our village excrement laid. It stank, and I smiled. Let the putrefaction of this place stink them all out, I thought. Wherever I was going would be better than this. I hurried on to the crossroads and sat on a milestone, exhausted, hoping I was too early for The Fixer. Hoping someone would come by and offer me a ride. I would go wherever they were going, away from this place, somewhere, anywhere and I wondered where on earth that would be.

Part Two – Just Tia

19. Tia

I had taken a leap into the unknown, and in that dawn light I looked back at my village where soon the sun would make its slow curve around the mountain. A morning mist was rising, and through the grey I saw the pale mass of white houses, tumbling down the hill, like milk spilt from a churn. I strained to see our own house where Ma and Pa would still be huddled together fast asleep and wondered if I would ever see my parents again. I sat on the milestone for over an hour, watching the men arriving at the tannery for their early morning shift and listening to the chirrup of birdsong. I watched the bushes quiver as the little creatures shook the night-time from their wings. It was such a familiar sound and such a glorious sight that a feeling of extraordinary peace rose within me, as if my heart was filling with something new which was yet to be revealed.

I looked left and right. There was a long straight highway and a signpost. Seville to the west and Gibraltar to the east. Which way should I go? I had no choice. I would have to go wherever a traveller might take me, but that didn't stop me from dreaming. I remembered Incarna's descriptions of Seville and those bright, hard-working women at the Royal Tobacco Factory. Surely west would be best? Then I looked the other way, across the great chunk of mountain that restricted my view. What lay beyond it? I had no idea. In my heart I hoped for Seville, where the future seemed so golden and bright, but the choice was not mine to make. Then out of the dawn light came the clatter of hooves. Was it The Fixer come to collect me? I crossed my fingers hoping that it wasn't him and stood there, tensed and ready to run. But then the familiar smell of hides wafted through the air and for once they smelt wonderful. Pepe pulled his horse to a halt and backed it into the tannery yard. Doors opened, men came forward, shifting their weight as they hoisted the skins onto their backs. Their grunts reminded me of Don Francisco, the thin curtains and the full moon and those terrible three nights. Pepe threw me a friendly glance, looking me up and down, and taking in the battered suitcase at my side.

'Are you going to Seville,' I asked, but he shook his head.

'Going east to fetch bark, then on to Gib.' He saw my disappointment. 'You can come if you likes but no moaning. The road's rough and my cart ain't no landau.' I had no choice. I had to trust him. Besides, it was Pepe who'd rescued us from a town full of cholera. It was Pepe who'd helped me through the trials of the tannery. Pepe was not like other men, whose manners were rough. He was quiet and gentle and separate from the rest. So I mounted his cart and arranged my skirts across the seat as he flapped the reins, and his beloved Jefe jerked into a trot. We swung out onto the main road and into the soon-to-be rising sun, knowing that I would miss The Fixer because he would be travelling up from a different direction. So, if only for a few hours, I would be safe.

A while later Pepe broke our silence.

'Rather have this animal any day,' he said affectionately. 'Better companion than the wife, that's for sure.' I laughed as Jefe trotted on; carrying me away from my troubles, away from my old life, away from the city of Seville where I'd imagined I might fulfil my dreams. Pepe must have read my thoughts. 'Seville ain't as grand as they says it is, you know.' I looked at him in surprise. 'There's plenty o' trouble over there, with layoffs and stuff, people forming unions, 'n' demonstrating in the streets.' I knew this wasn't empty gossip. Pepe travelled this route several times a week and picked up all sorts of news. 'Everyone's smoking them new 'cigarillos' now. Cheaper 'cos they're rolled on machines. So, all them girls was made redundant, forcing 'em onto the streets, deciding should they stay or should they go?' He waited for my response, as if I had understood his meaning. But I looked at him blankly so he carried on. 'Go back to the countryside or stay in the wickedness of the city? Now there's a question!' But still I didn't understand what he meant. 'Girls' hostels, Tia, built hard against the city walls, turned into brothels to please them rich industry gents.' He looked over to see if I'd taken this in. 'You had a lucky escape my girl, dodgin' that pimp Jimenez Torres.'

Again we rode on in silence but this time thoughts came crashing in. If Pepe was right, then the man who called himself *Don Manuel* - whom others called *The Fixer*, whom Ma called *The Chameleon*; and Pepe was now calling *that pimp* - must have been weighing up my potential when he'd pressed me against the wall of our house. He must have been wondering if I was best working in a factory rolling tobacco or lying on my back satisfying a man. Perhaps he couldn't decide and I couldn't help wondering. Was I a good girl or bad? It seems a woman is either one thing or the other, but never both.

The sun was coming up, and as it began to warm my bones I wondered if perhaps I'd been unfair to Incarna. What if, when she'd turned up on our doorstep that morning with new gossip, it wasn't to retell my shame with Don Francisco? Perhaps Incarna had found out about Jimenez's new tricks and had come to warn Ma. And if so, Ma had chosen to ignore her. So, when Ma pulled the envelope containing that wretched man's bill towards her, did she already know that I might end up as a prostitute? If so, why was she willing to let me go? Surely she wouldn't put her daughter into the hands of a pimp? As we moved further away, this question raced through my mind, but there was no way of knowing the truth. I sat upright in the cart, facing forward, trying not to think of what I'd left behind - trying to erase the possibility of my mother's double treachery. But those thoughts stuck. They nagged at me and tried to bring me down.

Hours passed before we reached a viewing platform where I peered over at the sea, thundering against the rocks, then across to where it was calmer, to the pale grey strip on the other side of the Straits, where Tangiers loomed out of the mist. I remembered my daydream up on that mountain - *working in a rich household for a good family* – and I wondered if my dream might come true. We rode on, shielding our eyes from the oncoming sun, its brilliance reminiscent of that thin street in my beloved town where we'd rushed from the darkness of the boarded-up church, to the radiance of the ocean. I shivered at this new trajectory and at what I might find at the end of our journey.

Eventually we turned inland, where afternoon shadows and woodland silence calmed my mood. We rested in a clearing, sharing Pepe's bread, whilst local harvesters loaded his cart with bark from the cork trees. I watched them pile it high whilst Pepe stroked Jefe's muzzle, and whispered endearments into its ear. He was so caught up with his animal that I had time to study his features. There was a leathery texture to his skin caused by being out in all weathers, I supposed, and the rough stubble on his chin gave the impression of an older man. Now, though, as I saw his face illuminated in that soft forest light, I realised he was much younger than I had thought. Perhaps the same age as Ma. He patted Jefe one more time and looked over.

'Reckon you'll need some work then?' I nodded. 'Well I'm going to a factory close to town. You might find something there.'

Now Pepe's cargo was stacked so high that the cart swayed unpredictably from side to side and we travelled so slowly that the light was already fading as we picked our way through a small town near Gibraltar and arrived at some factory gates. The cart swung into a vast yard where tall doors opened into an interior filled with artificial light. Men were using ladders to stack cork so high that it was impossible to see where it stopped. I shivered with the freshness and ambition of it all. Pepe took me to the office by the shoreline where the manager offered me work for the next day.

'Name?' he asked, writing in his book.

'Sebastiana,' I said, embarrassed. 'But call me Tia.' My life was changing and I was determined to change too.

That night, with no bed to sleep in, I rested under a tarpaulin in Pepe's cart, listening to the soft comings and goings of the unseen waves out there in the darkness. I remembered Ma's mantra about waves and sorrows and hoped that I would be safe from her preoccupations and that I could create my own destiny instead of hers. Now though, with the journey ended, my fears had nowhere to hide. I began agonising over those three nights with Don Francisco. Why hadn't I resisted? Why did I just lie there while that awful man touched me? Over and over, my thoughts tumbled and each time they came to rest with the same calculation. It had been my fault. No matter how I tried, I found no answer other than self-reproach. Yet I was determined to force this from my mind. So I turned to get comfortable on the floor of the cart where the lingering odour of hides merged with the sweet aroma of fresh cork in a cocktail of old and new, decaying and fresh, until gradually the stench of yesterday gave way to the fragrance of an unknown tomorrow and I fell into a deep sleep. Those few hours were full of dreams, of new beginnings as promised in the brilliance of those illuminated factory doors.

20. Tia

I peeped out from the tarpaulin and saw the wide curve of a perfect bay and the enormous rock of Gibraltar looming out of the mist. It seemed so close I could almost touch it. I looked around and in that early morning light, the full extent of the factory was now visible, stretching right down to the shoreline. Waiting outside the doors, still open from the night shift, was a long queue of mules, weighed down with panniers of cork. They swished their tails quietly alongside their owners and it seemed such a friendly sight that I slipped eagerly out of Pepe's cart, desperate to begin something new.

'This will be your bench,' the manager explained. 'First the corks come out here.' He walked over to another bench where thick slabs of bark were being fed into a machine and cork stoppers were emerging and bouncing into a basket. He collected one and placed it into a contraption on my bench. 'This is an embosser,' he said, 'and this is where you press. Here.' He took my hand and held it over the lever. I felt his palm against the back of my hand, warm and firm. Then he pressed down with my hand under his, forcing the lever until there was a click and the stopper fell out into a basket. He retrieved it and pushed it into my palm. An image had appeared on the top of the curve, and I ran my fingers over the precise golden indentation, so wondrously neat and clean and shiny. 'When your basket is full, you take it to the despatch department where they are sent to Jerez to seal thousands of bottles of sherry that are exported from the ports of Cadiz.' He waved his arm across the room as if showing me the world, and I imagined with delight, all those corks being pulled in so many faraway places.

I settled quickly into the factory routine because the work was easy – not like Pa's workshop - but I didn't mind the monotony. Here, no one knew my past. I was a girl from nowhere and it suited me fine. But then, as I stood mindlessly at my machine, memories would sneak through, like serpents in the grass. I tried to shut them out, to shed my old skin and slip into the light, all shiny and new. But guilt leaves a trail. I'd deserted my parents, leaving them with a huge debt to The Fixer. They would be at his mercy for the rest of their lives. And then there was Pa's twisted desires and Don Francisco's lunacy under that harvest moon, and worst of all, Ma's decision to send me away because I was a hussy. Was this me? Was I this person? And had I brought her with me from the west? As much as I tried to let her go, I couldn't. This girl wasn't even a snake. She was nothing but a tiny snail, clinging to every pathway, leaving a slimy trail of who I was and where I had been. To ease my guilt I decided to save money each week in order to repay our debt to The Fixer, and although it would take me years to achieve, I was determined to try.

'Take this to Ma please,' I said to Pepe when he was back from one of his trips. I offered him an envelope with a month's worth of savings. He must have realised it contained money.

'Your parents don't need it, Tia. Talk is, they got an even better contract with Don Francisco so they should be rakin' it in soon.' I shivered at the man's name but insisted.

'Pepe. I have to repay my debt.'

Pepe raised his eyebrows. 'Tia, it's them what owes a debt to *you*,' he said, but if he knew the truth he wouldn't have said that, so I thrust the envelope into his hands making clear what I needed him to do.

I was proud of my new employment, discovering that the factory had nine thousand square metres of vaulted space, equipped with the latest machinery for steaming, drying, flattening, slicing, and stamping the raw cork into submission. We made a hundred million stoppers a year and, in return for our high production, the owners had built a school for workers' children and employed a doctor too. For our safety they had installed a fire-prevention system that could pump two hundred litres of water per minute of water into the plant in case there was a fire. We had to be careful when handling any combustible materials and smoking was only allowed at the far end of the yard.

Pepe was impressed. 'Should be safe enough 'ere then, Tia,' he said.

I ventured into town with three other girls who, like me, had recently joined the factory. We peered into shop windows, packed from side to side and top to bottom with women's blouses.

'Try these, Tia,' Eva said, holding up a pretty blouse and a woollen skirt. Eva was older than me and seemed to take charge of my wellbeing.

'Isn't it a bit grown-up?' I said, remembering Ma's dress and how I had made myself look like a hussy. But I tried them anyway, and as I looked in the mirror I saw a respectable girl wearing a high-necked blouse with puffed sleeves, and a high-cut skirt that showed off my narrow waist. I paid and made a note to buy thick petticoats to keep me warm in the winter. We four girls lived in a hostel near the factory and on Sundays we pinned our hair into wide-brimmed hats and promenaded in the tree-lined avenues of the town, eyes down but ever-watchful for boys walking on the other side of the street. We clustered together, arm in arm, deciding which of the boys was the most handsome, and who looked the richest. After a while, I began to scoff at my mother's saying, *sorrows, and waves, never arrive alone,* because here there were no sorrows. This place and this factory, had given me another chance at happiness and I was determined to take it. The girls and I became close. I'd never had friends before. We thought we were invincible, showing off in front of the men, walking coquettishly across the yard where they sat smoking. They used to cat-call us, saying, 'Here come 'Las Gaviotas.'

We lapped up what sounded like a compliment from these worldly men, - but it wasn't. One of the older women explained that *Las Gaviotas* was a taunt - a joke at our expense. It was a name given to prostitutes who sailed behind merchant ships, providing comfort to sailors, like hungry seagulls following their wake. But above the click-clack of the machines, we couldn't hear the men's sniggers and the more we strutted, the funnier their little joke must have seemed. In truth, I was still the same ignorant country girl exchanging one silly error for another, unable to escape my own foolishness.

21. Tia

Despite a four-year age difference Eva and I became a partnership. Bored with life in the countryside, she'd packed her bags and come to the bay looking for work, and as I got to know her, I realised that she was like a runaway horse with no particular direction in life. She just wanted to have fun, and had no time for my seriousness.

'Pass me that sheet' she shouted as I tried to hang it on the line. Then, as I came close, she grabbed it and threw it over my head, all wet and cool. 'There, that should get rid of your frown!' she said, turning me around until I got dizzy. Eva's self-confidence was contagious, and even when clouds rolled over the sun, her world seemed bright with colour and so different to the melancholy of my mother. I began to adore Eva and her audacious ways.

It was Sunday and we were resting in the hostel when she cornered me in the salon. Between the fingers of her right hand was a long sewing needle, and in her left was a cork stopper. 'Sit down,' she said.

'Why?' I asked, suspicious.

'Just there, by the fire,' she said. 'It's about time you had your ears pierced.'

I looked at her in fear. 'Won't it hurt?' I whined.

'Course not. And even if it does, so what? All the girls get their ears done whether they like it or not.'

'All right,' I said, nodding. Being like everyone else seemed like a good idea.

Eva pulled a bottle of the hostel owner's brandy off the sideboard.

'You can't take that,' I said.

'Yes, I can. Now quiet while I concentrate.' She took a swig then tipped some of the liqueur onto a cloth, wiped my earlobe back and front, positioned the needle between some tongs and held it over the fire. Flames spluttered around the steel, turning it red. Then she handed me the cork. 'Here, hold it tight against the back of your ear.' I took it from her, trembling, and noticed that Eva's hand was trembling too. Was this a good idea after all? She drew up a stool and pulled me towards her. 'Keep still, Tia. It won't hurt.' Before I was ready, she had pushed the needle in. The sizzle of melting flesh rebounded through my ears, and a second later, I smelt it too.

'No!' I squealed, but it was too late. The deed was done. Eva sat back, pleased.

'That went well for my first try,' she said, grinning. I looked at her sideways.

'So you thought you'd try it out on me first!' I screeched, clutching my ear.

She laughed. 'So what? I've seen it done loads of times. Just the other one now.' She repositioned herself to my other side and heated the needle again. I braced myself; determined not to cry. When she'd finished, I ran up to my bedroom, clutching my ear lobes, already seeping with pus, and lay there sulking at the way Eva had tricked me. But then she appeared and sat on my bed. 'Peace offering,' she said and handed me a little box. Inside was a

90

pair of gold studs. 'I had two pairs, Tia, so we've got one each now.' She smiled and even though I resented being her guinea pig, I was overcome with happiness at being on the receiving end of her love.

The hostel owner's nephew came to stay and Eva took a fancy to him. She would wait till the end of supper and they would walk together along the shore. One evening she came back dishevelled and shaking. I asked her what had happened and she shook her head. 'Men are no good Tia,' she said. It seemed the boy must have assaulted her, but she said nothing, and when the hostel owner asked what the matter was, she smiled as if it had all been a joke.

With such distraction, neither of us had noticed that the end of a century was upon us. Workers marched the streets, raising fists in protest, demanding improved employment rights and fairer rents, telling anyone who would listen, that the twentieth century was going to be brighter and better than all that had gone before. There were other groups too; religious and fanatical. One evening Eva and I were sitting in the church square when a procession came by, each person solemn-faced carrying a placard declaring 'The End is nigh.' A man with a long beard was calling out. 'Beware the last chime of midnight eighteen ninety-nine, when judgement will be upon you.' Eva giggled but I wasn't sure. 'Save your soul before it's too late,' he shouted, and villagers crossed themselves in panic. 'The Rapture is coming,' someone called out, as if, soon, we would be in the presence of God and others ran around the square wailing 'The End of days!' Eva mimicked their tone. 'Oh lordie, the End of days.' And we both laughed.

In December the whole neighbourhood was obsessed and the owner of our hostel dragged the four of us to church where the congregation had doubled in size. Eva sat next to me and I felt her nudge me in the ribs as the old priest made his way, with faltering steps, towards the pulpit, wiping spittle away from his mouth as he prepared to speak.

'God has made some of us Good and some of us Evil,' he whined. 'He has made us what we are, and when the end comes, He will unmake us too.' Eva stifled a giggle and began nudging me again as the old priest quoted from the Book of Revelations: 'He that is unjust, let him be unjust still. He who is filthy, let him be filthy still.' He raised his frail voice to a higher pitch and Eva put her hand over her mouth to stop herself from laughing. 'For amongst you there are dogs, and sorcerers, and whores.' Then I saw him look over at Eva with a practiced eye and for a moment I felt her shoulder tense against my jacket.

22. Tia

On the last day of the century, houses were boarded up to prevent the devil from entering and a solitary man with wild hair and vacant eyes marched along the streets carrying a placard announcing the end of days. Our factory put up a notice announcing a temporary closure, saying we workers were too distracted by our anticipated fate to execute our duties properly. Gulls fled across the bay, heading for their nests, and smaller birds gathered under rooftops seeking shelter. The owner of our hostel lit every lamp she could afford and made us huddle in a corner, waiting for the new century to arrive and plunge us all to our doom. Pepe dismissed it all as nonsense and invited me to take a walk with him along the deserted promenade where we found a cafeteria whose owner had not succumbed to the mass hysteria of the town. We sat by a blazing fire and a waitress came along with pastries on a trolley. Pepe chose one.

'Here, take this, Tia. You looks like you need a treat.' Pepe was right. Despite Eva's attempts to cheer me up, I'd been thinking about my parents. Did they miss me? Had they repaid The Fixer's debt? I pushed another envelope of money across the table. Pepe tutted and shook his head, but by now he'd learned not to argue. I was going to pay them back or else. We sat in silence until I asked the question I'd been too scared to ask before, saying the words quietly as if they were the most precious of things.

'How are they?' I asked, and the sound of my voice felt deafening. Pepe looked at me and grinned.

'Thought you'd never ask,' he said. 'Your Ma asks about you every time I goes, and I always tells her the same. You're workin' in a steady job in a decent factory, and that she's not to worry.'

'And Pa?' I asked, remembering the horror on his face in my moonlit room.

Pepe sneered. 'Still got a lovin' for the drink. And your poor Ma, well...' His voice tailed off, leaving me wondering what he might have said next. But I didn't ask. My timid question had been enough for now.

A sudden gust battered the thin windows of the cafeteria, and outside, black clouds were forming in front of the sun. The room went dark. Customers gasped. I heard someone say, 'It *is* the end of days,' before dashing into the deserted street, no doubt intending to race home and lock all the doors before midnight. Pepe looked out of the window. 'Gettin' dark over them hills,' he said. The café fire had reduced to embers. I pulled my shawl around me to keep warm. 'Let's go. Looks like a storm's comin',' Pepe said. Outside, the earth smelt damp and the air was agitated by a constant wind as darkness folded around us. We hurried back to my hostel where Pepe took my hand. He must have seen the worry on my face, wondering about Ma and Pa, and about whether or not the storm would pass, and hoping that by tomorrow, the world would still be turning as it always did. 'You stay steady 'n' count your blessin's, girl,' he said gently. 'Like I says to your Ma, that factory is a gem of a place here in the bay, and you got this hostel here to keep you safe 'n' warm, and friends to look after you.' Then he gave me a friendly smile and left.

Dear Pepe, what a kind and thoughtful man he was. And right. I *did* have friends and I *did* have people around me who seemed to care, and above all I was lucky enough to have steady employment in that wonderful factory in the bay. But as I slipped under the covers of my bed in a hostel filled with the owner's fear-laden lamps, Pepe's reassurances seemed to disappear. What did he mean 'your poor Ma'? Was she in trouble? But I had no sympathy, after what she'd done to me, why should I care? But in my heart, I knew that I shouldn't judge her badly. She hadn't been thinking straight. Jealousy had distorted her mind, turning her almost insane. I pulled the blankets over my shoulders. Poor Ma, nothing went right for her and perhaps there was some truth in her mantra. Maybe those sorrows would always be coming, as if our family was jinxed, and even though I had run away to a better situation that Pepe had described so well, perhaps I would never escape our family misfortune either. I thought about my grandmother, a woman I had never met, the one whose name I shared. Why had Ma called her a tortured soul? And would some evil fate happen to me too? I pulled the blankets in tight. Stop thinking like this, I told myself, but the sense of doom wouldn't go away. I looked at the clock. An hour to midnight. Outside, the wind was pushing the air around like mischievous spirits, and in my semi-sleeping state I imagined them cavorting on my pillow, keeping me awake. And I wondered if my namesake, Sebastiana the elder, was watching me lying there in my bed. Was her spirit alive? Perhaps we never die, I thought. Perhaps our ancestors appear whenever we living ones need them. Maybe, unwittingly, we pull them out of limbo to help us find our way and they stay beside us, gently pushing and pulling us like the to-and-fro of the tides.

When I eventually yielded to sleep it was filled with nightmares. First came butterflies, trapped in an ornate box, their wings tattered where they'd tried to escape. I saw my own hand reaching up to release them, but I was too clumsy to open the clasp and

95

their wings were too fragile to fly. One looked like Eva and she was laughing at some silly joke. I tried again to loosen the clasp, but with every turn it got tighter, and with every movement I felt my stomach churn. Then came a multitude of crows sitting on thin wires. They were screeching like out-of-tune violins and with each note came a stab of pain. One crow, as black as soot, turned its head towards me and the moon lit up its face to reveal a bright-red beak stretched into a mocking grin. Then it was the mouth of a man wearing a black cape. The Fixer was in my dreams and there was lipstick smeared across his cheek. And all this time the clasp on the box kept turning and the butterflies kept struggling against the side of the box, trying to get out and The Fixer was grinning and the pain in my belly was grinding.

I woke up. Between my thighs was warm and wet. I jumped to my feet and something oozed down the inside of my thigh. Blood.

I knew this was coming. I knew that one day my life would change forever. Even so, seeing that red liquid seeping from inside me was too much. 'Ma, help me,' I cried into the empty room. Eva must have heard because she came bursting in and as soon as she saw my problem she burst into laughter.

'Well, girl. Now you're a woman like me.' Eva was only eighteen but seemed so much older. She pulled my bloodied nightgown off and gave me an old cloth. 'Put this between your legs to catch the flow.'

I stood there in that ice-cold room, naked and unprepared. The night air was sharp and cold draughts were whistling through the thin glass of the windows. The clock downstairs chimed midnight. I started to cry. I was faint, but after a few moments, this helped to calm me. I went to the sink and doused my nightgown in cold water as Eva had instructed.

23. Tia

Pepe was right. The first day of the new century was no different to any other. No devils came to take away sinners, the righteous were not despatched to heaven as the priest had suggested and there was no storm either; just a wind that blew all signs of rain away leaving a cold January sun in an endless blue sky. The only difference was that, for once, Eva had been thinking about her future. We took our usual walk along the bay and when she asked me,

'Tia, what do you want in life?' I was taken by surprise.

'I don't know,' I said, because truly I did not. Life had thrown all kinds of things at me and I had simply responded. It didn't occur to me that I could make my own destiny. Besides, women and girls weren't given much choice. 'I suppose I would like to get married and have children,' I said. But as soon as the words left my mouth, I realised how mistaken I was. To be a mother was a tricky thing - Ma and I were strangers. Why would I be any different towards a daughter of my own? Besides, as I looked out across the bay, I could see the coastline of North Africa and the city of Tangiers. People said it was an exciting place with opportunities for all nations to thrive. I saw a steamship slipping across the horizon and wondered where it was going, perhaps to Buenos Aires where people were emigrating to find their fortune. 'And you, Eva? I asked. 'What do you want in life?'

'Me? I want fine dresses and someone to cook for me, and make my bed,' she said and we both laughed at such a thing.

The factory reopened for production and as usual the manager strolled through our floor, laughing and showing off his pure white teeth. He approached my bench and after he'd passed, he turned back and winked, making blood rush to my cheeks, but I avoided his eyes and he walked on, leaving me gawping from my bench. The girls saw what had happened and warned me.

'You want to watch out, girl. Alfonso's twice your age and double the trouble.'

At the factory gates he stood watching us leave, smoking a cheap cigarillo, waving it about like a magician creating illusions with puffs of smoke. One evening he asked if he could walk me home. I kept my head down, scared to look into his so-blue Gypsy eyes. 'Well?' he asked. 'Aren't you going to answer?' I looked up wondering what to say. If I refused, I might lose my job.

'All right,' I said.

He took my elbow and steered me out of the factory into the evening sun. 'You're a funny little thing,' he said, and when I heard his mocking tone, I wondered if I should have said no. We walked towards my hostel, him doing all the talking. 'My father owns all the stables in the bay,' he said taking a deep puff on his cigarillo. 'And I have a special way of breaking in our horses.' I stayed silent, my body tense and my lips clamped shut. I was scared to engage with this man. He was old and I was young. He was loud and I was not. 'I begin with praise,' he continued, without bothering to check if I was interested, 'telling the creature how lovely she is, grooming her, rubbing her slowly with a soft brush. Then I take her into the yard and use a lunging line till she tires. But all the

98

time I am whispering and all the time she is blinking and listening to the murmur of my voice.' He finished talking and turned to me as if expecting a response. I didn't know what to say. What was my place in this conversation? The man's personality was overbearing. How could I make myself heard? Then I remembered the effect Don Francisco had had on me, rendering me passive and unable to resist his fumbling persistence, unable to say no. I bit my lip. Where had all that childhood defiance gone - arguing with my mother, standing my ground, or the petulance of adolescence when I'd altered that dress? Where was the disgust I'd felt at The Fixer, and that ultimate defiance when I'd escaped from home? I was losing my confidence again as if all that had happened to me under that harvest moon had lodged itself inside my soul, filling all the gaps with dread so that there was no space for my spirit to survive. We reached my hostel and I said a quick goodbye, but as I reached my room I realised that the man had got to me. Alfonso was interesting. He was a clever talker, so well informed, knowing so much more than I. So the next day when he leaned over my bench and whispered, 'Tia, you are graceful like my horses,' I liked what he said. And when he walked me back to my hostel and explained how he used a martingale to hold the horse's head down or a gagging-bit if the animal was difficult, I didn't realise he was talking about me.

Then it started - the gossip that brought me down. Each day Alfonso made his rounds and as he approached my bench I could hear my fellow workers whispering just loud enough for me to hear. 'Look at her, grinning like an idiot,' and 'Did you see the way he touched her as he passed?' Soon, they concluded that I was their manager's young mistress, voicing their disapproval openly as if it were an obvious truth. And as if to prove it, two of my new girlfriends began to snub me.

'I don't care if those girls don't talk to me anymore?' I said to Eva, and she frowned in sympathy.

'Be careful, Tia. Gossip can be cruel,' she said and I nodded because even though I said I didn't care, I knew she was right. I remembered how Incarna had talked to Ma, every word laced with disapproval and glee, and recalled my feelings in the *paseo* with everyone watching and judging. I remembered those bells in my village, announcing the return of the church with its relentless censure, and I resolved to act tough to fight the girls' malicious condemnation.

Alfonso began his rounds. I watched him circle the floor, chatting to each girl, leaving my bench until last. He approached, moving slowly, whistling until he reached me and picked a single cork from my basket. He tossed it into the air, winking as he caught it neatly in the palm of his hand. I saw the girls watching and I raised my head in defiance. Then he grazed my forearm with his finger and a glorious sensation ran through my skin. I couldn't control it.

'You're blushing, Tia,' he said, laughing, as he took my elbow and led me gently into a cloistered yard where piles of shredded cork were waiting to be delivered to the linoleum factory in Algeciras. He moved closer and took a deep breath as if he was going to smell me. Then he cupped his hands around my face and kissed my cheeks. I closed my eyes. The tang of his body was sweet. When I opened them he'd backed off and was lighting a cigarillo. I watched, mesmerised as coils of smoke spiralled upwards. He moved forward again, holding the cigarillo between his so-white teeth. The smoke curled up gracefully as he rubbed his palms slowly up and down my back as if grooming his horse. I stood completely still. My eyelids flickered. He removed his cigarillo and put his lips on my neck. A blast of pain - or was it pleasure? - shot to the space between my legs. I let out a sigh, and as soon as he heard it, he took my hand and steered me, like a filly to her stable, into a small storeroom at the back of the cloister. As he turned to close the door, he flicked his still-smoking butt onto the floor outside.

100

The storeroom was dim with only a small fanlight for illumination, but his eyes were gleaming and moist. He pushed his body against me and I felt him hard against my skirt.

'No,' I said.

'Come on, Tia,' he said, grabbing my arm.

'Let go,' I shrieked, but he gripped even tighter.

'Don't pretend you don't want to,' he said, bending down to lift my skirt. I gasped, not from his actions but because, over the curve of his back, white smoke was curling in from the base of the door.

'Look,' I said. His hands were gripping my thigh. The smoke billowed in. 'Look!' I shouted this time. His hand moved up. Hadn't he seen it? Smelt it too?' I tried to push him away but he held me against the wall, grabbing my wrists and twisting them so tight that I whimpered in pain. I had to resist or else we would burn, so I shoved my knee into his groin and he buckled. I grabbed the door handle. The metal was hot.

'You bitch!' he said, doubled over and drawing in a lungful of poisonous air. I yanked the door open and dashed into the production room where thick black smoke had filled the space. Sparks were flying and soon they would be on the benches where piles of cork stoppers lay in tinder-dry baskets, waiting to ignite. Where were the water hoses? Embers were dropping like fireballs at my feet. Workers were running in all directions, disorientated, choking on the smoke. There was a crack and a surge of flame leapt down, catching the benches, licking them like tongues. The corks went up with a roar and people squealed as they fell. Flames engulfed their bodies and screams of agony rang out everywhere. There was only one door that led to safety, swinging wildly on its hinges, exposing the light from the bay then closing to the darkness of death. It was then that the hose system started, but weakly, not like it should have. Steam rose, making it difficult to see. I had to get to that door. I had to escape. So, dropping to my knees, I fumbled blindly across the sodden floor, my skirt caked in a mulch of cork and soot. The hoses trickled to a halt. Alfonso was beside me now. 'Get me out of here,' he bleated. The door swung open. A gust of air blew in, reigniting the flames. They rose like lions, and all I could hear was their roar. I saw the door, still open, still swinging. Beyond that was the safety of the shore. I had to get there, but my skirt was heavy with dirt and steam. I tried to lift it but Alfonso was clinging to the hem. I tugged. He wouldn't let go. I had no choice. I pulled it off, petticoats too and ran in my bloomers, as low as I could towards the exit. Bodies were strewn everywhere. I tripped and fell. Alfonso passed me, holding my sodden clothing over his head. I raised my arms to him for help, but he sneered and turned away. The door was still open. He would be saved. He reached up to release the catch. But at his moment of triumph, it slammed shut and I heard him yelp. Flames devoured the back of his hand. Then the door jerked open again, and someone was dragging him out.

Now I was alone. Sparks fell like blazing rain, burning my face and singeing my hair. The roar of the fire made my head pound and blackness overcame me. I couldn't breathe. I let my body go. Surely this was the end. I sank to the floor, too weak to fight. But next to me was Eva. She reached out and held my hand. We helped each other up, the strength of one feeding the weakness of the other. The door was open. We burst through, running for our lives, away from that burning building, along the shoreline towards the sea. Then we fell together by the water's edge and I looked up and saw dark embers floating down like black snow, casting a tainted veil over the whole of the bay. Through the gloom I glimpsed Alfonso clutching his burnt hand and demanding to be seen by the doctors, raising his voice above the screams of the dying and the silence of the dead. How pathetic he looked. And all the while they were bringing out the charred bodies of our fellow workers and laying them out, one by one, onto the sand.

Part Three – Just Mariangeles

24. Mariangeles

Mariangeles opened the door to Tia's bedroom. It was empty. She ran downstairs and searched the kitchen and then the pantry. She went to the salon and the workshop and searched there too. Where was the girl? By now she should be getting ready to meet The Fixer. Then she saw the strongbox in the hall. Its lid had been forced open. She peered inside. Their money had gone. 'Sebastiana?' she called. No reply. She went to the back door. The bolt they snapped shut at night had already been opened this morning. Oh Sebastiana. What have you done?' she wailed, going into the kitchen and sinking into a chair. Their daughter had vanished. Their daughter had gone.

Later that morning, the sun was streaming through the kitchen, illuminating The Fixer's bill, still on the table. Two bowls of cooling porridge sat between Mariangeles and Bartolome, untouched, as they contemplated their daughter's unplanned departure. Mariangeles was distraught.

'She should've been on the way to Seville by now,' she wailed.

Bartolome nodded. 'What was she thinking, leaving us like this?' There was no need for an answer. They both knew why. Their whole scheme had been selfish, agreeing to The Fixer's plan to suit themselves rather than their daughter. And what exactly was his plan? All Mariangeles knew was that he would have taken Sebastiana to a hostel in Seville and the next day he would have introduced her to her new employer. But who was that employer? The owner of a cigar factory, she supposed, just as Incarna had described, but Mariangeles hadn't bothered to ask. Her only thought had been that the girl would be gone from their household and Bartolome would fall into her arms once more.

And then there was this bill, sitting there on the table. It had all seemed so simple. First, The Fixer would deliver Sebastiana to her workplace, then he would return to collect the payment for his services, and after that, bit by bit, Sebastiana would send them a proportion of her wages so that her parents' outlay would be repaid. It was a good plan, with which Bartolome had firmly agreed, but now the girl had run away and the entire scheme had gone wrong. Now they would have to pay and get nothing in return. Mariangeles scooped up their uneaten porridge and tipped it down the sink.

'How in God's name are we going to pay?' she wailed.

'That's easy,' Bartolome said. 'Don't!'

The porridge got stuck in the drain so she turned on the tap.

'I have to pay, Bartolome. You don't understand.'

'Of course I understand, woman. Don't pay him. It's as easy as that.'

Mariangeles hesitated then spoke over the running water, as if this might conceal her folly. 'I borrowed the money to pay The Fixer,' she said, forcing the porridge through the narrow gap in the drain.

'You did what?'

'I got a loan from that Garcia man and promised to pay him back bit by bit.'

'Why in God's name did you do that? '

'I had to. We needed money quickly.'

'Well, return it then,' Bartolome scoffed, but Mariangeles could see that her husband was out of his depth. She handled the money, not him.

'I can't,' she said quietly. 'Sebastiana took it all with her.' Bartolome stared at his wife as if he couldn't quite take it in. 'She stole the money from our strongbox before she left,' she added, and Bartolome dropped his head into his hands.

'My poor Tia,' he said. 'What did we do to make you act like this?'

'As if you didn't know,' Mariangeles snapped back.

'It wasn't my fault Don Francisco took a fancy to our girl,' he retorted.

'And you! What about you?'

'That wasn't my fault either,' he said.

'So, whose fault was it then?'

'It was yours, woman. You drove her away with your constant condemnations.'

'But you agreed to our plan, Bartolome. Don't blame it all on me.'

Bartolome got up from the table and turned to go. 'I'll have no more to do with this,' he said, retreating to his workshop and locking the door. Mariangeles slumped onto a chair. Oh, the treachery of the man; so hypocritical, so irresponsible, so immature! And how quickly her plan had gone wrong. She'd been anticipating this day for so long, when, alone in the house at last, she would reach out to Bartolome, touch his arm and caress his chest. He would turn to her and peck her on the cheek, then little by little they would re-enact the rituals of their lovemaking and afterwards she would rest in his arms, satisfied and content. This was her dream but it was turning into a nightmare. She went upstairs, sat on Sebastiana's bed and picked up the nightgown her daughter had abandoned in haste. She held it to her face and inhaled deeply, drawing in the natural scent of her daughter's body, and sighed. Oh, Sebastiana. What have we done? But part of her was still mad. The girl had spoiled everything, first with her flirting and now with her escape. She pulled the nightgown away from her face and stared at it. Was she holding the garment of a harlot, or was it that of an innocent child? And although she searched for an answer she could not find one to satisfy her agitated mind.

Later that day The Fixer came.

'I've been waiting at the crossroads, madam. Where is she?'

'She's gone, Father. She's left.'

'Left? After all I have done to secure her employment?'

'Sit down, please. Would you like a manzanilla? Bartolome, fetch him a drink.'

The Fixer slumped so violently into the wicker chair that Mariangeles thought it might break. Then he crossed his long legs in the space between them, gulped back the alcohol and slammed the glass back onto the table. Bartolome refilled it.

'Doña Mariangeles, these plans don't get made on their own. There are people I have paid for their time and dedication, deposits for securing a place in a hostel, persuasions to employers for your daughter's employment. Do you expect me to take on these financial burdens myself?' The Fixer drank again then leaned forward in the chair speaking first at one and then the other. The chair creaked with every move. 'Doña Mariangeles, you overestimate my patience. Don Bartolome, I am not a simple man. You must pay what you owe or...'

'Or what?' Mariangeles responded but she knew what he meant.

106

The Fixer was a cruel man and she had no doubt that he could find a way to hurt them. Bartolome refilled the man's glass and Mariangeles offered him a platter of ham. For half an hour The Fixer devoured their food and drank their liquor, and bit by bit he relaxed. Eventually he spoke and his speech was slurred.

'I am not unreasonable, my friends. I can appreciate your dilemma. I want you both to be content. Therefore, I propose that you pay me by instalments.' He stopped and looked Mariangeles directly. 'But, madam, I require one of those payments – however small – right now, or else there will be trouble.' Mariangeles nodded. Once more the man had put her under his spell and she could no longer argue.

'Keep our guest company, Bartolome,' she said. 'I'll be back in a moment.' She went into the pantry, closed the door quietly so that Bartolome couldn't hear, and hauled a sack of almonds out of the corner. She untied the string and plunged her hand into the dusty contents until she found it. Shaking the pouch free, she pulled it open. A few duros was hardly enough, but perhaps it would keep the man quiet for now. They were both drinking when she re-entered the kitchen, The Fixer with his feet on her table and Bartolome leaning forward with reddened cheeks. 'Here, take it,' she said throwing her last savings onto the table. Bartolome looked surprised but said nothing and poured himself another drink. The Fixer counted the cash and tucked it into a chest pocket then stood unsteadily and turned to Mariangeles.

'Madam, you are very wise. I will leave now but will return next month for the second instalment.' He bowed low but there was a new dynamic to his actions - no longer bowing graciously, hoping for a contract, as he had when they first met. This time, beneath his low-bent back, Mariangeles thought she saw a smirk.

25. Mariangeles

Incarna knew everyone in the district, and when Mariangeles had asked, as casually as she could, about money lenders, Alberto Garcia's name had been the first on her lips.

'Operates near the harbour, Mari, from an old wooden cabin between the fish market and the tavern. Clever bugger gets the ones on the way there, already too drunk to earn anything off the boats, and the fishermen on their way back from the tavern, who's drunk all their wages.'

Mariangeles stood outside Alberto Garcia's cabin clutching her basket. The harbour was busy with fishermen returning with their catch, and gulls were fighting with each other for scraps of abandoned fish. The air smelt foul, but she took a deep breath and prepared to enter. Last time she was here she'd been struck by the melancholy in Garcia's eyes. He hadn't stop sighing as he talked, as if the whole world was on his shoulders or that he hated his job so much that he was continually about to abandon it. Poor man, she thought, having to listen to every excuse for non-repayment and watching so many men plunge themselves into ruin, that he had lost all reason for joy. What a life. Day or night, desperate men who stank of booze rapping on his door.

She opened it and peered in. There were no windows so it took a moment for her eyes to adjust, but he was still there, smoking his pipe and counting a pile of notes and coins on his battered pine table.

'Good morning, Mr. Garcia, she said brightly, hoping her manner would smooth the path for what she had to say.

'Is it?' he said.

She closed the door behind her and immediately the busy world of the harbour disappeared as the interior was plunged into darkness. Garcia lit a lamp with what looked like a practiced hand, and it seemed to Mariangeles that negotiations probably worked best in the intimacy of this cabin where no one could disturb him and where his clients felt untouched by the judgements of sobriety.

'Mr. Garcia, I've brought you some produce from our garden,' she said, placing her basket on the table.

Garcia peered in and sighed deeply. 'Madam, do I look like a man who eats vegetables? Where is my money?' The lamp flickered over Garcia's face. It was chubby and pale, no doubt from spending all day in this dark, fetid cabin.

She coughed. 'I err… I've come here to tell you that my first payment will be delayed.' She smiled as convincingly as possible, knowing that Garcia usually dealt with men, not women, so perhaps her charms might save her from embarrassment.

'Madam, this is not acceptable. You know my terms.'

'But Señor Garcia, I am a woman of my word. I will not let you down. A few days are all I ask.'

'Three, madam. I will give you three days and no more.'

When Mariangeles emerged from Garcia's cabin, Bartolome was still hiding round the corner where she had left him.

'What happened? What did he say?'

110

'I have three days to find the money, or else.'

'Well, *I* haven't got it,' Bartolome said defiantly.

'Hasn't Don Francisco paid you for those bridles?' she asked, and when Bartolome hesitated, Mariangeles knew. 'How many? she asked. 'How many cases of booze did you buy this time?' They argued all the way back to the crossroads and when they reached the tannery she thought about Sebastiana and how they'd sent her to work there when she was only eleven. Bartolome should have gone instead. 'Why don't you see if they've got work for you here? she suggested.'

'Who me? A skilled craftsman working in a tannery? I fashion artisan products using the finest cured hides and you want me to work at the dirty end of the business? No thank you!' he said, marching ahead so fast that Mariangeles found it hard to keep up. She spent the rest of the day in the kitchen as far away from Bartolome as possible. It wasn't her fault that they were in this mess. It was her husband and their constant dilemmas, dipping between times of plenty and times of none. She sighed, disappointed at the disarray of her plan. With Sebastiana gone, she'd been hoping for a loving reunion with her husband; a chance to rekindle their love and resume their passions in the marital bed. But she no longer had the appetite for his caresses because her heart had been broken all over again. How could he be so irresponsible buying all that booze without consulting her? He knew that next month they would have to pay The Fixer, and, together with the loan from Garcia, they would have managed it. Besides, it was she who controlled the expenses and it was she who had spent the last two nightmare days trying to pacify The Fixer and now old man Garcia, whilst her husband did absolutely nothing. She thrust her head into her hands and stared at the bleach-clean tablecloth, so stiff, so barren and dry. What on earth was she going to do?

It was only then, at the lowest point in her thinking that her mind strayed to Sebastiana. It had been two days since her daughter's unexpected departure and only now did Mariangeles wonder where she had gone.

Incarna knocked at the kitchen door.

'Hello, Mari. Thought I'd come and see how you are.' She looked around the kitchen. 'Sebastiana's left then?' she said and Mariangeles coughed to clear her throat. She'd been expecting this and had prepared her answer.

'Yes, Incarna, she left a few days ago.'

'Well, I never thought you'd do it, Mari. How is she getting on?

'She's doing very well in her job at the cigarette factory, and earning plenty of money.' Mariangeles spoke quickly to conceal her charade and Incarna seemed satisfied, at least for now. But if Incarna discovered the truth, then the whole neighbourhood would hear about Sebastiana's flight and their debts not only to one, but two very dangerous men. Then they would be in danger of losing the confidence of their new and hard-won customers. She had to keep Sebastiana's flight a secret and she had to make some money to pay off the two debts. But how?

Bartolome was still snoring in bed when Mariangeles slipped out of the house. In her basket, concealed by a cloth, were several shoe lasts from his workshop. There was a cobbler in town who might buy them for good money and she hoped she had selected the ones that Bartolome hardly used. As she walked down the hill to the crossroads, the basket seemed to grow heavier with every step, so when she reached the place where east met west, she rested on the milestone and looked out across the glittering sea. Far off, a steamship was silently crossing the horizon like a swan gliding across a pond. Nearby, wagtails were flitting in the bushes then alighting at her feet, hoping for scraps. She felt a breeze on her

112

cheeks and this gentle airborne caress rendered her vulnerable.

'Mama,' she called into the air. 'Mama, you poor soul. Can you see me now? Selling off our possessions to survive? Can you see your wretch of a daughter who ignored your advice?' She remembered the day Bartolome had asked for her hand in marriage and her mother's slow consideration of the matter. Her mama had moved through most of her life in slow motion, her elegant neck supporting a troubled mind, and her head inclined slightly to the side as she declared a firm, 'No!'

Mariangeles shook her head. Why had she ignored her mother's decision? Why had she run away with the once-so-charming Bartolome and ended up like this? 'You were right, Mama,' she said to the breeze, 'and I was wrong.'

The steamship had almost completed its passage across the liquid horizon before Mariangeles got up and shook herself off. This thing had to be done. Selling their valuables was the only answer - starting with Bartolome's possessions, not hers. By the time she reached town her arms were aching, but she negotiated a good price for the old lasts and, fortified by a morsel of good luck, she decided to take a walk down Main Street towards their old shop. As she strolled between the tall houses, memories of her old life swooped in like a sudden wind and threatened to dislodge her resolve. She sighed. Perhaps this was a bad idea, revisiting the place where she had once been happy. From the end of the street she heard the sound of voices and hurried on wondering what was happening. When she reached the end, she saw a group of well-dressed men, women and children, waiting to enter the church. They were exchanging greetings and laughing together as if the world was theirs and the world was good. Mariangeles shrank into the shadows, not wanting to be recognised because here were the same bull breeders and cotton growers and stud farmers gathered together as they always did, and the same children, grown a little now, who had played with Sebastiana. She frowned. It wasn't Sunday, but then she realised that tomorrow was All Souls' Day; and tonight was the Mass where people honoured their dead. She'd been so busy with her problems that she'd barely consulted the calendar. Strange how she had remembered her mother on this special day while sitting on that milestone, and she made a note to think of her again on the journey back. The group entered the church and their voices became muffled as the door slammed shut, leaving her alone in the square, standing next to their dear old shop. Dusk descended and in that darkening silence she could hear her own breathing. Slowly she raised her eyes to take in the façade. Her heart fluttered as she read the sign hanging over the doorway, rusting now, but its letters still decipherable in the twilight. *Luxury Goods for Gentlemen and Ladies.* She closed her eyes and listened through the muffled sounds of the choir singing in the church, to other noises emerging from the past: Bartolome's shears snipping into hides; his hammering of studs into fancy harnesses; the rattle of her sewing machine on the uppers of crisp tan brogues; and the cry when she pricked her finger embroidering suede slippers for a banquet at the town hall. How did we lose it all? she asked herself, trying to expel the memories that were causing her such pain.

Sighing, she walked away from the shop, away from the town and out into the darkness of the countryside, towards their modest and now daughterless home. At the crossroads she sat on the same milestone as before, except now the only light came from the tannery building where the night shift was just about to start. Through the bright-lit windows she saw men preparing hides for soaking, and others at benches, creating oils to nourish the skins. In the shadows of the yard she saw a familiar figure. Pepe had finished unloading and was feeding his animal. She smiled, remembering his generosity in taking her family and all their possessions away from the cholera-stricken town and asking only a pittance for his fee. Not all men are bad, she thought, only the one I married and the one my mother married too. What was it about the women in her family who repeatedly made the wrong choices? Grandmother, great-grandmother - they all had a story to tell. The light from the tannery cast a muted glow over the landscape so she closed her eyes, deliberately maximising the darkness, trying to evoke the image of her mother and her grandmother standing together at the well. Her mother's head was inclined to the side as always, her elegant neck stretched into the light whilst her grandmother wiped the blood from her daughter's swollen cheek. Across her jawline was a bruise.

'You can't go on like this,' she remembered her grandmother saying. 'He'll kill you one day, I swear.' Mariangeles put her hand to her own jaw, as if feeling for a bruise that would bring her closer to her past. Poor Ma, who'd endured her husband's cruelty, but continued to sew beautiful dresses with her steel needles and silent strength. 'Dear Ma, you could have been much more,' she whispered into the night air. Then she crossed herself in remembrance of that fatal blow that had put her mother in her grave, and shook her head as she remembered, once again, her family's lament. *Sorrows and waves never arrive alone.* Was it really her turn to experience sorrow? Wasn't escape from cholera, and the shame of Don Francisco enough? She trudged up the hill, opened the door to their home and listened to the sounds of Bartolome still snoring in their bed. He must have spent the whole day in there. She laughed a sad little laugh, remembering how, until recently, she had desired him to the point of obsession. What had she been thinking? Had she been insane? Then she remembered her raging jealousy of Sebastiana. What an utter fool she had been. How quick she had been to blame her daughter for things out of her control. She shook her head. Perhaps her feelings were nothing to do with Sebastiana. Perhaps her jealousy was really some form of envy at the girl's burgeoning beauty and the loss of her own.

She tiptoed into the pantry, pulled out the sack of almonds, and retrieved her pouch. Inserting the money from the lasts, she pushed it as far down the sack as she could and tied the string. This was *her* secret, nothing to do with Bartolome; a problem to solve on her own, without the intervention of her hapless husband. Besides, he probably wouldn't notice that his lasts were missing, so perhaps she could take something else tomorrow.

26. Mariangeles

Blunt shears, templates for boots that had gone out of fashion, an assortment of dyes, and waxed threads that he didn't use anymore, shiny eyelets, studs, buckles, and laces of differing lengths and widths, were all placed in her basket and transported down the hill until, day by day, bit by bit, the pouch in her almond sack grew fat.

It was almost a month before she'd accumulated enough to visit Garcia. As she entered, he was sitting with his feet propped on a small stove that heated the November air, making the cabin seem even stuffier than usual.

'Three days, I said, madam. Not three weeks.'

'Señor Garcia, forgive me, but I have done my best.' Mariangeles placed her savings carefully onto the table and while he counted them, she took in the gnarled and stained surface where countless transactions had taken place before. She smiled. Garcia's face was pale and smooth, yet this table was not. The two didn't match, as if the man's baby face was the outward representation of a character that was damaged and stained inside.

'Is this it?' Garcia said.

'I cannot bring you more, but I'll be back next week with another instalment,' she said hopefully. Garcia sat back in his chair and reached for his pipe. He didn't appear angry.

'Interest, dear lady. It will cost you double for your delay.' Mariangeles nodded. She was expecting this, but what else could she do?

On the way back she took a detour along Main Street, and, once again, she stood in front of their old shop. This time she peered through the mullion-glass window. Through the grime she saw cobwebs in every corner and what looked like mouse droppings on the floor. Why hadn't the bank found a tenant to keep the place nice? she thought, remembering the warren of rooms above the shop which she had kept so neat and clean for them to live in. She remembered the day she gave birth to Sebastiana, and all that hope for a better future, and how everything had gone so very wrong. But at least here she'd felt alive and connected. At least here in this town she'd had a life. Her shoulders dropped, picturing herself so calm before and now so frantic, scurrying about trying to pay off debts to two unpleasant men with nobody even noticing her efforts. She wondered if she wasn't just fading away, dissolving into the atmosphere, becoming a nobody, almost numb. Then she remembered The Fixer. He was due to collect her second instalment in a few days and she had just paid her secret savings to Garcia. In all this mess she hadn't been thinking straight. What was she going to do? Perhaps Bartolome had received his monthly payment from Don Francisco, and perhaps she could get hold of it before he wasted it on booze again. She hurried up the hill eager to find out, but she would have to be careful. Confrontation made Bartolome angry. She would have to ask nicely so that he would oblige.

When she arrived she was surprised to find Pepe sitting at their kitchen table. Bartolome's eyes were shining as he poured himself a drink.

'Pepe's brought us this,' Bartolome said, pushing an envelope across their table. He'd already opened it. 'It's from Sebastiana.'

Mariangeles gasped. 'Where is she Pepe? Is she all right?' She grabbed the envelope expecting a letter, but money fell out instead. She stared at it. 'Is this from her?' she asked, frowning. She looked over at Pepe who answered carefully, and it seemed to Mariangeles that he was holding something back.

'She says she wants to pay off her debt. Forgive me, Mariangeles, I told her she didn't need to because of your contract with Don Francisco, but she insisted.'

'But where is she?' Mariangeles's heart was full, and this rush of unexpected emotion made her giddy.

'She's fine. Living in a girls' hostel with steady work and says you're not to worry.'

'But where, Pepe? Please tell me where.'

'Forgive me again, Mariangeles, but she asked me not to tell.'

Mariangeles slumped in a chair. She deserved this humiliation, driving her daughter away with her accusations. But now she was thinking. How did Pepe know all this? And how did he know where she had gone? Then she realised. It must have been Pepe who took Sebastiana to her new destination. Yes, she decided, that was it.

'Did you take her east or west, Pepe? At least you can tell me that.' Pepe looked down at his feet.

'I can't, Mariangeles. I promised.'

That night Mariangeles waited for Bartolome to settle in bed, then coughed to get his attention.

'Have you received Don Francisco's payment?' she asked carefully.

'Of course, woman, and he was very pleased with my work. Said my bridles and breeching straps were superb and that he wants me to provide a dozen extra cinches this month 'cos his drivers are so careless.'

'So, where is it?'

'Where's what?'

'The money, Bartolome. I must have it to pay The Fixer.'

'Why do you need *my* money when we've got Sebastiana's? We can pay him with that,' he scoffed. Then he turned away, pulled the covers over his shoulders and immediately started to snore. Mariangeles closed her eyes in exasperation. What was the point in arguing with the man? She rolled over as far away from him as she could and thought about Sebastiana. Thank goodness she was safe and able to send them money, and thank goodness for Pepe taking an interest and looking after her like that. Then she smiled to herself, because during the conversation with Pepe earlier that day, he had addressed her, not once, not twice, but three times by her full name. *Mariangeles* He had spoken it gently and respectfully so that, just for a second she felt whole again. For once she wasn't fading away. For the first time in a long time, she felt real.

27. Mariangeles

December arrived. Mariangeles took the last items she dared from Bartolome's workshop and sold them in town. After that she would have to sell her own things instead. She visited Garcia and he took her modest payment without complaint. Was he beginning to fall for her charms? Afterwards she took a detour to the old shop again. It seemed to be calling her, enticing her back to her old life every time she visited. Why had no one taken on the lease, she wondered, then realised. A new shopping development had opened on the other side of town, so, apart from churchgoers, this area was almost deserted.

Mid-month, The Fixer arrived, moving slowly around the room, picking up her ornaments, turning them over to read the potter's credentials, turning them around to check for cracks. Flustered, she fetched Sebastiana's money and handed it to him, trying to avoid his eyes. What was it about this man that paralysed her? He counted her payment slowly, as if checking that she hadn't tricked him then looked around the room as if expecting something else. Mariangeles fetched a plate of ham and set a bottle of manzanilla beside him. Was this what he wanted? He sat down at her table and spoke with his mouth full.

'Don't think you can bribe me with your wares, Doña Mariangeles.' You still owe me a lot of money and will do so for some time yet.' She nodded, unable to speak, unable to look him in the eye. He knew her secret. He knew that she had tried to despatch her daughter into the care of a stranger without checking his credentials, without making sure her daughter would be safe, and this unwholesome connection between them felt like glue. Would she ever detach herself from this revolting man? And now here he was in her kitchen, clutching her daughter's money in his nasty, thin fingers. Not Bartolome's money, as it should have been, but their daughter's hard-earned wages, sent to make sure they could pay her debt. She tried to hold The Fixer's gaze, but the burden of her betrayal was too much and she bowed her head in shame. He must have caught her mood because he stood up and advanced as she retreated, until her back was against the wall. The odour of his body overwhelmed her and when he spoke his breath was dank with their wine. She braced herself as he pushed his bony hips against her waist and raised both his hands - the right holding Sebastiana's money, and the bony fingers of his left wrapped around her neck. 'If you don't pay all that I am owed, I'll wring your throat.'

When he left, Mariangeles's heart was beating so fast she had to sit down. Her head was spinning with The Fixer's threat. She felt sick, she felt lonely and desperate to share her burden with someone who would understand. But whom could she tell? Whom could she trust? She heard Incarna call from outside.

'You in there, Mari?' her neighbour said. Mariangeles jumped up, brushed down her apron, put on a smile and opened the door. Incarna bustled in and sat in her usual chair. Mariangeles remained standing, hoping her neighbour's visit would be brief. 'Everything all right?' Incarna asked. 'Only I just seen that Fixer man leaving?'

'We were concluding our business, that's all,' Mariangeles said, flustered at her neighbours unexpected arrival. 'Would you like some cake?' she added. Eating pastries seemed the only way to distract her neighbour, but Incarna would not be distracted.

'I've heard a rumour, Mari, and you might not like what I have to say.' Mariangeles sighed. Had her neighbour discovered her lie about the whereabouts of Sebastiana? Her heart was thumping again. Was her falsity about to be disclosed? And as a result, was client confidence in the family business about to tumble? Incarna popped a lump of cake into her mouth and leaned forward. 'Some say The Fixer's not who we thought he was. They say he fixes things all right, but instead of putting them girls into factories, they end up in brothels instead.' She swallowed then continued. 'You see, Mari, our Fixer, our Manolo Jimenez Torres, is nothing but a pimp!' Incarna sat back and smirked. Mariangeles gasped. Surely this couldn't be true? But if it was, then she would have sent her daughter to a terrible fate. She stared at Incarna and Incarna stared back. There was a moment of stillness between them; two women so very different, two women so unaligned. How could she explain to Incarna that Sebastiana hadn't gone with him? How could she admit that she'd lied? Then something was happening. Her vision was darkening. Her head was spinning. Her legs felt heavy. They buckled and she grabbed the side of the table to stop herself from falling. The burden of these last few months had been too much. She was falling. She had to let go.

'Here, Mari, take my seat,' Incarna was saying and through the fog, Mariangeles thought she heard kindness in her neighbour's words. She reached out. Incarna grasped her arm and led her to the chair. Mariangeles' head was still reeling and her stomach dipped. What was happening? She felt sick. Incarna fetched water and placed a rug over her lap. She gently touched her forearm. 'What is it, Mari, dear? Something is troubling you and I want to help.' Mariangeles allowed the cool water to travel down her throat and it seemed to revive her. I have to tell someone, she thought, or else my heart will burst. She looked up at Incarna who seemed different now; more respectful, more kind. I might as well be honest, she thought. What was there to lose? So, for the first time in their fragile friendship, Mariangeles talked and Incarna listened, and with each revelation Incarna squeezed her arm and rubbed the back of her hand to comfort her, as tears fell down Mariangeles's cheeks and dissolved into her apron. When everything had spilled from her lips and she had stopped sobbing, Incarna made them both a pot of tea and sat beside Mariangeles.

'You'll find her, Mari, don't you worry,' she whispered and it seemed to Mariangeles that her neighbour was sincere.

The rest of December passed quickly. Incarna brought her own cakes now, which the two women devoured with genuine conversation and a pot of tea at the kitchen table.

'You know, Mari, I always thought you was a bit stuck up for my liking, but now I can see that you're not,' Incarna said.

Mariangeles managed a smile. 'I just don't like your tittle-tattle, that's all.'

'Fair enough but I'm not like you, Mari. Aint got no hobbies, can't read, so what else can I do all day but talk about this and that?

'Well, all I ask is that you don't bring it to my door, all right?'

Incarna nodded. 'I promise,' she said and Mariangeles sighed with relief. There had been a softening on both sides and Incarna seemed to accept her criticism, but she doubted her neighbour could keep her promise if another juicy dilemma were to arise.

Bartolome spent all day in his cellar and when he did emerge, his gait was unsteady. It seemed to Mariangeles that he had retreated into an alcohol-laden world that she could not enter - and why would she want to anyway? The man was so self-absorbed that

124

he seemed totally unaware of his surroundings. Not once did he question how Mariangeles was paying off their debt to Garcia. And not once did he notice the absence of his tools and materials. In fact, they hardly spoke until one evening he thrust a list of dishes into Mariangeless's hand as if she was the cook and he was the client. Bartolome had decided to celebrate the beginning of the new century, inviting Don Francisco and a few other customers to his home.

Crates of alcohol filled the cellar and she had prepared platters of food that she'd covered in muslin and left on the cellar table. Mariangeles had done her best. The party started at eight and just before midnight she went down to the cellar where several men were lounging on the floor and Bartolome was standing in the middle, boasting about his workmanship. No one noticed her gathering up the dirty plates and no one addressed her as she cut the celebratory cake that she had prepared so carefully. She went back upstairs, feeling invisible again, and retreated to bed where she lay listening to the racket two floors below. She closed her eyes and let out a long, deep sigh. She'd had enough of their noises, she'd had enough of her husband's idle boasting and the drunken arguments that seemed to rattle the entire house. She rolled over and pulled the covers over her body. She'd had enough of everything.

In the grey, morning light of the first day of the twentieth century, Mariangeles made a decision. Why should they use their daughter's money to pay The Fixer's debt? It wasn't fair. My soak of a husband can pay it off instead. After all, his contract with Don Francisco had brought in enough money to survive, if only he would stop drinking it all away. So, when Pepe arrived later with another envelope from Sebastiana, Mariangeles went straight to the almond sack, slipped the money into the pouch and plunged it deep inside the almonds with extra force, as if to confirm her resolve. Then she stood in the shadows of her cool pantry and put her hands together in prayer. Please, Sebastiana, come back, she thought. Then I can return this money to you and we can start again. She wanted this to happen. She wanted her daughter back. She wanted to make amends. But then she frowned. In the back of her mind she still wasn't sure of the girl's character. If she hadn't been so coquettish, flirting with Don Francisco, then none of this would have happened. Mariangeles shook her head, trying to fathom her daughter's motivation but when she couldn't, she gave up, closed the pantry door and returned to the kitchen. Pouring Pepe a cup of tea, they settled down for a brief chat. It had become a habit to talk for a while and each time he came, Mariangeles was tempted to ask him the question he had sworn not to answer. *Where is she, Pepe?* But she knew how unfair her question would be, both to him and to her daughter, so she remained silent, and as they chatted, she realised that Pepe had shaved his face more closely and was wearing a new tweed jacket.

28. Mariangeles

Mariangeles rifled through her wardrobe and selected a shawl that no longer kept out the wind, a belt that no longer reached around her waist, and a pair of boots she'd been saving for best. They weren't worth much but they would have to do. Then there was the flamenco dress she had made for the *paseo*. She pulled it off its hanger and held it close to her body, considering its worth. The burgundy-red background matched the thread she used on her embroidered suede shoes and the raspberry-red polka dots made her smile. She inspected the seams and admired the stitching along the ruffled hem. How could she sell something that she had made so beautifully, just like her mother had taught her? So, she returned it to the rail and closed the door to her wardrobe. Selling her dress would be the last resort.

Snow had fallen on the mountain when she set off to the crossroads, and the sun was yet to fill the village with enough heat to melt the ice on the hill. She slid and stumbled and skidded her way down until she reached the milestone by the tannery where, as usual, she rested to catch her breath. In the yard, men were collecting hides from Pepe's cart. She watched for a few moments, standing still so that no one would notice her, and saw that as the men went to and fro, from inside to out and back again, they slapped Pepe on his back and made jokes as if they liked him and enjoyed his company. How pleasant it all seemed and how much nicer than the conflict and anger raging through her home. She sighed and hurried on to the crossroads. Her toes were cold, her fingers pinched and her exhaled breath made regular bursts of pale mist as she pounded along the curved lane that led into town. Behind her she heard a cart.

'Mariangeles, need a lift?' Pepe asked.

She laughed. 'You're not going my way,' she said, and her voice sounded youthful, like a teenage girl.

'I could if you wanted me to,' he said, but Mariangeles shook her head.

'It's all right. I'll see you next week when you visit.'

Pepe flicked the reins to turn Jefe back to the crossroads. She watched carefully. Which way would he go? When it reached the end, the cart turned east and Mariangeles smiled because she had worked it out. Pepe was travelling east to collect cork from the forest of the Alcordonales and a month later he would come to visit her with Sebastiana's money. So her daughter hadn't gone west to Seville as Mariangeles had thought. She'd gone east to the Bay of Gibraltar.

Next day Incarna came.

'Perhaps you could go over there to find her,' she said as they sat together with their pot of tea. 'You could have a little adventure.'

'Sebastiana doesn't want to be found, Incarna. So, I think I should let her be.'

'As you like, Mari, but there may come a time when you need her and she will need you.' Mariangeles wondered what her neighbour meant, but she didn't like to ask. Their new-found trust was a delicate thing, like the vegetables that grew in her garden; ready to

128

flourish but subject to the whims of winter beyond their control. If their situation got any worse, would Incarna remain her friend? If they became destitute, would she still help her out? Still, she made a note of her neighbour's suggestion. Maybe, when the time was right, she would ask Pepe to take her on his cart and she would be reunited with Sebastiana. And this time she would hug her and hold her tight, and try not to think about her daughter's character. And this time she would address her as Tia.

The month passed. Pepe was due. Mariangeles removed her apron, arranged her hair and waited. All morning she waited and again in the afternoon. Bartolome made frequent trips through the kitchen and down into the cellar but she ignored him. Pepe was much better company than her husband now. She waited throughout the evening too, but still Pepe didn't come. She made supper, ate it alone at the kitchen table and went to bed. Perhaps he would come tomorrow. She awoke feeling hopeful, but there was no sound of Jefe coming to a halt outside her door. She began to worry. Had there been an accident? Was there something wrong with Sebastiana? She tried not to think about it, concentrating instead on how she was going to tell Bartolome he would have to pay The Fixer's next bill. She had two weeks to convince him before that horrible man came, so she would have to be firm; she would have to insist. Bartolome would argue, but she would stand her ground. At last she would fight back. Then she heard shouting from the workshop. She crossed the yard and stopped outside to listen. Don Francisco was in there sounding furious.

'These are no good. My men would tear them apart in an instant!'

Bartolome was almost crying. 'But you have to take them, Francisco.'

'*Don* Francisco to you, Bartolome. I am your client not your friend.'

'But you came to my party.'

'Yes, to sample your wife's cooking and drink your wine, not to listen to your boasting. Fine workmanship, my arse!' Don Francisco strode out of the workshop, flinging a bundle of cinch straps to the ground, then rode away. Mariangeles bent to pick them up and immediately saw the problem. The edges were uneven, causing weak spots along their length and where the buckle bar was inserted, the holes were too close to one edge. She sighed. The straps were useless.

Bartolome came out. Mariangeles had hardly looked at him for weeks and was shocked by what she saw. His face was flushed and he could barely stand. He belched and staggered into the kitchen where he sat down with his head in his hands.

'Oh, Mariangeles,' he wailed. 'What shall we do?'

'About what?'

'Don Francisco refuses to pay.'

Mariangeles shook her head. How could she ask her husband to pay The Fixer's debt now? And how were they going to live? She looked across at Bartolome. He was beyond redemption. Drink had stolen his looks; drink had stolen his skills, and now it was stealing his soul. She sighed. It was over. There was nothing else she could do for him. She went into the garden to check that her seedlings had not suffered from the winter frost. She would need every one of them to flourish if they were to survive. Then she went to the hen house and pulled out two eggs for their supper. It was all they had to eat.

29. Mariangeles

Pepe hadn't visited for more than a week, but that was all right, she kept telling herself. Perhaps he was sick, or his cart was being repaired. He would come soon, she was sure of it. In the meantime, the pouch containing Sebastiana's last contribution was still lodged safely in the almond sack and she refused to touch it. Instead, Mariangeles looked through her wardrobe again. There must be something left to sell. She picked out her remaining blouses and stuffed them in her basket. Bartolome's jackets and waistcoats had already gone to the pawnbroker last week. What was the point of keeping his clothes, when he remained in his overalls night and day? She pulled out her flamenco dress. Should she sell it this time or not? It was such a beautiful thing and she'd been proud of her workmanship, stitching flounces that seemed to have no end. They had flicked playfully as she'd walked up the hill on that morning of the *paseo*. Who cared if no one had noticed her? She loved her creation so much she couldn't bear to part with it. So, she put it back in the wardrobe again. The dress would stay.

Walking down the hill into town, her legs felt weary and her mind was distracted. She sat on the milestone to rest, and once again looked over to the tannery, hoping in vain that Pepe would be there. She considered walking into the yard and asking the men about Pepe's whereabouts so that she could collect Sebastiana's money, but by now the whole village knew their circumstances and she didn't want to seem desperate. So she lumbered on into town hoping that Pepe was all right and that nothing bad had happened to him, or to Sebastiana either.

On her return she saw The Fixer's horse lashed to a post outside. Peering into the kitchen, she watched him lift her ornaments off the shelf, turning them over and over, almost dropping them with his uncoordinated limbs, and then putting them in his bag. He continued doing this on every shelf, alcove and drawer until they had all disappeared before she dared speak.

'What are you doing?' she asked.

'Redeeming my debt, madam,' he answered without looking up.

'I told you I would pay,' she said showing him the money from her sales in town. The Fixer scoffed.

'That's not even half,' he said and he was right. Mariangeles had split the payments between Garcia and The Fixer and hoped the consequences would not be too severe. The Fixer took the money and walked out leaving Mariangeles looking around her bare kitchen. She allowed herself a smile. Those knickknacks had little value. They were out-of-date rubbish she'd bought on a whim when she'd had money at her disposal. She was glad The Fixer had taken them. They reminded her of her foolishness. At least he hadn't got his filthy hands on her dress. It was much more valuable than those silly ornaments he'd carried off in his bag.

When Incarna arrived, she went straight to the stove and lifted the kettle to make a pot of tea. She didn't ask Mariangeles to explain her sadness. Instead, she sat beside her and said.

'Saw that Fixer bloke carrying off your stuff, Mari, but I reckon you paid your debt months back.'

'He says I still owe him, Incarna.'

'Rubbish. He only comes here to humiliate you because he knows he can.' Mariangeles looked up. How perceptive of Incarna and how foolish of her to let it happen.

After Incarna had left, Bartolome staggered into the kitchen.

'I need money,' he said.

Mariangeles sighed. 'We don't have any,'

'Yes we do, woman. I've seen you with that pouch.'

Mariangeles took a deep breath. 'I'm not giving you a penny of that, you old drunk.'

Bartolome appeared in her vision. She saw his arm raised in front of her. Pain screamed through her head, followed by a weird silence as if she was dead. Everything was black. The floor was cold. Had she fallen? She struggled to her feet, hardly able to breathe. A strange weight in her eyes made it hard to see. Leaning on the table for support, she touched her chin and winced with pain - Bartolome must have struck her.

She looked about and realised he had disappeared. How long had she been out? She stood still, trying to control her breathing, closing her eyes remembering her grandmother wiping blood from her mother's cheek and putting ice on the bruise on her jaw. She shook her head. This was the first time Bartolome had struck her, but it wouldn't be the last. Groping her way to a chair, she dropped into it and sighed. 'Sorrows and waves never come alone,' she said. It was the family curse that just wouldn't go away. Her grandmother had said it and her mother had said it too. 'The women in this family are doomed,' she announced to the room, and hearing those words aloud and disconnected seemed to confirm their central importance. Then she closed her eyes, trying to summon the energy to fight the downfall that seemed destined to come her way.

Pepe came the next day and she rushed out to meet him.

'Where have you been? I missed you,' she said.

He stared at her bruised chin and the bump on her forehead where she'd fallen to the floor.

'Mariangeles, what happened?' he asked.

'Nothing. I fell, that's all. Do you have news of Sebastiana? How is she?

Pepe seemed to understand her pretence and answered as if nothing was amiss. 'I haven't seen her. And sorry I didn't come before. I was looking for work.' They sat together at the kitchen table. Pepe talked and Mariangeles listened. There had been a fire in a factory where he delivered cork and it had closed down so he had lost his delivery work and had to find something else. Mariangeles nodded in sympathy.

'And Sebastiana's money?' she asked, trying not to sound desperate.

'Like I says, I haven't seen her so there's no money, Marieangeles. Sorry.'

Mariangeles frowned. Something wasn't right. Then she realised. 'Sebastiana worked in that factory, didn't she?' Pepe looked down, avoiding her eyes. 'And that's why she hasn't sent her money, because she can't.' Pepe shook his head, but Mariangeles could see it all now. 'Oh, Pepe, is she all right? Did she survive? Tell me she did!' Pepe sighed and Mariangeles pleaded. 'Please, Pepe, you have to tell me.' Eventually, Pepe smiled.

'I suppose you have a right to know. Tia is fine, Mariangeles. They say she survived the fire and has moved out of the hostel, but forgive me, I don't know more than that.'

'So, where is she now, Pepe? Tell me!

'Mariangeles, I'm sorry, but I really don't know.'

134

Part Four – Tia and Mariangeles

30. Tia

My limbs were burned. My mouth was full of soot. When I coughed, black mucous fell from my mouth onto the scorched sand. Eva lay beside me, unmoving. I prodded her shoulder.

'Eva, wake up.' She opened her eyes.

'You look a sight,' she said.

'So do you.' And in the chaos we laughed. But it was hysteria not joy that triggered our laughter because all around us was the horror of death, survivors running into the sea to ease their burns, the half-dead dragged from the smouldering building and placed somewhere quiet where they would surely die, bodies covered in cloth to conceal the horror of their incineration. The building, too, was a skeleton; its iron girders the only parts left standing. There were no piles of cork waiting to be processed. They had been consumed by flames. There were no big old doors that let in the light. All that was left was a pile of black debris. We watched as a solitary and final curl of smoke rose slowly from the embers, rolling and twisting away like a genie let out of a bottle. The factory had simply disappeared. Over by the fire engines I saw Alfonso pleading for attention, bleating about his burnt hand, but the rescuers ignored him and eventually he gave up. A journalist wandered around asking survivors what had happened? how it had started? who was to blame?. One of my old girlfriends pointed in my direction and the journalist turned his head.

'Ignore him,' Eva said, but my stomach dipped.

'Let's go,' I said and we hurried away, trembling, to our hostel where we dived into the bathroom, pulling off our blackened clothes and using carbolic soap, rubbing it furiously to create a lather. We scraped a pumice stone on our legs to remove the embedded grime and washed our hair, one, two, three times in a mixture of vinegar and water. When we'd finished, we wrapped ourselves in towels and went into the salon where the hostel owner had lit a paraffin stove to warm our bones. Eva started coughing - a deep troubling cough - and I sat still, trembling at the horrors of that fire and listening to her struggling for breath. Then I remembered the girl pointing and the journalist staring. I couldn't bear it. Guilt came creeping in; that old familiar snake of self-reproach was sidling up beside me. Was it my fault? Had I led Alfonso on? Was it my foolishness that had started that fire and caused so many of my fellow workers to die?

A knock on the door early next morning woke the whole hostel. I had a visitor, and when I went to the salon, the same journalist was waiting with a notebook in his hand, his face eager for a story.

'How did it happen, Sebastiana?' he asked, and the use of my name felt like an accusation. Eva came and stood beside me.

'It wasn't my fault,' I protested.

'Some people say it *was*,' he replied with no emotion. Eva stepped forward.

'Why don't you ask Alfonso? He was the one with the cigarillo,' she said.

'We have,' he said and beneath the man's unconvincing smile I could see his smirk.

136

'And what did he say?' I asked.

'He talked for half an hour or so about the girls under his care and how they became infatuated with him, and how it wasn't his fault that you did too.' Eva raised her eyebrows and was ready to speak, but I put my hand on her arm.

'Leave it, Eva, please.'

The next day's edition carried the story in detail. The hostel owner didn't want to show me, but I insisted, and there it was - reports on fire damage and statistics about the number of deaths and injuries. Below that were several eye-witness statements including Alfonso's. *That Tia girl got me going. How was I to know she would drag me into the dark and provoke such tragic circumstances?'* My heart raced. I felt sick as I searched the columns for my protestations of innocence. But they were not there. The journalist had denied my voice, but not my name. There it was in print as black as soot, for the readership to see. He'd even mentioned how I'd come from the east, and that maybe I was escaping from something terrible back there. I had never disclosed my past to anyone, but perhaps my old girlfriends had picked up the scent of my misdeeds as if it was an odour carried upon my clothes, and perhaps they had speculated and insinuated whatever they thought I had done. So that was that. The jury had decided. The judge had passed sentence. I was the girl with a dubious past. I was the girl who had started that fire and there was nothing I could do to correct their assumptions.

We had no work. We had no wages. We couldn't pay the rent. By the end of the month Eva and I left the hostel. We stood outside with our packed suitcases full of the pretty clothes we had bought with our once-so-secure wages. The owner of the hostel came out to say goodbye.

'I know a place in town. The people have almost nothing, but they will always help someone worse off than themselves,' she said. So, we set off on foot to a series of buildings close to the river. They were no more than *chozas* – shacks with roofs made from roughly hacked branches and held together with clay, then layered with palm leaves to keep out the rain. One was empty and when we entered, the light was dim because there was no glass in the windows and the shutters had been closed to keep out the cold. There were two rooms, one with a fireplace in a corner, two raised beds in the other, and a dirt floor covered in straw Outside was a shared toilet, a small garden that had a space for growing vegetables, and an empty chicken coup with food still left in the trough. Someone had abandoned this place just before we had arrived and I hoped they had found work, like we intended to do.

'It's only temporary,' Eva said and I agreed. We were young. We would find work soon. An old man came by. He introduced himself as Jose and offered us bread, and the next day he brought us two chickens.

'Wife sent you these. They're a bit old now but they're still producing,' he said revealing a toothless cavity behind his lips. We cleaned out the coup and begged for peelings from a neighbour. We named the chickens Maya and Mena. The older one - Maya - was always sick and produced fewer eggs than Mena who seemed to understand our hunger and would give us two eggs every day without fail. They were such friendly creatures that we brought them into the house overnight where they slept on our beds. But we needed more sustenance than eggs could give us so we sold our fancier clothing to a second-hand dress merchant who looked us up and down with distaste, but we didn't care. We needed to eat.

'We have to do what we have to do,' Eva repeated daily and even those few words set her off into a bout of coughing. Residue from the fire was sitting in her lungs. From time to time her coughing would bring up globules of grey-black mucous, but most of the time her chest was tight and she could hardly breathe.

138

'You need a doctor,' I said, but we both knew there was no money for that. I went out each day searching for employment, but thanks to the journalist, word of my misdemeanour had got around. No one wanted to employ the girl who had started that fire. I returned one afternoon, despondent at my lack of progress, to find Eva tending our garden. She was bent over, hoeing the soil, and I saw the bones of her shoulder blades sticking through her dress.

'Eva, leave that,' I said. When she turned around I saw that she was crying.

'I have to do something,' she said.

Eva and I walked along the promenade where several families were enjoying a walk in the evening sun. We approached a corner and saw Alfonso standing under a lamppost, and he saw us too. As we came towards him, he shouted,

'You bitch. Thanks to you I've lost my job.'

'What's that got to do with me?' I asked.

'The owners said that when they rebuild they don't want me. Said I'd lost the respect of the workers. Couldn't they see I was injured?' He held up his hand, still bandaged from the fire. Eva shook her head.

'Tia told me you left her for dead on that floor.'

'What do you know? You weren't there. But *she* was, the bitch,' he sneered pointing at me. As we walked away, he shouted after us, 'You two will regret this, you wait and see.'

On our way back along the promenade we saw that Alfonso was still standing under the lamppost, but now he was surrounded by a group of survivors. When he saw us, he raised his voice again.

'Threw herself at me in such a passion that I must've knocked my cigarillo to the floor,' he said loudly. I stopped dead. That's not how it was, but no words came because my mind was full of doubt. Eva held my arm.

'Don't take his bait, Tia. He's not worth it,' she said, but I kept thinking. Maybe the fire *was* my fault. I was there, wasn't I? I could have discouraged him, but instead I led him on. Alfonso hadn't finished. He turned to the survivors.

'I tried to help, but the stubborn little madam ignored me.' The group looked angry and I wanted to tell them that Alfonso was lying, but I couldn't speak, and Eva couldn't either. She had a bad coughing fit and had taken herself off to the shoreline to recuperate. I stood there alone and silent as, one by one, they approached me, deliberately taking turns. A young woman dressed in black, came right up to my face.

'I lost my husband because of you. He was only thirty-four.'

Another spat out her comments like bullets from a gun.

'No work, no money, no life. We're all going to starve.'

Then someone waved the newspaper article at me, and when I didn't speak, she swiped it across my face.

'Bitch,' she said walking away. I lowered my eyes, remembering how gossip had brought me down before. I remembered the villagers at the *paseo* thinking I was a hussy and the girls in the factory assuming I was Alfonso's mistress. Now the press were at it too. It was all so wrong but it was also true, because my behaviours had made them think those things. It wasn't them who had behaved badly, it was me. They must have seen the misgivings on my face because another woman came up to me.

'You deserve to die in agony like the rest of them poor souls,' she said. I gasped. How could she be so cruel? I went to speak but her face was so twisted with hate that I lowered my head and they all laughed.

'Nothing to say for yourself, bitch?' one asked and I shook my head. As I closed my eyes, tears squeezed out and fell down my cheeks, and those tiny innocent droplets seemed like the greatest confirmation of my guilt. The women walked away, sneering. Alfonso's artful performance had succeeded. I was the witch who'd devastated families and caused the factory to close, rendering a whole community destitute. I was marked - as if an ash-laden cross had been drawn across my forehead for all to see. Eva saw what had happened and hurried back. She put her arm around my waist and we walked back to our little shack in silence.

A new cork factory had opened not far from the charred remains of the old. I left Eva wheezing in the shack, and set off to find the manager to try to get work there. He laughed when I told him my name.

'You've got a cheek, since you're the one who started that fire,' he said. However, I pleaded with him, and it worked. 'All right, you can sweep up the dust on the factory floor, right here where we can keep an eye on you,' he said. I did so but it wasn't a good atmosphere. No one spoke to me for fear I might jinx the place with my presence, and by the end of the week the manager let me go. 'You make my workers nervous,' he said.

That evening, in order to raise my spirits, I returned home along the water's edge where the sea lay flat, waiting for the sun to slip its moorings, and the landscape became tinged with a golden hue. Tall pines had taken on a ruby-red brilliance as the sun started to drop into the horizon. Could anything be more beautiful than this? I stood as still as I could, immersing myself in the sunset and evoking memories of my childhood. How could everything have gone so wrong? I thought about the harbour in my old town and the steamships and the fishing boats and the wild untamed wind, and how I had dreamt of a life in grand places such as Seville, Gibraltar or Tangiers. The world had been full of possibilities then. Who knows what I could have been doing instead. I missed my parents, too, and wondered if Pepe had told them about the fire and what I was doing now. But then I shook my head. Pepe wouldn't do that. I'd made him swear never to reveal my location and he was a man of his word.

It was summer and our neighbourhood began teeming with travellers from Cordoba, Seville and Madrid who came to their second homes by the sea. I walked along the promenade admiring their pretty balconies filled with expensive flowers and the well-dressed children playing in their gardens. Behind the shoreline was where the gardeners and the cooks and the maids lived, relying on summer money to get them through winter. And behind them were the *chozas* where we, the beggars and the jobless, scavenged for a living. None of the holiday-makers knew me, so when I knocked on their doors and offered to wash their bedlinen and their fancy clothes, they agreed. In our modest shack I lit the fire and heated water in a vast copper pot that I shared with a neighbour. I pummelled the clothing with a dolly, rinsed it under a standpipe outside and pegged it out in the breeze. The steam from all this washing seemed to ease Eva's chest and help her to breathe so that gradually she regained her strength, but something had changed. She had a haunted look as if something was troubling her.

'I can't bear to see you working like this, Tia. I need to find work too.'

Poor, joyful Eva had lost her sparkle. Guilt and infirmity had made her sad.

There were many changes in the area. Jose told us that navvies were being employed to build a second harbour in Gibraltar and new steam ships from Liverpool docked overnight before sailing off to ports in the Mediterranean. Coming the other way, merchant ships sailed in from India, passing through the Suez to trade in Europe. We didn't go out at night for fear of the sailors roaming the streets, as well as soldiers from the local barracks, fists clenched, ready for a fight. There were rich people, too, - new factory owners and Englishmen who hunted on our soil and gambled at the racetrack in the no-man's-land between us and Gibraltar. Then, when they opened up a railway from Algeciras, even more money flooded into the area.

Jose explained as we sat together on his porch. 'Attracts punters from all over the place. Them girls in the brothels are making a packet.'

A few days later Eva hugged me, and when she waved goodbye, my heart sank. I had lost my companion; I had lost my friend and Eva had lost her way.

At the end of the summer my customers returned to their winter homes and once again I had no work. A new bar had opened just down the road so I went to ask if I could wash their dishes. As I approached, I saw a man in old-fashioned English tweeds leaning on a silver-topped cane at the entrance, and above his head, swinging in the breeze, was a sign: 'Venta Alfonso.'

'Hello, Tia. Come begging for a job?' Alfonso said. I froze as he raised his hand in mock sincerity and I saw that it was still scarred from the fire. Then I smiled to myself, realising that even with his fancy tweeds and silver-topped stick, Alfonso was just as self-centred as ever. I turned around, listening to his laughter as I walked away, unable to bring myself to ask for work from such a cowardly liar.

The bar thrived and Jose came by to explain how Alfonso made his money.

'His men run small boats across the bay and return overloaded with spirits and tobacco stolen from merchant ships anchored off Gibraltar. You see, Alfonso's got distribution routes high up in the

Cazorla hills where he sends Scottish whisky, Caribbean rum and Cuban cigars to places like Seville and Cadiz, and inland towards the sierras. It's a pretty impressive operation.' And it was true. His bar was attracting people from all walks of life. I saw hawkers, bootblacks and street musicians touting for business and heard many arguments that went on throughout the night. Jose said it was because the staff only got paid in tips, so they short-changed the customers and when they got angry, Alfonso had to offer one of the girls he kept upstairs as compensation.

Evenings in my shack, just metres from Alfonso's bar, became unbearable. I could hear the sound of the cook chopping octopus on the block - the thud of the knife on a wooden block, then the sizzling of those glorious circles of white flesh laid on the griddle. The rich aroma drifting along the street was so intense I could hardly bear it. I licked my lips at the thought of dropping 'pulpo asado' into my mouth - the skin charred and crisp – the inside soft and creamy. Oh, the torment, oh, the pain - jagged and cruel – as hunger prowled through me like a wolf. I should have done something about it – taken in washing from the locals - cleaned people's houses – anything would have done. But no one wanted the hussy who'd started that fire. Yet I was determined to stay positive, so one evening I took a walk along the shoreline. As I listened to the rhythms of the ocean, its waves rolling in one by one seemed to match the rise and fall of my breathing. I inhaled the salty sea air deeply and smiled. I was alive, I was young, and I was relishing nature. Then, in the distance I saw a figure, thin and black against the sinking sun. The person saw me, too, and turned to go, moving rapidly across the sand. But I recognised her gait.

'Eva,' I shouted and she stopped. There was no escape. She knew I could outrun her, so instead she dropped to her knees on the sand. There were no words. I held her tight as she sobbed into my chest and when we pulled away from each other, I looked into her gaunt, dazed face and knew for certain what I had guessed at before. I took her hands in friendship, studying her nails - all chewed to the quick - and her skin ingrained with dirt.

'Don't, Tia. Please don't look,' she cried, and I stroked her palm to ease her trembling. Everything about Eva had become restless. A dog barked and she jumped. A ship's bell sounded in the harbour and she gasped.

From thereon in we met every evening, but when the sun dropped over the horizon, she was quick to turn inland, leaving me alone in the twilight. That was the worst time for Eva; when she was most in need of her evening dose of Chinchón - an aniseed liqueur that charmed and soothed her through the trials of the night. We never talked about her life as a prostitute. I think our daily walks beside the sea gave her a sense of normality and perhaps even enchantment in what must have been a cruel and unending routine. Poor Eva. Like me, she had been an innocent who'd come in from the countryside looking for work. But life had tricked her into this terrible existence and, remembering my lucky escape from The Fixer, I tried my best to alleviate her suffering and give her some joy. One day I found a pebble in a rock pool. It had blue veins running through it and a soft brown edge. I reached down and handed it to her. 'Keep it safe, my friend. It may bring you luck,' I said, and Eva smiled as if she had never heard anything so positive. Then she buried it deep in her pocket. Of course, in the morning its colour would have disappeared; the bold contrast would have merged into shifts of grey. But I hoped she would remember my words and the sense of hope that went with them.

I tried my best to survive, remembering how Ma used to tend her garden and, with Jose's help, my vegetables began to grow. Mena continued to lay her eggs, and when I lifted them from the straw they were as well rounded with freckled beauty as they always were. But when I pressed them, the shells fell apart, and inside, the liquid was pale and insubstantial. Like me, on my journey from prosperity in that harbour, to the granite hillside village, to leaving home and finding work, then ending up in this shack, my lovely creatures had withered inside. I held them to my chest, not wanting to leave one without the other, and whispered, 'Goodbye my little ones.' Then twisted their necks and prepared them for the pot.

Winter came and stillness entered the vegetable garden as everything went to sleep. I watched the birds sitting in the carob trees, lining up on the branches, turning this way and that, swapping positions and planning their route to Africa, and I longed to fly with them to somewhere warm and safe. Then one day they were gone, leaving empty skies and the anticipation of that long hunger-ridden interlude of winter. I had to get out of there; I had to find a job. Jose's wife understood my desperation and went inland and asked around for me, until finally someone said yes.

'It's up on the hill - prettiest house on Main Street - and the housekeeper's a good'n,' she said, and then leaned in to whisper. 'No one knows you up there, girl. No one's heard the gossip about you and that fire, so keep your mouth shut and all should be well.'

I gathered my few belongings into my suitcase, thanked Jose and his wife for their kindness, walked away from the cluster of *chozas* and took the long road up towards the village on the hill. This was the second time I had moved from the coast to the interior, but this time I hoped the people might be friendlier than in my old village and that up there things would not go wrong as they had before. My mind raced with possibilities. Would they be kind? Would they pay me enough to send money home to Ma? Then I remembered her words so often repeated: *'Sorrows and waves never arrive alone'* and I hoped that this time things would be different, that this time I would break the family spell.

31. Mariangeles

Mariangeles came back from town to find the pantry door wide open. She rushed inside kicking away the mass of almonds scattered all over the floor and lifting the empty sack. No pouch. Sebastiana's precious last payment was gone.

'Not just a drunk but a thief too!' she shouted loudly so that Bartolome would hear her from wherever he was skulking. That was it. She gathered up her sewing machine, shears, buckles, needles and buttons and threads, pushed them into a cupboard together with rolls of fabric and locked the door. Bartolome would not get his hands on these to sell for booze. Then she rushed upstairs, dashed into her bedroom, opened the wardrobe and pulled out her flamenco dress. She stuffed it into a suitcase, added whatever else would fit, flew down the stairs and out of the house, running and stumbling down the hill, breathless and giddy. This was the flight of her lifetime. Nothing else mattered - she had to go.

At the crossroads she sat on the milestone, panting and heaving until she'd calmed herself enough to think. The tannery lights shone. Was Pepe there? She couldn't see him so she dusted off her clothing and started walking again, crossing the highway and striding into the curved lane that led into town. Her legs were sturdy and her mind was alive. Keep moving forward, she told herself. Keep on this path. Finally she reached the ancient stone gateway to the city. How many times had she passed through this gate in order to sell her possessions for a pittance? She looked up at the archway showing the construction date of 1292. For centuries travellers had passed through this gate, some coming, others going. But where was *she* going? Where would she stay?

Her pace slackened, she took a deep breath and as she walked, slowly now, through the narrow streets, her question seemed to be answered. She turned into Main Street and picked up speed, striding along its narrow length towards the end. It had to be empty. It had to be hers. Then she stopped and let out a deep sigh. The window was still bare and the sign *Luxury Goods for Gentlemen and Ladies* was still hanging overhead. She remembered the wooden gate that led into the back yard, and it sang a rusty song of welcome as she turned the latch. Knowing where to look for the door key, she ran her fingers across the top of the frame, hoping it was still there, until she found it covered in cobwebs and grime. She pulled it into sight, inserted it into the lock, and, as if destined to do so, it clicked open with ease.

The place was damp and very cold so she gathered wood from the yard – brittle-dry from years in the sun – and lit a fire in the stove in the salon upstairs. At first the flames surged and crackled loudly as if waking up from a deep sleep and black smoke billowed into the room. But after the chimney had burned off years of dust and dirt, it settled into a soft glow of embers that kept her warm for the rest of the evening. It was getting dark but she had thought ahead and placed an old lamp on the dresser. She lit it now and it spluttered into life, casting a warm glow over the old familiar room. Then after inspecting the beds and deciding they were too dusty for sleep, she fetched an old chair, sat by the stove, closed her eyes and dropped into an exhausted but liberated sleep.

She was woken at dawn by mice scurrying under the floorboards. The whole place was a mess, but it didn't matter. She was free. She was happy. And above all, she was home. Searching for the implements she needed and finding them in the same cupboards where she had abandoned them years ago, she now set about cleaning her old residence. She dusted and scrubbed and stretched and squatted and filled endless buckets of water from the well. Her legs ached, her forearms, too, and by nightfall she settled in the same old chair and immediately fell asleep. Tomorrow she would start on the shop below.

The morning was bright, but the energy that had carried Mariangeles out of that house, down the hill, and into the shop, had disappeared. She sat by the now-cold stove and pondered her situation. This wasn't her property. It was owned by the bank. Soon they would discover she was there and demand she pay rent. Until then she would pretend it was hers. But she had no money, she had no clothes and her stomach was sore - she had to eat.

She went to the harbour, taking care to avoid Garcia's cabin. How in heaven was she going to pay his next instalment? She took her place at the back of a long queue of down-and-outs, and watched the fish wives gutting fish and shouting to one another over the wind. At the front of the queue, children with no shoes and men with no work were pleading for the heads and tails of tuna or sea bass. They were probably *sin techos,* she thought – homeless men who had lost their homes and their families to drink, They stood there, knees bent to keep themselves steady, and she thought of Bartolome up there in that house. Was he eating? Would he come down here begging like the rest of these men? Would he be joining this queue? As she waited, she glanced carefully over at old man Garcia's cabin. She wasn't ready to face him yet. With his outrageous interest rate, her debt was mounting, but every week he had seemed pleased to see her, even when her payments were less than required. Now, though, she had nothing to give him so what would he do then? The boys left with their scraps, no doubt carrying them off for their mothers to boil on stoves to make a thin stew. Slowly the queue shortened until she reached the front. She lowered her head, desperate not to be recognised, anxious not to be identified by her sins. After all, she was the once-prosperous owner of that luxury goods shop on Main Street and she was the mother who had tried to send her daughter away with a pimp. And now here she was begging for food like all the others. They would say it was divine justice and laugh in her face. Her stomach dipped as she lowered her head and extended her upturned hand, waiting for their charity.

Back in the yard, Mariangeles hauled water from the well. After years lying dormant there was no way to tell if it was safe to drink, but she filled a pot and placed it on the stove. Then she added the meagre pile of fish scraps and some thyme that was growing in the yard. She waited a few minutes for the scraps to concede their flavour, but hunger was the enemy of patience and she could no longer wait. She grabbed a cup, dipped it into the premature soup and brought it to her lips. It burned her tongue, but she drank it anyway.

Fortified by the soup, she set about cleaning again. The display window had several glass panels and each was full of dead insects and grease. She dusted and scrubbed inside and out with an old bar soap she had found under the sink, then rinsed them with cold water until they sparkled. When it was dry, she removed a yellow damask curtain from an upstairs bedroom, shook out the dust and laid it onto the base of the window. Then she pulled her flamenco dress out of the suitcase and hung it in the window, suspended on a thread. She went outside. Now the window sizzled with red and yellow - the colours of Spain. Now there was a small chance that someone passing by might stop to take a look.

Next morning every muscle was aching and every bone creaked as she eased herself off the uncomfortable chair. Soon she would need a proper night's sleep but she dreaded the thought of dragging one of those old mattresses down the stairs, into the yard, and beating out the dust. Without food inside her, did she have the energy for such a task? She went into the kitchen and looked in despair at the empty pantry. Then taking a deep breath she went outside to the big old doorway of the church, sat on the step, lowered her head so that no one would recognise her and extended her upturned hand. There was no other way. She had no choice.

A stranger stopped and placed a few coins in her palm. She looked up.

'This isn't me. I'm not like this,' she heard herself saying and the stranger made an effort to smile, but she could tell that he wasn't listening. He was sniffing the air as if there was an unpleasant odour. Perhaps she needed a bath. She hurried off to the bakers to buy bread, and to the slaughterhouse to buy a bone. On the way back along Main Street she saw an old woman sitting in the threshold of her house with a tray of vegetables. She bought a potato and some greens, and if the woman recognised Mariangeles as one of her old neighbours, she didn't say so. But her smile felt warm and her eyes were so tender that Mariangeles started to cry.

'Thank you,' she said with as much grace as she could muster.

Back in her kitchen she stuffed bread into her mouth while the vegetables swirled in the bubbling water and fragments of red meat fell away from the thick, white bone. 'Bit by bit, day by day,' she said out loud and waited a little longer this time to satisfy her hunger.

Church bells rang. It must be Sunday, she thought, as, once again, she tried to straighten out her limbs for the day. Then, nourished by yesterday's stew, she fetched a mattress out of a bedroom and hauled it down the staircase into the yard. For two hours she bashed and battered and whacked the thing until there was no dust remaining. She beat the mattress as if she was beating herself. She was bad. She was wicked. An obsession with her husband had led her to the point of madness. A desperation to be held and loved, an untamed jealousy of Sebastiana, and the fear of losing her body had ruined the relationship with her only child. When she had finished she sank to her knees. How foolish she had been and how terrible the consequences of her folly. It was only when she'd calmed down that she realised what she had to do, and spoke her thoughts aloud in the yard as if the walls could hear her.

'I must find Sebastiana. I must ask for her forgiveness. I must make amends.' But first she needed to earn money.

The bells were still ringing, but beyond the cavernous noise of the clappers on the brass crowns, she thought she heard another sound: a rap of knuckles on wood, short and sharp followed by another, then another. Someone was knocking at the door. She went into the shop and through the glass, saw two women peering into the window. They appeared to be admiring her dress.

Mariangeles invited them in and they looked around the empty shop with caution. She was quick to reassure them. She had to take a chance.

'My equipment is in storage whilst I renovate the shop,' she said quickly, 'but don't worry, ladies, I can take your order and have them ready within the month.' She smiled over the lie as they inspected the dress both inside and out, testing its seams and admiring the cut. The mother wanted one the same colour but in her size, and the daughter wanted the same style but in blue. Mariangeles took their measurements and accepted a small deposit, then the women hurried out of the shop, already late for Mass.

Mariangeles fell into the chair, beaming at her first success

152

then frowning as she wondered how she could fulfil the order. Everything she needed was locked away in a cupboard in that house on the hill and there was a chance that Bartolome had already discovered them and sold the lot. Besides, even if he hadn't, how was she going to bring such a heavy load down into town? There was only one person who could help, but she didn't know where Pepe was. Then she remembered that Sunday evening was delivery time at the tannery where he still had the contract to bring in hides. So she waited all afternoon before setting off once again through the town and into the countryside, hoping that Pepe would be there and that he would agree.

She could smell the tannery before she got there and see from a distance a horse and cart in the yard. She hurried on through the darkness. Pepe would help her collect her things. They would go to the house together and he would distract Bartolome while she retrieved her equipment from the cupboard. But when she arrived, she saw that it wasn't Pepe who was standing there, and it wasn't Jefe, his horse, shaking its head in the tannery yard. It was a younger, slimmer-built man who held the reins of a small pony, and he was smoking a cigarette.

'Where's Pepe?' she asked.

'Doesn't work here no more. It's my round now.'

'Yes, but where *is* he?' she asked again.

'How should I know,' the youth replied.

Mariangeles left her address with the manager, then fled. She was cold. She was hungry. She was disappointed. Oh, Pepe! Where was he? She missed him.

It was time to face Garcia, so in the morning she went to the harbour, hoping to appeal to his apparent good nature and ask him to extend the length of her loan. She found him seated at his table as usual.

'Ah, dear lady, you visit me at last,' he said without his usual smile.

'I've come to ask a favour,' she said.

'I don't do favours, Madam. I do business transactions.' He leaned over the table with narrowed eyes. 'Where is the money for this week and the three weeks before that? Mariangeles wiped her cheek. Some of his spittle had landed on her face.

'I have a little,' she said, offering half of the ladies' deposit. She would need the rest for food and materials. Garcia scoffed.

'This is not enough, dear lady.'

'But my circumstances have changed, Señor Garcia. Soon I will pay you more.' She spoke quickly, trying to lighten the mood.

'But thanks to you I am out of pocket.' He got up and came round the side of the table. He was shorter than she'd expected. 'Perhaps a different arrangement could be made to tide me over?' he said, pushing his belly against hers, and shoving her backwards over the table. Her legs flew from under her. He leaned forward with his lips squeezed together as if coming in for a kiss. She struggled. 'Don't resist me,' he said, but she *did* resist. She bit him hard on the side of his cheek and when her teeth sank into his fatty flesh, she tasted blood. He pulled away, screaming as she opened the door and fled.

Back in the yard she swilled her mouth out then ripped off her clothing and washed herself in the well. The water was cold but she didn't care. Removing the man was all she wanted. Then she dressed and went inside to heat the rest of the stew. It was meant to last two more days but she had to eat it. She had to fill her body with goodness to eliminate the bad.

As she slept she heard a voice calling through her dreams.

'Mariangeles, you in there?' She woke up and looked about. It was midday. She must have fallen asleep. The voice called again, 'Mariangeles?' She knew at once it was him. He had found her. She rushed to the back gate. Pepe raised his hat in greeting and she flung herself at him, burying her head in his chest. She felt his arms come slowly around her and she pressed in harder, took a long deep breath and began to sob, short deep sobs of remembrance; of how she had escaped from Bartolome, how she had queued for scraps and surrendered her dignity begging for money and how she had been assaulted. She sobbed and sobbed, wetting Pepe's jacket but he didn't seem to mind. At last, she pulled away and invited him inside

'Where have you been?' she said when they were seated by the stove.

'I've got work back east, Mariangeles. *Two* jobs so I don't have time to deliver them hides no more. Only came back 'ere to collect my pay.' Mariangeles smiled. How lucky she was to have visited the tannery just in time, and how lucky she was to call this man her friend. 'They say The Fixer's left the area,' he said. 'Something about Englishmen coming into Seville and taking over his patch. So, you've no need to worry about him no more, Mariangeles.' She loved the way he said her name. It made her feel she could trust him with almost anything, except telling him what had happened with Garcia. Some things were too personal, even between friends. But she wasn't so sure about being safe from The Fixer. The man enjoyed his power over women, just like Incarna had suggested, so perhaps he would be back. She sighed, hoping that Pepe was right, that she had seen the last of him, and that she could relax.

There was no problem collecting her sewing equipment. She and Pepe slipped in quietly through the back gate and heard Bartolome snoring upstairs. Mariangeles stared with contempt at the dirty crockery and the grime on her kitchen table, and put her handkerchief over her mouth to stave off the stench of drink.

'Let's get out of here,' she said when they had finished. 'I can't bear to see this place again.' They descended the hill with a cart full of equipment, and Mariangeles let out a huge sigh. Behind her, piled into the cart, was all she needed to make those two dresses and after that she would make more. Right now, she didn't care about profit as long as she could eat. Slowly I will recuperate, she said to herself, and after that I will go with Pepe and together we will find my daughter.

32. Tia

Jose's wife was right. It *was* the prettiest building in the street, with bright blue shutters and balconies crammed with ceramic pots of vivid red flowers. It was so different to that grubby little shack by the bay that I couldn't believe my luck. I stood opposite admiring the way its sturdy white walls were braced against the steep incline of Main Street and decided it looked like a sailing boat battling the winds. There were five steps leading to a carved central entrance and in the left-hand corner was a servant's door. I took a deep breath and pressed the bell. A middle-aged woman appeared, smiling.

'My name is Agnes,' she said, and I saw that she had kind eyes and that her hands were red and dry from years of washing and cleaning. 'I'll take you through the main house so that you can see the whole building, but keep your eyes down so you're not tempted to stare. Don Diego doesn't want to be bothered with his servants.'

We went up a main staircase and I barely touched the balustrade - made from finely wrought iron with shapes twisted to look like branches and leaves - because it looked so delicate. We reached the top where a floodlit atrium cast a warm glow over the floors below. Agnes saw me admiring the view and warned, 'Remember never to stare down at the family, Tia. This is their private space.' Then, as we passed through a small door into the servants quarters at the very top of the house, her tone softened. 'You'll sleep in this room, girl, next to mine.' She handed me some sheets and a pillowcase and we made the bed together, adding a soft blanket for when a winter wind would rattle through the thin windows. 'You'll be working in the basement. It's a long way down mind.' Then she disappeared down the service stairs to the floors below. 'Follow me when you're settled,' she called up from the darkness.

I leaned over and whistled into the depths. An echo bounced up. It seemed a long way down. Then, placing my foot on the first step, I began to descend. On the middle floor the stairs dropped even more steeply and twisted out of sight. I took a deep breath and this time went faster, missing a few steps as the momentum caught me. Down I went, flying through the air until I reached the basement, breathless and very much alive. When I arrived, thick with joy, I saw that I was in the wash house. There was a washtub and a machine called a mangle that I didn't know how to use. It was very impressive. Even so, carrying damp washing up all those stairs was going to be a chore.

'You're very young,' Agnes said.

'But a hard worker,' I said, eager to please.

I soon realised why they had offered me the job. There was to be no pay and I had to work every day of the week with only one Sunday free at the end of each month. There was no time off for illness, either, but I got meals and a room of my own, and I thanked Jose and his wife for my renewed fortune. Every day I boiled and scrubbed and rinsed and wrung the family's clothes, and day by day my arms became stronger and my calves became shapelier as I hauled the piles of wet washing up all those steps to reach the terrace where I hung them out to billow in the wind. I became happier too. Somehow, the process of converting clothes from dirty to clean and wet to dry, had lifted my spirits and unleashed the girl I was within. I began to smile, and this reminded me of Eva - my lovely Eva - and the way we used to laugh together as free as birds. Of course, we no longer met in the bay but I saw her from time to time, coughing continuously as she waited in the street. But whenever she saw me she turned her back and swaggered away, as if she no longer wanted to be my friend. This hurt, but I knew Eva. I knew she would have her reasons and that beneath those horrible clothes was a young and beautiful person who used to laugh and joke and call me her friend.

One day Agnes and I sat sipping hot chocolate in the scullery.

'This house is like an ocean liner, Tia.'

I frowned because I'd never seen an ocean liner except from a distance and couldn't imagine it. 'Us below deck, all the passengers on the middle decks and me organising things from my room up top.' Then I realised she was right. The family and I lived in two separate geographies. Mine ran vertically up the windowless staircase that twisted through the rear of the house like a distorted backbone, connecting the coldness of the attic to the heat of the laundry below. Don Diego and his family lived horizontally across the middle floors in cool, spacious rooms illuminated by a filtered sun and warmed by winter fires, lit by my anonymous hand. They didn't know me and I didn't know them.

Once, I caught a glimpse of Don Diego when he returned home early and retired to his study. I had just finished setting his fire, and scurried out quickly so that he wouldn't notice. This suited me well, coming and going whenever needed and never meeting the person who paid for my keep. To him I was invisible.

However, there was a boy in the village whom I wanted to meet. Every day I watched him from the balustrade on the upper terrace, as he was on his way to the slaughterhouse. Once he looked up and waved, and I waved back. Then, three weeks later, on my day off, I emerged from the servants' door and there he was.

'Hello, Tia. I've been waiting for you to come out,' he said, smiling.

'How did you know my name?'

'I asked the housekeeper, of course. Will you walk with me?' he asked, offering me his arm. We went up the hill and into the church square where we sat on a bench. Tiny particles of dust had been raised by carriages arriving at the church, and they lingered in the rays of the sun, making everything seem magical. To break the ice, he offered me one of the pamphlets he'd been distributing in the village, but I kept my hands in my lap, not daring to accept something I couldn't read properly, my schooling having been suspended by the arrival of cholera. The dear boy realised and withdrew it immediately.

'It's from the Syndicate of Workers,' he explained gently. 'My father and I are members.'

'But what is your name?' I asked. In his nervousness he'd forgotten to say.

'I am Pablo but they still call me Pablecito even though I'm seventeen,' he said, and I laughed at his childish protestation.

'Then I'll call you Pablo,' I replied and my voice sounded more assured than I felt.

We met every month on my day off, walking arm in arm into the square where children ignored us as they played hopscotch and tag. Adults frowned as we strolled past. It was not proper for a girl of fourteen to be without a chaperone in the company of a man. Of course, I was aware of the protocol, but I was an exception. Those rules didn't apply to a girl from the *chozas*, the girl who had started that fire. Besides, I liked this boy. He was a thinker and a gentleman who only worked at the slaughterhouse to make a living.

160

I could see the unhappiness in his eyes when he said, 'I must get out of that place soon, Tia, before it steals my soul.'

'At least you get paid.' I blurted out.

'You get paid too, don't you?'

'No,' I said quietly, suddenly feeling ashamed, as if I was only fit to be a slave. But the truth was that the only reason I needed money was to resume my payments to my parents.

Pablo looked angry.

'That's not right, Tia. They must give you something. It's only fair.' I could see that he was on my side as he continued in a fervent voice. 'Food and a room are not enough. You must demand a wage.'

I shook my head. 'But I'm happy there, happier than I've ever been.' I said without explaining why.

Pablo was outraged. 'Tia, come to the next syndicate meeting. Perhaps others can persuade you better than I.'

We were soaked when we arrived at the farm-worker's hovel just outside the village. The family mule had been brought in from the corral to shelter from the deluge of rain that had descended, leaving little room for the group of men and women who sat, dishevelled, around a meagre fire. Steam rose from our sodden clothes, as hot almonds lashed with honey were passed around on a plate. The smell of the mule and the damp clothes and the sweet nuts made me choke, but I held it back and sat in the shadows where I felt more at ease. Rain fell like thunder onto the iron roof, making it difficult to hear what was being said. One by one, speakers stood to tell their stories. Some were wracked with pain and others were wheezing with consumption, but here, in this tiny place, their words were expansive and passionate. I listened in horror as they spoke of cruel employers and dangerous machines and not enough to eat. Each speaker showed a conviction that I'd not heard before, men and women moved to distraction by their circumstances, some spitting onto the earth as they spoke or raising their fists like warriors. There was no room for submission.

Pablo asked me to speak. 'Tell them, Tia. Tell them your situation.' But I shook my head. I couldn't. I was tongue-tied, or maybe my wounds were too deep, or perhaps I didn't deserve their sympathy. Whatever it was, I lacked the confidence to speak from the heart and couldn't connect with these people, nor empty my heart in anger. Pablo looked disappointed but I didn't know how to explain. So I avoided his eye and turned away to watch the flow of dirty water sliding down the thin glass windows, leaving smears of rust-coloured debris behind.

Back in my room I regretted my shyness. Ma would have known what to say. Ma was a strong woman who always thought ahead. Even sending me away with The Fixer had been planned carefully in advance. Me, though, I was a mouse, pinned down by my past follies so that now I dare not commit to anything real in case I spoiled it again, in case this new life vanished completely like that factory in the fire.

I tucked myself into bed wondering about home, remembering all the things that had gone wrong before. I recalled The Fixer's last visit to explain the arrangements for my removal, and the way Ma and Pa had walked away arm in arm, leaving me standing alone and frightened in the kitchen. Was Ma happy now that she had Pa all to herself? Would they really be close again after all that had happened between them? Was it worth it, Ma? Trying to send me away, perhaps to a pimp? How could I forgive her after what she had done? But as the night closed in and a wind rattled the window, I pulled the blanket over my shoulders and thought again. I wanted Ma to comfort me, sleeping here, so far away from home in a strange bed. Perhaps I *did* miss her and our old way of life. I wondered if I should forgive her and part of me said yes, but most of me said no. I was happy in this employment and pleased that Ma didn't know my location. This suited me fine. This was my revenge because she owed me a debt and I was making her pay.

Pablo and I continued to meet on the last Sunday of every month. I listened politely as he talked about the syndicate and its importance to the people of our village. He didn't notice that I was waiting for the subject to change, that I was hoping he would turn to me and say something nice. He was a kind boy but he often spoke as if addressing a crowd.

'It started in our great cities - in Barcelona and Seville. Men who work till they drop, women who walk the streets and go with men in order to feed their families, children as young as eight bent double in factories. We've had enough, Tia. We want equality and justice, and what started in small bars in quiet neighbourhoods, is multiplying so that soon socialism will be the only way. Soon we will have our revolution. Soon you will be free.' His voice rose as he spoke and fell as he tried to persuade me to become more active. 'Come with me, Tia. Come to our next demonstration and you'll see how ordinary people will change our land.' And because I liked him, I nodded and he grinned with delight.

It was dusk when twenty of us met on the main road, marching in giddy unison on the road towards Gibraltar. We held blazing torches and the whole procession was bright and noisy. Pablo's father was shouting the loudest, through a megaphone.

'Brothers and sisters, we must break free from the shackles of deference to the church and to the gentry. The second republic is coming and between us we will create a just society in which all can live in peace and harmony.'

'My father is a giant among men, Tia,' Pablo whispered as he leaned in towards me. 'He takes the theories of Marx and Engels and reinvents them eloquently at the factory gate.'

I didn't respond. I'd never heard of these people, and didn't know what to say. Instead, I moved to the back of the procession. Here the burning torches could not illuminate my hesitant face. Here, in the darkness, my ignorance was shaded in the tail-end of a father's shooting star.

'Our production is our strength,' he shouted, as we marched down the road in such a rush that suddenly we were outside a huge mill, lit by real electric light and on the top floor, silhouetted in an odd blue glow, were several people looking down at us from a large window. We must have seemed a terrifying sight, lit by primitive ragged torches, raising our fists in the agitated breeze. Then, as my eyes adjusted, I saw someone I recognised. Staring out through the flickering light was the face of my employer, Don Diego. I stepped back into the shadows just in case he recognised me, just in case he knew who I was, although I was fairly sure he knew nothing of the servant who lit his fires, cleaned his clothes and made life so comfortable for him and his family.

A siren started its piercing drawl. Doors opened and workers emerged into the yard. They'd just finished a twelve-hour shift and their faces were caked in flour, making them seem like ghosts. Pablo the elder stepped forward.

'Men, do not accept this oppression. We must unite.'

A few stopped to listen but most seemed too exhausted to think. They ignored him, pale-faced like the living dead, leaving a trail of white dust as they trudged through the gates and away to their homes. The older man persisted. 'Capitalists have destroyed man's liberty and taken away the dignity of our labour.' But it was too late. The men had gone, leaving his words hanging in the flour-ridden breeze. Pablo stepped forward.

'Come on, Papa. Don't be dismayed. You're a man before your

time.' He put his arm around his father's shoulder and I felt the love between them. 'One day things will change,' he said. 'One day people will accept your words as truth, Papa. You'll see.' We plodded home in silence, but Pablo the elder was striding ahead with determination. I could see that he was scheming and planning his next advance and I was pretty sure that it would not be long before he would rally the mill workers to his cause. Then everything about our world would change.

That night I lay in my room thinking about how fervent Pablo and his father had been, and how sad and weary those workers at the mill were. Perhaps this father and son were right and I should support their fight. But then I thought about how happy I was in Don Diego's house and how his profit from the mill paid for my keep. The labour of those worn-out men was keeping me alive. So who was I to judge? And who was right and who was wrong? Then, at midnight, I heard the outside door slam shut and Don Diego came in, bellowing as he made his way to his study.

'Damned idiots! Don't they realise I've got a business to run?' I knew he was talking about tonight's demonstration and became worried. Perhaps he *had* seen me after all. Was I in trouble? I had to know. So, wrapping a blanket around me, I ran barefoot down the servants' stairs to the first-floor landing where a door opened onto Don Diego's study. From here I could hear his ranting and his wife's gentle pleading.

'Come now, Diego, you know what happens when you get angry.'

'Came right up to the factory gates with those damned torches, trying to get at my men.' I heard a key being turned in a lock and his wife pleading,

'Don't do it, Diego. It will make things worse.'

What did she mean? I had to know, so I peered through the gap between the door and its frame. Neither husband nor wife took notice of their servants, or our efficient functioning of their

165

household, so I hoped they wouldn't notice me now.

I squinted. Don Diego was standing beside a safe and its door was open. In his hand was a pistol. His face was red with anger as he turned to his wife.

'These are treacherous times, Emilia,' he said, waving the pistol in the air. 'You can't trust anyone these days. Still I'm lucky the men didn't stop to listen. Turned their backs on Pablo Lopez and that idiot son of his, didn't want anything to do with them. Too damn tired I suppose.' Then he laughed. He laughed at those poor men who worked so hard to make him his money. And how dare he call Pablo an idiot? He was the most intelligent person I knew. I stared through the gap in anger. He was loading bullets into the pistol and muttering, 'I knew this would come in handy sometime.' Now his wife moved into my view, as pretty as anything, with her hands together as if in prayer.

'Please don't, Diego. I bought it as a gift from a trader in Toledo. I didn't expect you to use it.' I saw that the gun had been removed from an inlaid box and the interior was lined in green velvet. How could such a beautiful thing, lying in such an ornate box, be used in anger? His wife must have been thinking the same and she made her words sing like those of an angel. 'Look at its beauty, Diego. Look at the fancy damascene work along its edges and the shape of the trigger curled up so gracefully like a licking tongue. It's not meant for shooting. It's meant for love.' But Don Diego took no notice.

He slipped it inside his jacket and declared, 'The world is changing, wife. Besides, if you want fancy dresses and expensive trips to Seville, then let me handle things my way.' I watched her pull a shawl over the shoulders of her beautiful nightgown, and fold her arms against her chest, helpless to protest, as Don Diego pulled out a bottle of brandy from the desk drawer and slumped into his chair. He shoved his feet on the desk and swigged at the bottle as if he didn't care. I tiptoed back to my room, grateful that Don

166

Diego hadn't mentioned my name but I was worried too. Recently I'd grown bolder and more confident about my future. I was fit and healthy and the housekeeper treated me well. Now though, I felt sick. My stomach lurched and my head spun as I realised that everything I was beginning to take for granted was just an illusion. I was still very much at the whim of others, dependent on them for my very existence, and no matter how I tried to convince myself otherwise, my newly acquired self-assurance was a sham because everything - my food and my shelter, my very survival - was in the hands of a very angry man and his weak compliant wife. My only hope was to stay quiet and not make a fuss.

33. Mariangeles

Mariangeles decorated the shop walls with sketches of her creations, and stacked an old dresser with rolls of bright-coloured cloth, allowing them to cascade onto the newly scrubbed floor. Then she placed her sewing machine and her paper patterns just visible in the back room, so that customers could observe her at work and know that, thanks to the talents of her mother and grandmother and their mothers before them, she was a skilled craftswoman. Then she filled the shop with flowers from the meadow and warmed it with logs in the hearth. Her first order had been collected that morning and the mother and daughter had left the shop full of admiration. Now, other women were gathering at her window, hoping to see something they liked.

'Come in,' Mariangeles said, and as they entered, she recognized the wives of the bull-breeders and cotton-farmers whose children had played with Sebastiana years ago. Mariangeles smiled. From now on Sunday mornings were going to be busy.

Later that day she marched down to the harbour and, without knocking, went straight into Garcia's cabin. When he saw her, he bristled.

'You've come back then,' he said and as he spoke Mariangeles noticed the row of small indentations running across his cheek, still red from where she had bitten him.

'Here,' she said slamming her payment down onto his table. The same table where he had assaulted her; the old battered table that seemed to represent his soul. 'Count it and give me a receipt,' she demanded. 'And I expect you to deduct the extra interest you charged, or else I will go to the authorities and tell them what you did.' Her heart was thumping. She didn't know how he would react.

He stood up and coughed. 'Madam, it is an honour to do business with a woman such as you.' He bowed and Mariangeles raised her eyebrows. Standing up to this man was easier that she had thought.

'So we will resume our arrangement at the same rate as before?' she asked and Garcia nodded. Mariangeles left smiling. Her debt had been reduced, and she had stood up to her aggressor in a way she would never have done before leaving Bartolome. As she walked back through the busy harbour, she glanced over at the queue of down-and-outs waiting by the fishwives' stall. Amongst the barefooted children and the ragged men, she saw him - legs bent, shoulders hunched and his clothes in pieces. Her stomach dipped. Her heart jumped. What should she do? She stepped forward as if she might walk over and greet him. Then stopped. Above her, gulls were screeching. Were they warning her to hold back? It had been a long journey to get away from Bartolome and his drinking but it would be a short journey back if she took another step in his direction. She stood and watched for a moment as he shuffled forward in the queue but she didn't go to him. Instead she turned away and strode across the square, not looking back, not wanting to know more about his obvious misfortune. Disconnection was the only way to keep safe, to keep herself sane.

Pepe came to visit. He sat by the stove and sniffed the air.'

'Smells good, Marieangeles,' he said, leaning over a pan on the stove. She smiled at hearing her name on his lips. It felt good.

'Tell me about your new jobs, Pepe, 'she said stirring the stew.

'I'm doin' contraband now,' he said, and Mariangeles raised her eyebrows. 'We pulls our wagons out at dawn, travelling to Medina and then on to Jerez and Seville, then come back through the old smugglers' routes, crossing the sierras and the lake at Almodovar. It's quite an adventure.'

Mariangeles sighed. Why do men always get themselves into these situations? Why can't they be sensible like us? Pepe hadn't finished. 'We follows the twists and turns of the arroyos, and ends our shifts with a *copa* or two in Alfonso's bar. Then early the next day we goes the other way, collecting even more alcohol and cigars out of Gib and start all over again.' Mariangeles tipped the stew into bowls and Pepe sat back, cheeks radiant from the steam, his eyes shining and happy. 'You should see us, Mariangeles. Carts packed full of booze and those fat Cuban cigars. Alfonso has connections see - brings shiploads over. He makes a fortune.'

'So, who is this Alfonso?'

'He's... er... just a man with a flair for business, 'Pepe said but Mariangeles had noticed his sudden restraint and guessed.

'Does this Alfonso have anything to do with my Sebastiana? she asked.

'Can't say, Mariangeles but I'm not gonna keep working for 'im. I got plans.'

'What plans? Something legal, I hope.'

'The roads is full of ruts and when it rains we has to pay the Bullock Men to drag us out the mud, so I designed a new wheel with bigger hubs and shorter spokes that'll make driving easier over them muddy tracks. I drills only halfway through the hub

171

see, so the spokes are firm and the wheel is strong. Then I attach the metal tyre, hammering the band onto the wooden rim while it's still red hot, then dowsin' it with icy water so it shrinks to fit the wheel. It'll make me a fortune, Mariangeles. I'm sure of it.'

Mariangeles smiled as she collected the empty bowls and put them in the sink. Who was she to judge someone else's dream? 'Sounds good,' she said then asked 'and what about the other job? You said you had two.'

Pepe's face dropped. He pinched his lips as if holding in his answer. 'It's only a bit of this and that,' he said. You wouldn't be interested.

Mariangeles knew better than to push her friend to reveal his secrets so she changed the subject, asking the question she had longed to know the answer to.

'Have you seen Sebastiana? Is she still living near Gibraltar?'

'Told you before, Mariangeles. I don't know where she is but I don't think she's gone far. I see all sorts on the road and I ask them if they've seen your girl travelling and the answer is always no. So, I reckons she's still livin' in the same area, somewhere in the bay.

That evening Incarna appeared at the door. 'Found you at last, Mari' she said. 'Been to the house loads of time and you wasn't there. In the end Pepe told me you was here.' She looked around at the sketches on the wall and the sewing machine in the back room. 'Doing all right for yourself, Mari. Good for you. If you ask me, we're better off without men getting in the way, without havin' no one to answer to.'

'You're probably right, Incarna but it's nice to lay next to a man all naked and warm and have him hold you tight,' she said and Incarna laughed.

'Missing him already?'

172

'No, Incarna, I'll never go back to Bartolome now,' she said, allowing her mind to wander a little to another possibility. Pepe wasn't like her husband. Pepe was quiet, respectful and kind. Was he someone in whom she could trust? Was he someone who could be more than just a friend? After all, he had split from his wife years ago - on the road too much to keep their flame alive, he'd said. But Mariangeles kept all these thought to herself because Incarna was still the gossip she always was. And as if to prove it, she plonked herself in the chair by the stove.

'You'll never guess what's happened to The Fixer, Mari. They say he's left the area, been pushed out by the Gypsies, so he's had to go somewhere else to make his money. Reckon you had a lucky escape.' Mariangeles agreed but even from this distance, she still felt under his spell and she put her hand to her neck, remembering his fingers around her flesh and the strange movements of his limbs. The man was cruel; the man was a manipulator. The man was bad.

'So, where has he gone?' she asked, hoping it was far enough away for her to put him out of her mind.

'They say 'es gone East, Mari, somewhere Gibraltar way.'

Mariangeles shivered. East near Gibraltar was not what she wanted to hear. East near Gibraltar was near her girl.

The treadle on the sewing machine moved noisily up and down. The thread on its spindle spun swiftly round and round, and the shuttle in the lower compartment rattled in syncopation with the rest. Mariangeles worked on her creations from early morning until dusk dimmed the light. Word of her talents had spread across town and she was fulfilling orders before the *fiesta de caballos* began. Even Garcia appeared at her window and stared at her while she was cutting cloth. She wondered if he was checking her out as a potential client for another loan, or was it something else. She got up and closed the curtains, anxious to keep the man out and concentrate on her work. Later, she sat by the fire with a needle in her hand and with Incarna's words nagging her like a dog at a bone. The Fixer was in the bay of Gibraltar and Sebastiana was there too. Somewhere over there in the east was the man with whom she had so shamefully conspired to take Sebastiana away; to carry her off to, what she now knew, would have been a life of misery in a brothel working for that terrible, cruel man and she couldn't help worrying. What if they met? What if The Fixer recognised Sebastiana in the street, remembered her as the girl who ran away leaving him with an unpaid bill? The man was vindictive and would seek retribution and this would be his opportunity for revenge. She was sure of that. She had to find Sebastiana before it was too late. But how? According to Pepe, the bay of Gibraltar was a big place and she didn't know the area. But *he* did. Perhaps he would help her find her daughter. Or would he? He had kept Sebastiana's location secret for so long that maybe he was still keeping it now. And who was this Alfonso fellow he'd mentioned? She'd seen the disturbed look on Pepe's face when she had asked about him. Something was going on. She sensed it.

Just as she was closing, Garcia appeared at the window again but this time he knocked on the door.

'May I come in?' he said, removing his hat.

'Why? Your payment isn't due for a few days,' she said.

'I know, but this is a different matter,' he said looking down at his shoes. He seemed shy, twisting his hat in both hands, so she let him in and he coughed as he readied himself to speak. 'Dear lady, I have been thinking about our arrangement. Perhaps there might be another way.'

Mariangeles scoffed. 'What? Like last time when you attacked me?'

'Madam, I deeply regret what I did,' he said stroking a finger across the scar on his cheek. 'I have come to apologise for my gross behaviour and ask if you would be willing to take me on as a partner.'

'A partner?

'Yes, dear lady.'

'You mean a business partner?'

'No. I mean, no. I didn't mean that. I meant… a romantic partner if you see what I mean.'

Mariangeles stared at him. Was he serious? 'Do you mean marriage?' she asked.

'Madam, I am unused to these things, but any arrangement - married or not.'

'You mean living as man and woman instead of paying off the rest of my debt?'

'Yes, that's it,' he said excitedly. 'I would waive all rights to your payments if you accept my proposal. I would treat you well, dear lady. I would treat you right.' Mariangeles stifled a grin. How pathetic thc man looked standing there clutching his hat. But despite his clumsy attempt to kiss her the other day, she felt sorry for him. How lonely he must be, hidden in that windowless cabin all day with no female companionship to offset the behaviour of drunken men. But then she did a calculation in her head. What Garcia didn't know was that soon she would have enough money to pay off her debt completely. Soon she would be free from any further obligation. Besides she could think of nothing worse than lying next to him for the rest of her days.

She smiled a long extended smile to give herself time to think, then touched his arm as tenderly as she dared, and murmured 'Señor Garcia, I am an independent woman who prefers to live alone. I would be a fraud if I was to accept your invitation.' Garcia nodded, bowed to her in an old-fashioned way, and then left, stumbling a little as he exited the door. Mariangeles retreated into her workroom. She sat amongst her cloth and her patterns and her labours, where she felt safe. How curious men are, she thought. First assaulting her then proposing a liaison. She went to the mirror and studied her face. At fifty-six she had thought herself too old for love, but perhaps not. Perhaps there was a chance, but not with that clumsy Garcia who lacked social skills and had no understanding of how to woo a woman. The next day she went to his cabin and repaid her debt. She laid the money on the table and he counted it quietly without protest, then bowed one last time and held the door open for her to leave. It was finished. It was done. Outside, gulls were dipping and diving on the thermals and calling to each other over the spray. They seemed happy and so was she. Spring was coming and she felt the rise of something new, some opportunity she could not quite articulate but which was almost ready for her to touch. She walked over to the harbour and watched the waves gently lapping against the castle walls. Nothing violent today, everything soft and serene. She sighed deeply, remembering her mother's refrain; *'sorrows and waves never arrive alone'* and wondered if perhaps, at last, she had broken the family spell.

When Pepe came for his now monthly visit, she was prepared. 'Pepe, you must help me find my daughter. I have to find Tia before it is too late.'

34. Tia

My hands had become red and chapped like Agnes's and my stockings, held up with old pennies, were ripped and frayed. My boots were worn down at the heel and no longer fitted my feet. But life wasn't so bad as long as I resisted Pablo's advice to demand payment for my work. Don Diego seemed such an angry man that I daren't risk it. So, I kept my head down and got on with my work, becoming skilled at getting the fire to burn at the right temperature by adding just enough wood to bring the copper to the boil, then spreading the charred pieces to provide a constant simmer. Sheets, pillowcases and undergarments all surrendered to my attention and each morning I worked like a mule, pounding the dolly in the tub, scrubbing the clothes against the washboard, and rinsing everything in a huge tub before passing them through the mangle.

It was spring and the terrace looked beautiful in a cloudless sky. One by one I hung the wet washing on lines that crisscrossed the space, looping the corners of the sheets as Agnes had taught me. The rope line rasped against the poles as the sheets bulged and dipped in the breeze, reminding me of those ships I used to watch sailing across the bay. Then I started on the underwear, holding up a pair of men's all-in-ones with fancy buttons on their openings, front and back. I pegged the shoulders to the line and instantly they filled with air, re-assembling the form that had recently occupied them. I giggled, trying to imagine Don Diego's naked body inside. Then, as I stretched to peg out more clothes, my legs felt tired and my arms gave way. Needing a short rest, I leaned on the balustrade which overlooked an alleyway running along the back of the house, and listened to the flapping of sheets and the chirping of birds on the rooftops. Suddenly I heard an odd noise from the alleyway below. I looked down. Someone was crying.

'Don't hurt me,' the voice said.

And a high-pitched man's voice replied. 'Then give me my dues, girl.'

I stared down into the shadows. A man was gripping a girl's throat and she was struggling for air. He jerked her head to one side and she squealed in pain, then she started coughing a deep rasping cough that echoed throughout the alleyway. The man shoved her against the wall, bending her double as if to break her back. 'Let me go,' she cried but her arms were caught up inside his black cape so she couldn't move.

I leaned into the alley to get a better look. The girl's face was contorted with fear and her eyes were tight shut. But mine weren't. They were wide open in horror, as I watched the limbs of the man quiver as if he had an affliction. I knew at once it was The Fixer; the man from whom I had escaped all that time ago, and the girl whimpering in pain was my lovely Eva. Oh god! What should I do? I heard her cough again with that deep lung-filled sound that seemed to go nowhere. He dragged her into the street and I ran downstairs just as the two of them were emerging from the darkness. I went to speak, but Eva ignored me, pulling the man around and handing him a purse. Then she linked her arm into his and with the strangest swagger, sauntered away with him as if she was happy to be in the company of that terrible man.

178

I didn't understand. What was The Fixer doing here? I thought he worked in Seville where he had planned to take me all those years ago. So why was he here? And with Eva too? I thought she lived in Alfonso's place down in the bay. I watched them walk off, noticing his legs rising and falling so unnaturally and although I understood it was an affliction beyond his control, I couldn't sympathise, remembering how he had pressed his thin body against me in our kitchen and how it had smelt of a stagnant well.

I returned to my work but could not erase him from my thoughts. I would have to be careful. If I met him again, he might recognise me as the girl that had escaped from his clutches, the girl who had run away. I hoped I was wrong. After all, I was much taller now and my jawline had become more pronounced since last we met. Perhaps he wouldn't know who I was. Perhaps I was safe. Even so, from then on, wherever I went in the village, a streak of black would catch my eye and I'd look up to see a figure flash past, deadly dark against the white walls. Was it him? Had he come here to haunt me? He appeared at night too, darkening my dreams, sapping my energy, until in the morning I could hardly think. A feeling of dread passed over me and I knew that soon he would come. I could feel it in my bones and in my stomach too. I became sick and Agnes noticed.

'What's up, Tia? You look terrible.'

But how could I explain that this man from my past was waiting around every corner ready to pounce. I would have to explain how I'd escaped from The Fixer and come to the east looking for work and found it in the cork factory before it burned down. Half a story wouldn't do because Agnes was clever, she was sure to have remembered the newspaper article telling everyone that the girl who started the fire was from the west and had a troubled past. She could easily deduce that *I* was that girl. I had to speak to Eva. She was the only one who would understand. Besides, I had to know what was going on.

After finishing my work for the afternoon, I slipped out of the house and hitched a ride to the bay. The first thing I smelt was the familiar aroma of *pulpo asado* wafting from Alfonso's kitchen and the first thing I saw was how dilapidated his place looked; windows broken, roof rusting and the bar sign *Venta Alfonso* swinging on one hook like a dead fish on a line. Perhaps Alfonso didn't care about the state of his bar as long as men kept coming to buy his booze and pay for his girls. Why should he bother to make the place nicer? I stood in the sand, under the shade of a palm tree, where no one could see me, and called up into one of the bedrooms. A drunken female voice shouted through the dirty window.

'Hey girl, come up and join us.'

I shook my head 'Is Eva there?' I asked and very soon my old friend emerged from the building. What a state she was in. Her teeth were black, her hands were shaking and she was even thinner than before. I rushed to take her in my arms and as she rested her head on my shoulder, I felt her bones against me like a skeleton. We walked towards the shoreline.

'We'll have to be quick,' she said. 'The punters arrive soon and if I'm late Alfonso will refuse to give me food.'

'Eva, that man you were with in the village.'

'Who? Manolo?'

'Is that what he calls himself now?'

'He's been trying to get me to leave Alfonso and work for him. Says I'm skin and bone and that he will feed me well and give me somewhere nice to live.'

'And did you say yes?' I asked, worried that, like my mother, she would fall for his perverted charms.

'He said he wanted to try me out first.'

'Eva, I know this man. You mustn't trust him.'

180

'It's too late, Tia. I've decided. I'm going with him tomorrow.

'But he is cruel.'

'I already know that. His idea of sex is humiliation.' I was shocked to hear Eva talk like this. But what did I know? She must have read my mind because she sat on the sand and patted the place beside her.

'Sit down, Tia. I am going to tell you about the ways of men.'

She spoke of sex in every detail including the things she was asked to do. Dear Eva, she told me this because I needed to know and because my ma hadn't told me before. It sounded horrible.

'But, Eva, how can you stand it?'

'The power of the mind is a wonderful thing, Tia. We girls have a saying *When a man is on you, plunge yourself into darkness. When a man is in you, rise into the light.*' It was an act of enormous courage for Eva to tell me these things and all the while she was looking about nervously. I suppose she thought Alfonso would suddenly appear and make me his, and then he would punish her too. Despite this she went back to the bar and returned with a paper packet wrapped in string. She must have stolen it from the store where the girls kept their medicines. 'Here, Tia. Inside are tinctures made from thistles and ginger. The first will help you stay infertile and the ginger is to make you bleed. You never know when you might need them.' There was a small jar of olive oil steeped in rosemary too, and a lotion of marjoram to rub into my abdomen if my bleed was painful, and a tincture of herbs laced with rum to ease the cramps. And all this time I was praying for both our sakes that Alfonso wouldn't arrive. Before we parted, I put my arms around her waist and held her tight. Her shoulders relaxed and she folded into my embrace and sobbed like a child. Then we pulled apart and I walked back into the village, slipping quietly into my bed and hoping that The Fixer or Manolo as he was now called would not find me.

I was alone in the square, waiting for Pablo, when a voice from behind spoke.

'Permiso?'

A man came around the bench to sit beside me. He tipped his hat and when he wrapped his black cape around his bony knees, a sickly-sweet odour wafted up between us. Was this real? Was The Fixer really sitting here with me? Or was it my imagination? I trembled then bit my lip making blood seep into my mouth. It was warm. It was sweet. It was real.

'Good morning, miss,' he said and his voice was shrill like I remembered. And had he remembered *me*? I prayed not. 'My dear girl, may I be of assistance?' he said. I didn't reply. My body had gone rigid with fear. He leaned in and lifted my hand from my lap, then held it in his long cold fingers and kissed it with wet, tepid lips. 'Permit me to introduce myself,' he murmured. 'I am Manuel Jimenez Torres, at your service.' He stared into my face. 'Don't I know you?' he said, searching my features, searching his mind. 'You look familiar.' I looked down trying to hide my face. 'What's your name?' he asked but I didn't look up in case he saw the terror in my eyes. He waited a few more seconds and I felt him tense at my lack of cooperation. Then he released my hand and it dropped like a stone into my lap. He stood upright, towering above me. 'I'll go now but we'll meet again, I'm sure.' Then he strode off, sweeping his black cape behind him, just like he had in the square of our old town the first time we'd met.

When Pablo arrived, I was desperate. 'Let's get out of here,' I said.

'What's the matter, Tia? You're trembling.' 1 shook my head at his question, not wanting to tell him about my encounter with The Fixer because then I would have to tell him how I had escaped the wretched man's clutches back home, and explain my flirting with Don Francisco and then that foolishness with Alfonso and the fire that made me jobless and brought me to this village. I wouldn't be able to stop myself. What would he think of me if he knew all that, if he knew I was the girl who had started that fire? Everyone in the village knew about it, but no one knew it was me. I wanted him to care about this new girl, not the foolish one with a terrible past.

'It's nothing,' I said shrugging him off. We walked down the hill to the Alameda where the plane trees were creating silky shade that put me more at ease. We sat on a bench. 'Let's meet here from now on,' I said. Pablo didn't ask why, perhaps because I was still shivering. Instead he put his arm around me and for a moment I felt safe. But I dared not venture into the church square again, nor sit on that bench anymore, in case The Fixer sidled up beside me and remembered my name.

For now I had escaped his daytime encounters, but every night The Fixer sat on the end of my bed and every night he was wearing black plumage as if he were a bird of prey. He was my watcher, my keeper, and as I sank deeper into my dreams, his mouth transformed slowly and silently into a vicious red beak. And every night he stared at me, scrutinising my face as if he was about to recognise the girl from the west, the girl who'd escaped his plans. Each dawn I woke immersed in his evil, and I remembered Eva's account of men's desires and the things they made her do. Were all men the same? Surely not? What about dear sweet Pablo, with his earnest faith in the human spirit? Surely he wasn't the same as those hateful men? I wanted to love Pablo, I really did. But each month we met, these questions returned to haunt me and then I doubted everything. Was there such a thing as the real love of a tender man? And even if there was, could I love him? And more importantly, how could he possibly love me back?

Now nightmares dissolved into daydreams, making me unsure of what was true and what was not. I began to see The Fixer everywhere and I wondered if I was trapped inside my own nightmare. Agnes asked me again

'Are you sure you're all right, Tia. Is that boy you're seeing giving you trouble?' I shook my head but she wasn't convinced. A day later she approached me. 'I've been asking at the church. The priest said he will talk to you, and help you with your troubles.' Her tone was so kind and her intentions so pure that, although I had no interest in the church, I agreed.

It was the same priest that Eva and I had listened to at the end of the century, except now his gait was even slower and his skinny old hands moved rapidly in time with his speech as if conducting an orchestra. I suppose that was true in a way; him waving his hands like a baton, always in control of his congregation.

Agnes and I sat together on a pew as the priest talked and we listened.

'Life is a great circle, Tia. Take almond blossom for instance. It appears in April and by July their nuts will be ready for harvesting, then in November, the yellow-grey smoke of their bonfires fills the skies.' I frowned. What was he talking about? But I didn't interrupt. 'Everything has a beginning and everything has an end and sometimes the end is also the beginning.' I nodded respectfully but without comprehension. Was he trying to tell me to stop seeing Pablo? I didn't understand. 'Did our Lord not die so that we might be cleansed and reborn?' he said solemnly. 'Did he not suffer for our sins?' Agnes nodded gravely as if she agreed with everything he said but I left the church unconvinced. They were just words that meant nothing. I returned to my room and lay on my bed trying to fathom the old priest's meaning. I thought about how far I had come, from being accused of wickedness by my mother, to escaping The Fixer and coming to the bay, the tragedy of the fire and my exclusion by the rest, and how Eva and I had survived the poverty of the *chozas*. So many bad things had happened in my fifteen years and now they seemed to be getting worse. Eva was on a path to extinction, and I too, was at the mercy of men; dependent on Don Diego for my food and sleep; on Alfonso who had burned my reputation alongside that fire; and Pablo, too, whose love would certainly fade if he knew who I really was. And of course The Fixer. If he saw me again, he would surely recognise me. It was only a matter of time. So, perhaps the priest *was* right. Nature moves in cycles. It revolves. It comes back round. The foolish girl from the west who travelled east to start again was still inside me, waiting to resurface. Just as almond blossom lives its momentary glory in the sun then yields its beauty to a solid brown seed in order to start again, our past becomes our future, on a never-ending roll. I thought about my mother's refrain and I wondered. Was the push and pull of the tide too strong to resist? Was the family curse that had affected the women who came before me, about to bring about my own misfortune too?

Part Five: Mariangeles and Tia

35. Mariangeles

This year's *paseo de caballos* had been and gone. Mariangeles counted the abundance of money she had earned making beautiful dresses for the festival and divided it into two bundles; one for the safe-box hidden in her workroom, and the rest for her purse. She threw some travelling clothes into a bag, locked the door to her premises and went outside where Pepe was waiting in the whispering dawn light. Mariangeles gave Jefe an apple and mounted the cart.

'It'll take all day, Mariangeles,' Pepe warned.

'Don't worry. Take your time. I want to see where you took Tia. I want my journey to be like hers.' Pepe smiled, flicked the reins and Jefe headed out of town taking the road north to the crossroads, where they turned east into the slowly rising sun. How pleased she had been when he'd said yes. Bartolome would never have agreed to take time out to search, even for his own daughter. Yet here she was sitting beside her new friend, anticipating the joys of spending several days in his company and hopefully finding her girl.

Mariangeles felt every bump in the road. Every rise made her leap in the air, and every fall caused her buttocks to land so hard on the wooden seat that her entire body juddered. She could have hired a landau or travelled on one of Don Francisco's stagecoaches with its leather braces to smoothen the journey, yet despite the poor suspension on his cart, being with Pepe was where she wanted to be. She settled herself with a rug over her knees and relaxed. Jefe sensed the open road and soon they were picking up speed, travelling along the coast road where a heavy mist was lifting off the ground, obscuring their view and making the sound of Jefe's hooves seem dull and distant. Mariangeles could see nothing but the animal's flanks glistening with droplets of moisture, and his muscles moving in such a pleasing rhythm that she fell asleep. The screeching of an owl woke her and when she turned round to take a look, she saw another cart just like theirs and another horse just like Jefe riding behind them, grey and insubstantial like ghosts.

Her stomach dipped. 'What's that?' she shrieked and Pepe laughed.

'It's our shadows, Mariangeles. I often sees them coming up this way, when the sun's tryin' to eat its way through the mist.' Mariangeles laughed. Pepe was so knowledgeable and she was so naïve. When they reached a viewing place, the mist had cleared and they stopped to look out over the bay.

'That's Africa over there,' Pepe said pointing to the thin strip of grey in front of them, and somewhere along the coastline is the great city of Tangiers. Mariangeles smiled at Pepe's understanding of the landscape. She had seen so little of life beyond her locality. This was a real adventure. At midday they turned into the forest.

'Thought we could go up through the cork trees like I did with Tia,' Pepe said. When they found a clearing, they sat down to eat bread and drink wine. Nearby, men were stripping cork from the trees, leaving the inner trunk exposed.

'Those poor trees will surely die,' Mariangeles said.

Pepe smiled. 'Don't worry, Mariangeles. Them trees is perfectly safe if you knows what you're doing. In nine years that bark'll be

188

all grown back.' Mariangeles smiled. Her new friend was always so positive about everything. However, today he seemed sad.

'What's the matter?' she asked.

'Well, I reckons life was better when I was out collectin' bark. '

'Why?'

'Alfonso don't pay as well as the cork factory.'

'But didn't you say you had two jobs?' she asked.

'Yes, but…'

'So what is it that you do?' Mariangeles asked not realising her question would be difficult.

Pepe frowned then muttered

'I don't want to say, Mariangeles. Shall we go?'

They continued their journey, turning back onto the main road where the sun had burned through the mist. Pepe was quiet now as if her question had offended him, so she remained quiet too, holding her hand up to protect her eyes from the overhead sun. A giant promontory loomed up from the ocean; it was a rock that everyone talked about and which she had only seen from a distance, appearing like a pebble on a pond. Now though, she felt its huge presence; it was deep and solid and standing proud against the flatness of the mainland. Gibraltar was magnificent.

Dusk began settling around them, but they travelled on, the agricultural landscape giving way to the odd hamlet of workers' cottages, then the train station and finally they moved onto roads that felt smooth. They had reached the outskirts of a town. Street lights were being lit with tapers and people were gathering in the street or sitting in doorways observing.

'I'll take you to the bay first,' Pepe said. 'But I warn you, what you're going to see will be grim.'

By the time they arrived at the ruins of the cork factory, it was too dark to get a sense of their surroundings. All she could hear was the rhythm of the waves somewhere close by, moving slowly in and out like respiration, then exhalation. And all that Mariangeles could see, highlighted by a pale moon, was the jagged contours of iron girders distorted by fire, silhouetted soot-black against a midnight-blue sky. A shrill wind whipped up between them giving Mariangeles the impression of the rigging on a deserted ship, sailing crewless into a violent storm. Pepe sighed, staring into the wreckage devoid of human occupation.

'All the workers have gone now; dead or travelled elsewhere lookin' for work.'

'Like Tia?' Mariangeles asked, fishing for information.

'I told you, Mariangeles, I don't know where she went.' Pepe lowered his eyes and she looked at him critically.

'What is it, Pepe? What aren't you telling me?'

'It's nothing, Mariangeles, but I knows where Tia used to live. That might help.'

'Where, Pepe? Tell me.'

'We can go there now, and you can take a room.'

They left the cinder-laden factory and made their way to the hostel. 'I'll collect you in the morning,' Pepe said rushing off hastily, leaving Mariangeles certain that Pepe had a secret he didn't want to tell. At supper Mariangeles invited the hostel owner to join her, anxious to know as much as she could about Tia's stay.

'Do you remember my daughter?'

'Of course. What a sweet girl.'

Mariangeles smiled.

'Such a shame about that article in the newspaper, though. It tore her apart. '

Mariangeles frowned. 'What newspaper?' But the hostel owner was still talking.

190

'And that old wretch Alfonso, blaming it all on her.'

'What do you mean? Blaming her for what?'

'It was all just gossip, from what I could tell.'

'What was? What gossip?' Mariangeles could hardly speak or eat.

'All that talk about her being Alfonso's mistress and how she'd thrown herself at him in the cloisters.' Mariangeles's heart sank remembering the way Tia had flirted with Don Francisco and what had happened next. The hostel owner gathered up the plates of half-eaten food and as she went into the kitchen she added, 'So, now everyone calls her *the girl who started that fire*. Poor kid.'

Mariangeles slept badly; strange bed; terrible revelations knocking her off kilter, making her think the worst. Were those gossips right? Was Sebastiana really flirting with men twice her age, yielding to passions she shouldn't have? She turned over trying to sleep but she'd come here to find her girl - to hold her, to love her and apologise for her condemnations - and now this? She felt sick. Perhaps her daughter really was bad. Had she come all this way to discover this unpleasant truth? She tried to ignore it, remembering how Incarna used to gossip in her kitchen and how most of it was tittle-tattle rubbish. Some things are simply false, she said to herself as firmly as she could. But then she wondered if perhaps somewhere in their cacophony of spite there was a grain of truth.

36. Tia

I walked to the church square where a horse and a cart, covered in rosettes and ribbons, was waiting to take us to the fiesta. Agnes climbed up next to the driver and I sat with a group of servant girls in the back. The dress I'd borrowed from Agnes fitted well and when someone said, 'You look pretty, Tia,' I smiled. This was going to be a wonderful day. The horse began his careful descent towards Main Avenue, passing the museum, the doctor's house, the lawyer's, and then my own workplace where, in the servants' doorway, Pablo stood holding a bunch of flowers. He jumped out and ran alongside our cart.

'Tia, these are for you!' he shouted. I looked down at the running boy, flustered as he waved the bouquet up to my level. What should I do? Should I accept? I fussed with my skirts to give me time to think. Was it true what Eva had told me? Were all men bad? Not this one I thought. But how should I respond? Be thrilled or aloof? Show my delight or wait until I was sure? Pablo called up again. 'Take them please,' he shouted and I looked down at his earnest face.

'For me?'

'Of course.'

'But why me?' I was teasing him now. I couldn't help it. He grinned at my tone and I laughed a crystal-clear laugh of happiness. It was my first real laugh since before that fire and it felt good. Then I heard Pablo's answer, calm yet breathless as he ran alongside.

'Because, Tia, you are the most beautiful creature in the world.'

Agnes laughed.

'Poor boy. Put him out of his misery, Tia. Take the flowers.'

But I couldn't. Me? Beautiful? How could he possibly think that? Surely this was a trick and Eva was right - men were bad. Or was I scared that I wasn't good enough for him? Or that he was so much cleverer than me? Whatever the reason, I remained upright in the cart, eyes fixed forward, yet wanting to look down, as Pablo persisted all the way down the hill.

We turned into the square. The band was tuning up. Discordant notes from clarinets, oboes, trumpets, rose chaotically into the air. Children darted around the fountain, and men, dressed in embroidered jackets, sat on restless horses festooned in the colours of the rainbow. The men looked so handsome and mysterious sitting so high up with their wide-brimmed hats pulled over their eyes casting dark shadows across their faces. One man leaned over and offered his hand to a brightly dressed woman below. In a flash, he had hauled her up onto his saddle and there was a waft of cologne as the frills of her dress cascaded down the horse's flanks. Then other men did the same, hauling their women up beside them and snuggling their chests against the women's backs with a tenderness that I didn't quite understand. Whatever the sensation was, I felt a tingle of excitement. A musician waved padded sticks dramatically above his head, then crashed them down against the copper surface of a huge gong. The vibrations sent me into a spin. Suddenly the musical notes assumed a recognisable order as the first bars of a *sevillana* burst into the air. I closed my eyes. How could anything be more wonderful? When I opened them, Pablo

194

was standing below, holding the bouquet and catching his breath. I noticed that some of the heads of the flowers had drooped and the paper was damp. Agnes and I waited in the cart. Then the driver jumped down and swung Agnes to the ground. They laughed as if they knew each other and I smiled at their intimacy. There was a romantic feeling in the air that was hard to resist. One by one the other servant girls jumped down and I got up to dismount too. But then I stopped. Moving towards me was a white horse with its head restricted by tightened reins. From my position high up on the cart I could see directly into its eyes. They were edged in black, and within the thick, smoky rings they seemed gentle and kind. It blinked and tossed its head and I gasped at the elegant arch of its neck and its finely sculptured head. It was impossible to see the rider's face, shaded by the wide brim of his black sombrero, but he was dressed in black with embroidery running down the outer leg of his trousers with a colourful scarf thrown over one shoulder. The spurs of his high boots tinkled softly as he manoeuvred the horse between us. He leaned down and offered me his hand and without thinking, I brought mine up to meet it. In a flash he'd hauled me up and I landed heavily on the creature, making it misstep slightly as it adjusted to my weight. Then, before I could protest, the man wrapped his arms around my waist and I felt his chest pressed against my back. He leaned in to whisper.

'Tia, you do me the greatest honour.'

I knew that voice. I recognised the gravelly tone from smoking those cigars. It was the same tone he'd used with me in that cloister, and now I was seated on his horse with his arms wrapped firmly around my waist so that I could hardly move. What a fool I had been to raise my arm. Alfonso leaned over my shoulder and sniffed. 'You smell nice, Tia.' I shivered as he dug his spurs into the poor horse and we moved down the Alameda towards the bull ring. The movements of the horse forced my body against his - up and down, forward and back. I felt sick.

'Let me off,' I said, but Alfonso held me even tighter and when I struggled he pinched my arm then leaned in and whispered to me.

'These people don't recognise you, but if you make a fuss I can tell them. Shall I do that, Tia? Shall I tell them you are the foolish girl who started that fire?' I tried to wriggle free but Alfonso was holding me so tight now that I could only move my head. Then I remembered Pablo and strained to look over my shoulder, searching for him in the blur of faces. I found him in the distance, raising his bouquet into the air, holding it there for a few seconds to make sure I could see it. Then he flung the flowers into the gutter and walked away.

The horse sauntered along the Alameda and reached a group of men who watched as Alfonso jumped down and offered me his hand. Someone shouted 'Alfonso, you old tyrant!' He waved back then turned to me. 'Come on, bitch. Do as I say.' I hesitated but his tone was frightening and with everyone watching, what could I do? If the villagers discovered my identity, my reputation would be shattered and I might lose my job. The Fixer would surely get to hear about it, too, and discover that the girl who started the fire was also a stranger from the west. Like Agnes he would be sure to work out the connection, and even if he didn't recognise my face, he would soon realise who I was; the girl who had escaped his hands and left him with a debt. Then what would he do? I sighed and slipped down off the horse, placing my trembling arm through Alfonso's as we walked together towards the bull ring.

The doors were tall, with deep cuts where a century of padlocks and chains had gauged their way through them. We climbed a dark staircase and the echo of many voices vibrated like bees in a giant hive. I noticed that Alfonso was using a stick and that he was limping. How agile he'd looked on that beautiful horse. But now, as we emerged at the top of the stairs and he removed his hat, I saw that he was almost bald, and as we sat in the morning

196

sun, I noticed deep wrinkles etched into his forehead. He lit an expensive-looking cigar and puffed at it with a wide smile as everyone observed us. He hired cushions to make the stone steps comfortable and ordered beer from a boy.

'Here, Tia, have a drink,' he said but I shook my head and he laughed. We sat next to a balcony wrapped in red velvet, from where the mayor waved across at us and Alfonso waved back. Women with deep cleavages fluttered their fans towards him and men came to slap him on the back and give him a wink. I lowered my eyes and shrank into my seat, not knowing what to do.

The crystal-clear notes of a trumpet hit the air and a matador entered with his crew of toreros. The crowd went silent and I held my breath. A pasodoble started. There was a screech of metal as someone opened a gate and a bull burst in, its hooves pounding the dry sand, raising it like ocean spray. It stopped dead centre as the particles of displaced sand fell slowly to the ground and the creature took in its new surroundings, observing us as we observed him. The crowd cheered, and I did too, admiring his straight back and deep chest. He was magnificent. A torero waved a magenta coloured cape and the creature dropped its head to charge. What movement, what grace! It thundered forward and the man with the cape side-stepped with skill. Charge by charge, the bull attacked and over and over the bullfighter stepped away. And all this time the matador was watching, and I shivered as I saw him thrust his chest forward like a warrior ready for the fight. One by one, banderillas were thrust into the creature's neck, tearing its muscles, destroying its nerves. Now a necklace of its blood was dripping into the sand. The bull seemed in a trance, snorting and heaving, trying to raise its head. It retreated into a corner to catch its breath, weighing up the chances of success or defeat. The crowd went quiet and the bull remained still. The air felt heavy with the prelude to death. I studied the creature's expression - wide-eyed, staring, trying to work it all out - and remembered those skins in the tannery and how sorry I had felt for them. *'Poor things, they never stood a chance.'* The matador exchanged his magenta cape for red. The crowd began to chant

'Matale! Matale! They were demanding the kill. I covered my eyes as the arena fell silent. I heard the bull's hooves thundering forward. This was its last charge. I pressed my fingers into my eyes, imagining the sword concealed behind the matador's fluttering cape. Alfonso was on his feet and I was too. I couldn't bear to watch, but somehow I did. Something made me open my eyes and peer through my fingers. The matador raised his arm. The sword flashed and he plunged it in. There was a roar. The animal slid to the floor, gone, despatched, yielding to death and in that ugly moment something died inside me too. Shame came flooding in. Why had I looked? Why had I chosen to watch this creature's death? By looking I was complicit; a witness to the utmost cruelty, and it was as much my fault as the rest of that cheering crowd. I had to get away. I shoved past Alfonso, pushing through the applauding crowd and bolted down the stairs, reaching the ground just as men were raking the creature's spent blood back into the sand, already smoothing over the evidence of their latest crime.

With my head down, I hurried back through the village. What I'd witnessed was cruel, what I'd seen was bad. But Alfonso had been waving his arms and cheering above the rest and I hated him for it, and even worse, I hated myself too. Then with shame came fear. I looked about. Maybe Alfonso was angry that I had left without explanation. Everyone had seen me go, including the mayor and all those smiling women. He would have lost face. He wouldn't have liked it. So, I hurried on, not daring to look back in case he'd followed me. I passed the bar and glanced over. A man was standing in the doorway wrapped in a cloak. Was it The Fixer? I gasped, imagining his grin spreading slowly across his face then turning into a red beak like in my dreams. Had he been watching? Did he know what I had done? Did he know who I was? Now I was

198

rushing up the hill, my calves taking the strain as I looked back to check that neither Alfonso nor The Fixer were following. I reached the safety of the mill owner's house and stood outside searching for my key. Evening clouds were racing overhead, creating an illusion of movement. Just as I turned the key in the servant's door, there was a sudden flicker. Was someone standing across the street in a darkened doorway? I turned around and squinted into the dying sun. Was that Pablo? But my eyes were dazzled and by the time they adjusted, there was no one there.

I lay breathless on my bed, going over the horrors of the day. What an idiot I'd been, teasing Pablo like some haughty princess, then rejecting his gift of flowers. How naïve I'd been too, caught up in the mood of the fiesta with its stirring music, those brightly coloured costumes and the elegance of that beautiful white horse. How stupid I'd been raising my hand to someone in a fancy hat. And why didn't I escape when I found out who he was? I should have struggled more. I should have told him that I wasn't scared for my reputation. But that wasn't true. I was terrified. My life in Don Diego's house was safe. Agnes liked me and I liked her. What would happen if they found out who I really was, a girl from the west; a girl with no shame. I wrapped a blanket around me and new thoughts crept in on the October wind. Maybe our family had been doomed from the start, just like that bull in the ring today. It hadn't stood a chance and nor had we. Maybe there was a pattern to all this. Ma, Grandma, and the women before us, all encountering misfortune as if our lives had been pre-planned. It was as if my character was destined to be weak and submissive, allowing myself to be hauled up like a sack onto Alfonso's saddle, walking with him to the bull ring, taking his arm! Then I pictured Alfonso on his feet, applauding like a lord and me running away – a small resistance that gave me a glimmer of hope for my salvation. But I was scared that weakness was lurking inside me like a monster eating me from the inside out. I turned over in bed, trying to eliminate my worries and calling out into the air, 'Ma, please speak to me. Tell me it isn't so.'

37. Mariangeles

Next morning, when Mariangeles met Pepe outside the hostel, she was furious.

'Why didn't you tell me about Sebastiana's role in the fire? '

'I couldn't, Mariangeles. I didn't know how.'

'So you let me find out from a stranger!'

Pepe lowered his head. 'Forgive me, Mariangeles, but how could I tell you such gossip without knowing if it was true?' Mariangeles paused. Her friend was right. She shouldn't make judgements based on gossip. She went to pay her bill and the hostel owner spoke quietly as if she was ashamed.

'I spoke out of turn yesterday and I want you to know that I didn't believe what those gossips said. Your Tia was lovely and Eva was too.'

'Eva?'

'Yes, the girl who was with her. They left together and went to the *chozas*.

'The *chozas*?'

Pepe explained. 'They're rough shacks down by the river. I can take you there if you likes, but I warn you, it's rough.'

'I don't care about that. Let's go,' Mariangeles said, feeling so much brighter. The hostel owner had told her what she had wanted to hear - that her daughter was a good girl after all.

She was alert and excited as they made their way along the lane where, on either side, tall canes rustled in the soft sea breeze, and egrets, disturbed by Jefe's gentle canter, burst out of the undergrowth and coasted along overhead. A family of geese crossed their path and Mariangeles felt the enchantment of the place. Had Sebastiana felt it too? Yet despite the beauty of their journey, Mariangeles was shocked when they arrived, and saw the rough stone walls and roofs of palm where Tia had lived. Poor girl having to survive in this, she thought. She peered through the glass-less window. The floor was made of compacted mud and straw, covered in piles of leaves that had drifted in. The place was deserted. Leaning in the corner was an old broom and for a moment she felt inclined to go inside and sweep the leaves away in readiness for the next occupant but then she smiled at herself for being overzealous and instead went into the patch of garden at the rear. There was a chicken coop and the remains of vegetables fighting for survival and she thought of her own garden and her own survival that winter. She smiled. 'My daughter is a gardener, like me' she said proudly.

When she asked around, hardly anyone remembered the girls.

'In this place people come and go. No one stays for long,' a young man said.

And another said 'Old Jose might have known them, but he's gone too.'

A woman shouted across. 'Your daughter was the one what started the fire.'

Mariangeles bristled. 'You don't know what my daughter did.'

Another woman carrying a basket joined in. 'I shared my copper basin to do the washing. The other one turned pro.'

Mariangeles's heart sank. This is what she had been dreading - that her daughter might end up as a prostitute. Isn't that why she had come all this way? To make sure her daughter came to no harm, especially now that The Fixer was here? She shook her head. Please don't tell me it has come to this. But then she stopped because wasn't it she who was going to send Sebastiana away with that horrible man? Wasn't it she who hadn't bothered to ask what kind of employment Sebastiana was going to? How can I judge my daughter? she asked herself. How can I judge her without judging myself too? Her thoughts were interrupted by the washer woman. 'From what I hear she works with punters from that new bar over there,' she said pointing back down the lane to where they had just been.

38. Tia

At two in the morning Eva burst through my door. Her dress was ripped, an open wound bled on her forehead and bruises ran across her jaw. Poor Eva, her mouth was so swollen she could hardly speak.

She held her wrists up for scrutiny. 'Look!' she whimpered

I saw that they were red-raw from being twisted in someone's grasp.

'Eva, who did this? Was it him? Was it the man in the black cape?'

She nodded. 'I kept my mouth shut, Tia, but he said there was something about your face - something he recognised.' She coughed and grey mucous fell onto her chin. I wiped it away with the sleeve of my nightgown. 'He wouldn't stop, always the same question whenever we saw you in the street, over and over. *Who is that girl?* And every time I lied and said I didn't know. But then this.' She opened her mouth. Two teeth were crushed into her jaw. No wonder she could hardly speak. Poor Eva, holding my secret in for so long. 'Last night he saw you hurrying past the bar and he got angry and turned on me.' She felt around her wrists as if re-enacting the pain. "Oh, Tia I'm so sorry but I told him your name. He looked surprised but then he grinned as if he'd suddenly realised, and he rolled your name around on his tongue until his lip curled and he muttered something about 'a stubby little housewife called Mariangeles and her stupid husband Bartolome.' He said how they owed him money and how you had run away before he could get his hands on you. He looked so angry. Can you ever forgive me?' I held her hands to stop them from trembling.

'It's all right, Eva. I understand,' I said as I wiped tears away from her cheeks. How could I condemn my friend for her actions? She must have been terrified. But there was something I didn't understand.

'Why did you go with The Fixer if you knew he was so cruel?'

'He promised me good food and somewhere warm to sleep, Tia, and I was starving and so cold. Besides my cough was getting worse. I had to go.'

I nodded. Poor Eva, she was a mess. 'And did he do those things?'

'Yes. The place is warm and they feed me well, but I swear he hates us girls. It's as if he's trying to get revenge for something that happened in his past.'

Eva stayed until dawn when I took her up to the terrace to take in the fresh air. In that cold, bright light I saw that the blood smeared across her forehead had dried and turned black and her bruises were tinged with yellow. She looked in terrible pain so to distract her from her misery; I took her to the parapet overlooking Main Street. We looked across to the bull ring, then further out to the flat panorama that stretched towards a cluster of houses running alongside the road towards Gibraltar. Eva pointed.

'Down there, Tia. See? That's where I work now, in front of the race track.' I shielded my eyes from the rising sun and saw the rooftop of an elegant building rising oddly from the shacks around it. Further away were parallel lines of white fencing alonside a race

206

track and beyond that the funnels of ships waiting in Gibraltar harbour. Suddenly a whole world stretched out before me, so full of possibilities that I felt a rush of hope.

'Let's run away! We could become maids in a hotel.'

'Or I could marry a soldier!' Eva replied.

'In Tangiers,' I said.

'Yes, somewhere far away from here,' she whispered.

'We could go to Buenos Aires,' I said, but Eva looked at me blankly. A place she'd never heard of seemed beyond Eva's imagination and now she had her own faraway look in her eyes. She sighed

'I have to go back.'

'No, Eva. You mustn't'

'I have to'

'Why?'

'To apologise.'

'Apologise?'

'If not, she'll come and fetch me and lock me in my room.'

'Who will?'

'Sometimes she hits us or gets Manolo to do it.' Eva touched the bruise on her face and flinched.

'Who are you talking about? Who will do that?'

'I hear the keys jangling on her belt and think perhaps she's going to let me out, but then she goes to her room to sleep off the booze.'

'Who does, Eva? Tell me.'

She sighed, as if telling me would cause her even more pain. 'Mary Palmones. She used to live in town like us, but after the fire she went to Gibraltar to make her fortune and became obsessed with everything English. Changed her surname to Palmer and called her place *The Salon,* all la-dee-da like she was receiving royalty. It's beautiful – she spent a fortune furnishing the rooms with the finest silks.' It sounded horrible, but Eva tried to be cheerful. 'Don't worry, Tia. Mary will give me a shot or two of Chinchón and she'll tell me not to run away again. She won't do anything to hurt me. After all I'm getting to be her best girl.' She coughed mightily and I wondered how Eva managed to be so alluring to her clients when she was so ill. But then I remembered when the hostel owner's nephew had assaulted her and how clever she had been at pretending she was all right.

There was a raised window on the terrace, overlooking the atrium that dropped to the floors below. I'd cleaned it yesterday so it was gleaming in the morning light. A cloud passed over it and Eva peered in absentmindedly as the glass began to reflect her face. 'What a mess,' she cried, pushing her red lace bodice back into place, and brushing the dust off her green taffeta skirt. I supposed she wanted to look decent as she walked through the village in the light of day, but in truth her appearance was too gaudy for misinterpretation. As the cloud moved away, and her reflection disappeared I cautioned her about looking through the glass.

'Eva, we're not supposed to look down there.'

'Don't worry, they can't see me,' she said. 'Come on, Tia. Look.' I sighed. Eva still had that way of persuading me. Cautiously I leaned over and saw Don Diego's wife sitting on an ornate chair in the centre of the atrium. Her skirts had dropped softly onto the terrazzo floor where her children sat listening to her reading. Eva gasped. 'Look at that dress, Tia. It's the most beautiful thing I've ever seen.' It was made of pale-grey silk and as the woman adjusted her feet, I imagined a rustle of taffeta vibrating in the air. 'Mother of God! What a beautiful shawl too!' Eva whispered and I saw it was embroidered with flowers in pastel colours and that it was peppered with gold thread. Just then Don Diego came in, kissed his wife on her cheek and patted his children on their heads. I felt Eva move away as if she was leaving, and as I looked over to say goodbye she had already scooped up her skirts and was dashing towards the door to the servants' stairs.

'What is it?' I called but she didn't answer. 'Eva, what is it?' I tried again, but she was gone. I heard the echo of her footsteps rebounding up from the void as she flew down the winding steps to the street. I went back to the parapet to check that she'd left, and saw that Don Diego had come out on the pavement just as Eva emerged from the servants' door. She stopped for a moment to shield her eyes from a sudden burst of sunshine, then turned and disappeared down the hill. I knew that Don Diego had seen her. He folded his arms across his chest looking angry. I gasped and Don Diego heard it. He looked up. I ducked behind the parapet. Had he seen *me* as well as Eva? He went inside and I crept down to the half-landing where he had already entered his study and was whispering to himself as if demented.

'That whore in my house! How dare she turn up looking like that?' And I realised that he must have recognised the red lace bodice and the green taffeta skirt. Perhaps they were the same clothing he'd removed from Eva the evening before.

'What is it, Diego?' asked his wife as she entered the room. 'What's the matter?'

He shook his head and continued pacing up and down. 'That girl of ours was watching me from the terrace upstairs,' he said. My stomach lurched. He *had* seen me. 'She looked shifty, as if she was up to no good.' There was no mention of Eva. I suppose talking about me would distract his wife from the truth. Then he raised his voice even more. 'And what the hell was the son of that Pablo Lopez doing hanging about here last night too?'

So, I was right. Pablo *had* been there standing in the darkness when I arrived back from the bull fight. Oh, Pablo, my lovely friend. Even after I'd rejected his flowers in the square and even after I'd gone off with Alfonso, he obviously still cared because he was waiting for me. Perhaps he wanted an explanation for my behaviour or perhaps he wanted to make up and didn't have the courage to tell me. I sighed. How happy I felt knowing he had been there in the shadows. But Don Diego interrupted my joy.

'That girl of ours and Pablo Lopez are up to something and I'm going to fix this once and for all,' he announced.

I wasn't up to anything but he had to blame me for something now that he knew that Eva and I were friends. I peered through the crack and saw that the ornate box was lying open on his desk and Don Diego was opening his fancy pistol and checking the cylinder for bullets. His wife stepped forward.

'Don't do it Diego. Please don't.'

'These are troubling times, Emilia. Who knows what communist plan they've got hatched to get at me and my family? It has to stop.'

I had to warn Pablo about Don Diego and his gun. Returning to my room, I dressed quickly and, with huge strides, hurried down the hill, past the bar where The Fixer had seen me last night, along the tree-lined avenue where Alfonso had hauled me onto his horse, and behind the bull ring until I reached the slaughterhouse. The stench hit me hard, reminding me of the tannery. I covered my mouth and went inside. Through the dim light I saw six hides hanging from beams, their remaining flesh still sliding to the floor. On the right, suspended from huge metal hooks, were their carcasses and I realised they must be the creatures from yesterday's conquests. All around, blood was flowing into channels gauged into the stone floor. At the far end, a group of farmers stood in dark silhouette against the sunlight outside. Each held a bucket to collect the gore for use on their lands. I'd seen it before - watched farmers carve deep circles around their trees then pour the thick red liquid into the groove where it would sit glistening in the sun

210

like a ruby-red moat. Over the course of the day, the blood would dry into a thick crust and below this hardened surface, the liquid would seep into the roots, allowing the tree to prosper. *'Sometimes the end is also the beginning,'* the priest had said.

I couldn't find Pablo but there were several workmen sauntering about in the fetid air, each carrying an instrument of some sort and wearing aprons splattered in blood.

'Hey girl,' one of them called out. 'Come visiting, have you? Take a seat in the drawing room. I'll ring the maid for some tea!' A rumble of men's laughter came from the depths and then I saw Pablo walking towards me gripping a bloody saw. In his other hand, an animal's tail swished from side to side. Blood was smeared across his apron and his hair was tangled and wild as if he'd been working all night. Who was this savage in front of me? He took a step forward and I took a step back. This wasn't Pablo. This wasn't my dear sweet friend. This wasn't the boy who spoke with grace about the plight of others and who took my arm to help me across the street. I searched his face for compassion but found none. Instead, I saw a firm jaw and wild eyes glaring at me through the dim light. He opened his mouth to speak but I dared not hear his words. I panicked, forgetting everything I had come to say. Eva's words rang in my ears. 'Men are no good Tia,' she had said and perhaps she was right because Pablo looked like the devil himself. I turned on my heels and ran.

39. Mariangeles

Pepe stopped the cart outside a run-down bar. Is this where Sebastiana was working, Mariangeles thought, studying the rusting sign *Venta Alfonso* hanging on one hook above the door. Pepe pointed towards a building at the rear.

'I work here, Mariangeles. This is Alfonso's place.

'But it's just a hovel, Pepe.'

'Alfonso likes it that way. Says he makes money when the punters feel at home.'

'Is this the same Alfonso who blamed my girl for the fire?'

'Yes, I'm afraid it is.'

'Well, if Sebastiana is in there, I don't want to see her. If she's under the influence of drink or drugs I don't want to know.'

Pepe nodded and walked towards the bar. Mariangeles stayed in the cart, shaking her head in despair, expecting the worst. If her daughter had become a whore, what would she do? What could she do? Nothing. I will walk away, she thought. If Sebastiana is a prostitute, I will leave and never come back. Pepe went into the bar, leaving Mariangeles sitting high up on the cart, listening to the rustle of canes rubbing together in the marshes and the snuffling of geese about to take flight. She felt the chill of a sea breeze enter her bones and prepared herself for bad news. She waited. What was taking him so long? She clenched her hands into fists. Please don't be in there Sebastiana. Please!' If she was, then she would ask Pepe to turn the cart around and take her back home. Yes. That's what she would do. She would abandon her daughter to her fate. She shivered, wondering if that was true, wondering if, once again, she would desert her daughter as she had before. At last Pepe emerged.

'They've never heard of a Sebastiana, or a Tia either,' he said smiling. Mariangeles let out a sigh of relief. In her heart she knew she would never walk away. In her heart she knew she would do everything in her power to drag her daughter back home and care for her like a mother should.

'And this Eva girl? Is *she* in there?'

'She left a while back. Gone for good.'

Mariangeles sighed again. 'So how are we going to find Sebastiana now?' she asked sinking into her seat.

'The girls say Eva's gone to a house somewhere towards Gibraltar.'

'Do they know where? I have to know.'

'They said a man came trying to tempt them away, and that Eva went with him.'

'Who? What man? Where?' Mariangeles was desperate.

'They said he wore a black cape.'

'A black cape?'

'Yes. Says his name's Manuel Jimenez but he prefers to be called Manolo.'

'You mean The Fixer. Oh my God, it must be him.' Where is this place, Pepe?'

'They don't know. These girls are so far gone you can't get much out of 'em.'

'Poor things,' she said.

Just then a man on a white horse rode into the forecourt. Mariangeles looked him up and down. How ridiculous he looked in his English tweeds and a silver-topped cane jammed into the belt around his waist.

'What are you doing here, Pepe? It's not your collection day,' the man said, and Mariangeles knew immediately who he was. Her mouth twitched with anger.

'You are Alfonso and you lied about my girl, Sebastiana.'

Alfonso snorted. 'So?'

'So tell me, where is she?'

'How should I know, woman.? She abandoned me and my friends in the bull ring yesterday. Your daughter has no manners.'

40. Tia

I trudged back up the hill with the image of Pablo covered in blood, embedded in my mind. I passed the bar where The Fixer had seen me yesterday and looked up towards the house. All I wanted to do was throw myself into my work and not think of Pablo ever again. But when I reached what I thought was the safety of the servants' door, Agnes was standing there twisting her hands together looking anxious and severe. She pulled me into the quiet of the vestibule, where the only illumination came from a fanlight above the door. She spoke so quietly I could hardly hear her.

'I'm sorry, Tia, but you have to go. You have an hour to pack your things and leave.' I looked at her in disbelief. 'Don Diego says you stole his wife's shawl and....

'I didn't,' I shrieked.

Agnes was crying. 'Tia, I tried to defend you. Said you would never do such a thing, but Don Diego insisted. Said he'll throw you out himself if he has to.'

There was such certainty in her voice that I didn't protest. Instead, I slumped onto the bottom stair and threw my head into my hands. My mistress's shawl? I didn't steal it. Why do they think that I did? I shook my head trying to understand what had happened and realising that I was undone. Below me was the staircase down to the wash room, where I had worked like a mule, enjoying the process of making clean the family's clothes. Above me were the stairs winding up to the terrace where the breeze made me feel alive and where anything had seemed possible. But now all that was gone. My whole existence ruined and I didn't understand why. I began to sob and Agnes sat beside me and held my hand.

'I'm so sorry, Tia,' she said.

I couldn't speak, I couldn't think. Then I remembered my mother's lament and spoke it loudly into the dark corridor, as if everyone in the world should hear it.

'Sorrows and waves never arrive alone,' I cried.

Agnes squeezed my hand. 'I don't believe that, Tia.'

'My mother did. She said that all the women in our family were condemned to a life of grief and sorrow, and that no one could stop the curse from coming true.'

'Except God, Tia. We should surrender ourselves to his higher authority, confess our sins and beg for his mercy.'

'But I haven't done anything wrong,' I wailed, pulling my hand from hers.

'Perhaps not, but I have worried about you for a long time, Tia. What is it that you carry so heavily in your heart?'

I wiped my tears. This woman was thoughtful, bothering about me even though, in less than an hour, I would be gone from her life. Why should she take the time to care? Besides, I'd held onto my past so tightly, and protected it so carefully from the scrutiny of others. It was mine to suffer alone.

I shook my head. 'My sins are too great to tell,' I said.

'Nothing is that bad, Tia. Tell me, please.'

I stared into her face. What did I have to lose? There was nothing to protect anymore; no job to cling to, nothing remaining of my reputation to defend. All of that was gone. I was broken. I sighed deeply and suddenly my past was here in the present, rising to the surface, wave after wave of telling that burst from my mouth, and I couldn't stop it. I told Agnes about Don Francisco's fumbling in the middle of the night, and about Pa's desires and Ma's jealousy. I explained her decision to send me away with The Fixer, and how I'd escaped, but, like a fool, had fallen victim to Alfonso's trickery. I admitted that I was the girl who started the fire and how Eva and I only just survived the winter. I didn't pretend to be innocent.

'It was my fault – all of it,' I cried and Agnes held me against her chest and gently stroked my hair.

After a while she whispered, 'Tia, You were only a child. You cannot be blamed for the tittle-tattle of women, or the evils of a few bad men.'

I shook my head, still doubting my innocence, and wondered again about Pablo in the slaughterhouse. Was he really one of those evil men? But I didn't tell her about that. It was still too fresh in my mind to lay bare.

Don Diego's voice boomed down into the stairwell.

'Get that girl out of my house, now,' he said and we both jumped.

'Come on, Tia. It's time,' Agnes said. 'Collect your things.'

I didn't bother going upstairs to fetch my suitcase. I'd grown out of my old clothes long ago and, apart from the clothing on my back, all that was left was an old nightgown that wasn't worth taking. I walked to the door and paused, placing my hand on the latch ready to leave. Out there was uncertainty. Out there was ruin and no one to ask for help. Who would believe the innocence of the girl who started that fire? So, where was I going? What would I do? And how was I going to live?

A beam of midday sun entered through the fanlight and lit up the vestibule with its golden light. Then something caught my eye. A small red object was lying half-hidden in the corner. It was a rose with its long stem wrapped crudely in what looked like one of Pablo's pamphlets, and scrawled across it were the only three letters I recognised; 'TIA.' He must have left it there before I went to the slaughterhouse – before I had shamed him in front of those men. I held the head of the flower in the palm of my hand. Its petals were damaged, as if he'd retrieved it from the gutter, but to me it was the most beautiful thing I'd ever seen. My dear Pablo, sending me a flower as a sign of his affection even after I had gone off with Alfonso! He must have put it there last night and I hadn't seen it when I left this morning. And then what had I done? Shame rushed through me as I realised my folly at rushing from the slaughterhouse before giving him a chance to speak, allowing Eva's words to influence me and turning Pablo into the demon he never was. How could I have been so wrong? How could I have been such a fool? The rose trembled in my hand.

'My dear, dear, Pablo,' I said out loud. 'What have I done?'

Agnes must have heard because she coughed loudly, indicating that I should have left by now. But somehow, desperation forced me into action. Clutching the rose, I raced back up the winding stairs, past Don Diego's study where he was presumably waiting for my departure, past my attic bedroom where Agnes could surely see me, and up to the very top to the building where a tower stood sharp white against the blue sky. I'd never dared enter before, but now I pushed hard against the door and it opened abruptly, letting out a burst of trapped heat and the smell of old paints. I placed the rose on the windowsill, rearranging its bent petals to preserve its loveliness. It felt good to commemorate our innocence in the face of a world full of judgement. I decided that one day someone would find that rose, and on that day, a rounded joy might enter their soul, and they would speculate and wonder about who had offered it and how it had been received. Then I walked back down the winding stairs leaving my sighs lingering in the stairwell and opened the door to the harshness of the day.

41. Mariangeles.

Mariangeles had worked it out.

'According to Alfonso, Sebastiana was at the bull ring yesterday,' she said. 'So, where would that be, Pepe?

'There's only one bull ring near here. Up in the village on the hill.'

Come one, then. Lets' go!' she said, certain they would find Tia there.

They travelled through open countryside and as they entered the village, Mariangeles smiled at the similarities between her old village and this. Both built on a hill, both topped with an old church, and both overlooking a bay. She felt a flutter of excitement. Tia is here and I am too, she thought, certain that soon she would find her daughter and all would be well. They asked in bars; they enquired in shops. They consulted pedestrians in the street, but no one knew of a girl called Sebastiana or Tia or anyone who looked like her either. They walked along the Alameda studying all the young girls. They asked the boys. Did they know her? Had they seen her? But nobody knew, and no one had seen.

'Seems like Tia kept herself private,' Pepe suggested and Mariangeles was beginning to think he was right. Perhaps her opinion of her daughter was completely wrong. Perhaps, instead of being wild and wilful, her daughter was actually shy and timid and even lonely in this village, and she began to feel sorry for her. Pepe tied his horse to a hitching rail. 'Stay here while I fetch Jefe some water,' he said.

Mariangeles sat on a bench watching the animal rub its shoulder against the trunk of a plane tree. What a lovely creature it was, chestnut brown with white marks on his muzzle and a mane of softest cream. The branches of the plane trees were swaying high above her head and a robin was chirping out its territory. The afternoon sun was hanging softly in the air, like fruit on a bough waiting to ripen into the mellow heat of evening. A little further along, another horse stood swishing its tail, and when she glanced over, she saw that Pepe was leaning on the water fountain talking to its owner. Both men were fetching water for their animals. Pepe came rushing over with his new acquaintance. 'I've got news - some of it good, some of it bad.' Mariangeles sighed. She was getting used to being pulled in different directions, thinking one thing and then another. Either way she needed to know. 'This man says he had a load of girls on his cart yesterday.'

The man nodded. 'Yes, señora. Servant girls are rarely seen in the village because they work them so hard, but yesterday, being fiesta, they got the day off, so I took them down to this square and dropped them off right here.' He pointed to the ground and Mariangeles smiled realising that Sebastiana could have been standing on this very spot.

'So was Sebastiana one of them?' she asked. 'She uses the unusual name of Tia.'

'Tia? I overheard one of them being called that and I thought it sounded nice.'

'That *must* be her,' Mariangeles said and she took a deep breath of the air around her as if she was sharing it with her daughter.

The man hadn't finished. 'I saw her go off with a man on a white horse and all his mates cheered. There was a boy too, standing there with a bunch of flowers. He didn't like it one bit.'

Mariangeles sighed. First her daughter was a hussy then she was timid and shy, and now going off with one man and inciting jealousy in another. Who is this girl? Who is my daughter, she thought, shaking her head.

'No,' she said. Sebastiana would never do that, at least not willingly.'

Pepe intervened as if to calm her down. 'Do you know where this girl works?'

'Up on Main Street I think. With Agnes, my betrothed.'

'Let's go there now, Pepe. We're getting close. I can feel it in my bones.'

42. Tia

I trudged to the church square and sat on the same bench where I had met The Fixer but I was no longer scared because the risk of meeting him was the least of my troubles. Where was I going to sleep tonight? What would I eat? I watched children jumping in and out of the bushes and playing hopscotch on the pavement slabs. I moved into the shadows, sitting as still as stone, admiring their wildness, their pushing and pulling and running and chasing and hiding and seeking whilst I remained motionless, paralysed by fear. As people walked past, they seemed to stare in disgust, as if gossip about Doña Emilia's missing shawl had already reached their ears. Clever Don Diego getting rid of me with his false accusation. And all the while a little voice kept answering *'It's your fault. You deserve this. You are nobody.'*

Agnes came to sit beside me. 'I'm glad I've found you,' she said, then held my hand and squeezed it. 'Tia, I've been thinking. Let's talk to the priest.'

'What? That nasty old man!' I said, surprised at my firmness.

'The old priest died in his sleep, God Rest His Soul. There's a new one now, and he's bound to help.' Agnes crossed herself with the confidence of a true believer but I shook my head. I didn't want to talk to any man, religious or not. Agnes insisted. 'This priest is young. He will listen. He will understand.' I considered her proposal. What else could I do? Where else could I go? So, after a moment of hesitation, I nodded.

The priest was dressed in a robe, the hem of which was too long, with shoulders too wide, and he wore a hat that was too big. I watched him with caution as he passed a statue of the Virgin and crossed himself slowly with long clean fingers. Then, with a look of suspicion, he invited us both to sit. Agnes spoke first and her tone seemed to give the boy far more respect than I expected or understood.

'Father Benedict, we've come here for guidance. This young woman has fallen, but it's not her fault. Let me explain because the more you know of this girl's circumstances, the more you will understand.' I sat on the edge of a pew listening as Agnes talked on my behalf and I began to regret having told her my life story because she had remembered every detail.

'This poor girl was accused of enticing her father, and then an older man too, so she ran away from home to escape a man who turned out to be a pimp. Can you imagine it, Father?' I could see that the priest wasn't really listening. He was looking over his shoulder at the gilded wonders of his new parish church. I folded my arms against my chest. How dare he be so rude? Agnes hadn't noticed and carried on. 'Then she secured work at a local factory but it burned down and the poor girl was accused of causing the fire because of her passion for another man.' Agnes placed an innocent hand on my shoulder to show her support, but it didn't feel like support. It felt like treachery. By now the priest was wide-eyed. So he *had* been listening. Father Benedict brought his thumb to his lips and started to chew it. I supposed the talk of dalliances with older men and the prospect of incest disturbed him. Poor man! We had come to him for advice yet he seemed to have even less notion of the world than me. But Agnes didn't realise. 'Tia overcame all these things, Father, and came to work for Don Diego.' The priest looked up and nodded, relieved perhaps at a name he recognised. But his face was pale. My so-called sins were making him uncomfortable. I imagined him at night, checking the bolts on the huge nave doors to protect his church from the wickedness that lay outside it. 'And now she's been accused of stealing Don Diego's wife's shawl,' Agnes added as if this was the closing statement of her argument on my behalf.

'I would never steal a thing!' I blurted it out because this priest had to understand. This priest had to know.

Agnes nodded. 'The girl is innocent, Father. She needs your support.'

Poor Agnes, she had tried her best but now there was a long silence. The priest's eyes darted about in panic, and his face was even paler than the alabaster statue of Jesus above the altar. I waited for his words of wisdom and soon he turned to me and spoke.

'Child, I hear these tales of incest, lust, and debauchery, of abandoning your duties as a good daughter and I hear of your greed and wilfulness. You have brought several sins into my church so you will kneel here at the foot of the Virgin of the Seven Sorrows and say seven Hail Marys to cleanse this hallowed ground.' He led me towards the statue of the Virgin but I had stopped listening. Seven sorrows rattled inside my brain. Were these the sorrows of Ma's refrain? Was I chained to this mantra, never to be free? My cheeks flushed and my fists turned white with clenching. I would not be bound by moribund declarations and I would not be bound by this priest's notion of morality either. Angry words burst from my mouth before I could tame them.

'You speak of sins and a Virgin of the Seven Sorrows, but I have endured more sorrows than you will ever know - sorrows that have brought me to my knees. I don't need your stupid sins,

Father, and I don't need to pray either. All I need is your help.' Both of them gasped. Agnes stepped forward to calm me but I was already running down the nave, leaving them standing there in confusion, trapped within the confines of their so-certain beliefs. I charged through the big old doors, muttering like a lunatic, and marched along the street heading out of the village, I was furious at the priest's words, furious with Don Diego, furious with the world. Anger was my friend. Anger was beside me. She'd stepped out of the furnace and given me wings. Now I was flying down the road, past children pointing, women jeering, past the mill owner's house and the bar and down the lane into the woods. There was no thinking, just a raw force pulling me away from a village that didn't want me. A village where they judged me, spat me out, rejected me. I was moving away, moving forwards, moving onwards to somewhere – anywhere - and all the time I was gasping for air and this sensation thrilled me.

I set my sights towards the distance, like a soldier on a mission, but after several minutes I slowed to a quieter pace. Anger drifted away, her hot wings cooling in the breeze, and in its place came a tremor under my feet. A shudder as if the earth was displeased. A storm was coming. It started as a flutter then grew heavier as if someone had tossed me a boulder and I'd caught it unaware of its weight. I sank to the ground. Where was I going? How was this going to end? I was desperate for human contact, an arm around my shoulders, a hug; a look. The smallest kindness would do. I willed myself on, trudging now, slow and spare, into the woods where I might find some rest.

43. Mariangeles

Mariangeles banged on the servant's door. Sebastiana had to be there but who would she find? A sweet girl, timid and shy? Or a hussy with a wayward character? She was confused, but she had come so far. She had to know. A woman appeared.

'What do you want? We're busy.'

'Is my daughter here? She's called Sebastiana or Tia.'

The woman tried to close the door but Mariangeles shoved her foot in to keep it open. 'Is she here? Can I see her? If not then you have to tell me where she is.' Her heart was pumping. Her eyes were pleading. Oh how she wanted to hear that Sebastiana was as sweet as the hostel owner had suggested, not a hussy like gossips would have her be. Pepe put a hand on her arm and she relaxed a little and allowed the woman to speak.

'I'm afraid she's been dismissed.'

'Dismissed? Why'

'She stole my mistress's shawl.'

'Stole?'

'Well, that's what Don Diego says. The police are here, discussing it right now.'

Mariangeles removed her foot and backed away. My daughter a thief? On top of everything else, this was too much.

Pepe stepped forward. 'There must be a mistake. She wouldn't do such a thing.'

The woman leaned forward and whispered.

'I agree. Tia is a sweet girl but what could I do?'

Mariangeles shook her head. So, do you know where she's gone?'

'I took her to the priest but she didn't like his advice so she ran away.'

'Oh, Sebastiana!' Mariangeles wailed and the woman must have taken pity.

'Wait there a moment,' she said. They listened to her footsteps pounding up the stairs and when she returned she handed Mariangeles a garment. 'This is Tia's nightgown. Perhaps you can give it to her when you find her.'

Mariangeles took the nightgown and held it against her cheek, then buried her face into the fabric, inhaling the aroma so fresh and clean and smelling unmistakably of her girl. She remembered the last time she had done this, sitting on the bed the morning after Sebastiana had fled. She remembered her words then – *Oh, Sebastiana. What have we done?* And she repeated them now, but this time she used her daughter's preferred name. 'Oh, Tia, will we ever find you?' She sighed deeply. Just a few moments ago her girl had seemed so close and now she seemed so far away.

The woman began to close the door but then seemed to remember something.

'Tia has a young man who might know where she is. He works at the slaughterhouse.'

44. Tia

I arrived at a clearing, faint and exhausted. Trees were lurching back and forth, restless in the breeze. Clouds were darkening above me and the air had turned cold. The sun hid behind a cluster of clouds making the undergrowth shimmer with an unfamiliar light and I, a wretch of a girl, stumbled to a halt and sat down. I looked around at the unfamiliar surroundings and saw nothing but neglect. Between the branches of a blackberry bush I saw a stone carving surrounding a water spigot covered in lichen. Some of the branches had grown through, making the stone crumble. My head was spinning, and my stomach was sore with hunger. I reached into the bush and immediately was scratched by its thorns, but I didn't care. I grabbed a handful of berries, shoving them greedily into my mouth, letting the juice run down my cheeks. I wiped it away and saw a smear of bright red across the back of my hand. 'Oh, Ma,' I wailed, remembering the day we dyed Pa's lambskins in the kitchen. 'Why did you judge me so harshly? I asked. Why does *everyone* judge me so harshly? First Ma, then Incarna, and the villagers at the *paseo*, then the girls at the factory, and the victims of the fire - they all blamed me for something I didn't do. And now I'd been accused of stealing Doña Emilia's shawl. I shook my head and lay down on a patch of grass, closing my eyes to close down the questions with no answers, and tried to get some sleep.

Then the nightmares began. First, a vast ship with animal hides flapping like sails, moving towards a boy standing on the shore where I couldn't reach him. 'Pablo!' I shouted, but almond blossom was swirling and high up on the crow's nest sat a huge bird with a wide grinning mouth. A wave grew so high it darkened the sky and I was plunged into the ocean. Then a woman's face appeared; someone I didn't recognise smiling at me behind my eyelids, in front of the black. She was mouthing the words *hold yourself steady, Tia,* and I opened my mouth to speak. But no words came as my dreams surrendered to an empty, cavernous sleep.

45. Mariangeles

The sky was darkening. Clouds were accumulating overhead. Marieangeles sighed. How quickly the day had turned from hope to despair; from sunshine to storm. Then, like the turn of a switch, clouds burst and rain came thick and fast as Pepe drove the cart into the slaughterhouse yard. He dismounted, helped Mariangeles down, and pointed to a covered area.

'Stay under this canopy, Mariangeles. This place is not for ladies.' He dashed through the puddles into the building while Mariangeles waited, watching the rainwater dripping off the corrugated iron, and landing in rust-red puddles at her feet. There was a clap of thunder that made her jump, then a flash of lightning. The storm was overhead. She shivered and moved further under the canopy. From there she could see inside the slaughterhouse, where men shouted, saws scratched and hatchets were slammed onto blocks of wood. They were aggressive angry sounds that echoed around her brain whilst a wild wind raged through the trees. She shivered again. What she needed was peace. She needed to find Tia, not endure this relentless stress.

Pepe came out shaking his head.

'Sorry, Mariangeles. The men say this Pablo fella's gone off to help his father organise some demonstration near Gibraltar. Reckon there's going to be trouble soon.' Mariangeles shook her head in frustration. Was there to be no end to her searching? But Pepe was smiling. 'They did see her though. Said she came in here to speak to Pablo. Walked right in demanding to see him but as soon as she saw the blood she dashed off.' Mariangeles sighed deeply as if all this was too much. The good news was a sighting of her daughter but she was cold and exhausted, her clothes were damp and she needed to rest. She put her head in her hands and started to weep. Would they ever find Tia? Always one step away, as if fate was deliberately keeping them apart. It was all too much. Pepe put his arm around her. 'Don't worry Mariangeles, we'll find her, but let's get something to eat and we can start again tomorrow.

They went to the bar next to the Alameda and ordered *rabo de toro* - oxtail in a stew. The meat was soft and succulent, the sauce a rich shiny joy that ran down her throat with ease. Funny, she thought, how judgemental we can be, disliking the noise and brutality of the slaughterhouse whilst enjoying the fruits of their labours here with this stew. She wiped bread around the bowl to soak up the remains and sat back watching Pepe gulp down a beer. Here was a good man, she decided, not like Bartolome with his excessive drinking, or that arrogant boaster Don Francisco or the cruel, manipulative Fixer. She yawned, exhausted now that her hunger had been satisfied. All she needed now was a good night's rest, but where? With all the excitement of the day she had forgotten to arrange a room for the night. Pepe must have guessed her thinking.

'Look, it aint much but you can sleep in my cart if you likes. There's room for both without us being too friendly if you see what I means and the rain'll stop soon, I can tell.' She stared at him then laughed. Of course she would sleep in the cart with him. She couldn't think of anything nicer. They swung out of the village and took a track towards the woods where the trees would shelter them from the storm. Pepe hitched Jefe to the branch of a pine tree and pulled out blankets, a pillow and a flagon of brandy from a box beneath his seat. 'To keep out the cold, Mariangeles,' he said. Then he stretched a tarpaulin from the rear of the cart up to the back rest of the driver's bench and tied it to form a sloping roof that would take away the rain. Mariangeles wriggled down under the tarpaulin. 'Now we are cosy and dry,' Pepe said, offering her his flagon of brandy. They sat side by side, propped up against the bench, sipping brandy and listening as the last drops of rain dripped onto the tarpaulin, just as Pepe had predicted. Mariangeles yawned and rolled over into her blanket.

'Goodnight, Pepe' she said hoping she could rest. But sleep would not come. Her mind was full of the day; the trip to the *chozas*, to Alfonso's bar, meeting that housekeeper, and discovering that Tia had been accused of theft. She began to sob quietly, hoping that Pepe would not hear her, but then she felt his hand gently stroking her shoulder.

'It's all right, Marieangeles, we'll find her tomorrow,' he whispered and his words felt so warm and wonderful that she swung around and placed her arm across his chest. Then he pulled her to him and they remained like that for the rest of the night.

46. Tia

A pale morning sun fell through the branches, wriggling through the thicket, catching on droplets of yesterday's rain, making them shine like diamonds. I heard a gentle plop as each one fell onto damp earth, and felt a small breeze against my cheek. It was a gentle awakening made even sweeter by the singing of a dawn chorus as, from their rain-soaked nests, the birds rejoiced the passing of the storm. Now though, I felt the clammy wetness of my skirts and the wind cutting through my blouse, as a cruel realisation rushed in. I was alone with nowhere to go. I remembered the face that had appeared just as I fell asleep. *Keep yourself steady, girl,* it had said and for a moment I wondered if this was the grandmother I had never met; the lady whose torments Ma had never explained. Was this woman from my dreams looking out for me? Was she helping me with this ordeal? I was so desperate for kindness that I hoped this was true.

I stood up and brushed away the pine needles that had fallen during the night. A bluish light shimmered through the leaves and the morning frost stole my breath, turning it to mist. A squirrel bounded up a trunk with a nut between its teeth, no doubt ready to devour it as soon as it reached safety. And I felt my own hunger too, from the day before, and the day before that, and I walked along the lane hoping to meet someone who might give me food. But my heart was broken and my legs felt weak. Where was the anger from yesterday? Where was the passion that had made me defy the priest and power my way into the woods? I searched my heart for an answer, telling myself to bring back yesterday's fury before it was too late. But it had vanished, and in its place, a quiet determination seemed to take hold. I looked up at the Rock of Gibraltar covered in an early morning mist. It seemed to be hovering, detached from the ground, almost magical, and I decided. *This* was where I would go. After all it had dominated our horizon for so long, perhaps it had something to offer me now. Maybe working in a laundry or a smart hotel? Or better still, perhaps there was a ship in the harbour ready to take me away from all this to a new life in another world?

Along the roadside were signs of yesterday's destruction. Fences had fallen, leaves lay in soggy drifts against the verge and trees had been ripped from the ground exposing the root ball below. I came to a field enclosed by a dry stone wall. A girl was picking flowers from the hedgerow. She looked about my age and I thought she might be alone too. But then I heard her call out so I hid behind the wall.

'Will these do, Mama?' she said, handing her mother a bunch of wild hyssop.

'They're beautiful, my child,' the mother answered, and I saw the girl snuggle into her chest. Then the woman saw *me* and her eyes narrowed as if she knew who I was. 'Come on, my sweet. Let's go to your father's grave.' I felt her words tighten inside my heart and turned away. Then I saw there were other villagers too, heading towards the cemetery to honour their dead, clutching flowers to replace old with new. It must be All Souls Day.

My wet clothes still clung to my body, but they loosened now as the sun grew stronger, freeing my limbs, making my strides longer. Now I was moving forwards not back. Now I was on the road to a new future, leaving my past behind. Ahead, Gibraltar seemed to beckon, telling me to hurry because this was where my future lay. Perhaps here I could find hope. Perhaps here was the solution to my woes. And despite the hunger in my belly, I moved on, one step after another down the road towards that rock.

There was a sign for the *chozas*. Should I go there? Should I find someone to help me like they did before? But what was the point of returning to a place where we'd suffered so much, and where Eva had left me and turned herself into a whore? I stared at the sign and the pull on my heart was too strong to resist it. I turned off the highway and passed through the overgrown fields and marshes to our temporary home. It was still very early and no one was about, so I wandered the settlement until I found our empty shack. I remembered when Eva and I had come here desperate and how the people were friendly and no one judged us, but accepted us as we were. I went inside and the floor was covered in leaves. I saw our old broom leaning against the wall and without thinking began sweeping furiously until I'd shoved all the debris into a pile outside. It made me feel better clearing it off like that. But now I was exhausted. Those few minutes had been enough. I couldn't bear the emptiness of remembering, so I stood up and walked away. There was nothing there for me now.

Ahead, I saw a fork in the road; two directions - left and right. Which way? Right would lead to Alfonso's tavern where, yet again, *pulpo asado* would be crisping on the griddle. Should I go there? My stomach said yes but my mind said no. Someone was bound to offer me food but then where would the next meal come from? And the one after that? They would ask me to stay, tell me to go with a man to earn my keep, and I'd end up like Eva. I shook my head. No.

I turned away, avoiding the bar and all the temptations that lay within and plodded on. I had no plan; just a relentless hope that something better might be round the corner. Dizzy with hunger I arrived at the flour mill where I had seen Don Diego on the night of our demonstration. I looked up at the tall chimney bending like a giant finger, pointing at me, accusing me of stealing his wife's shawl. Was my mind playing tricks? The water wheel was turning and its giant paddles were calling *'Tia, you're a thief, Tia. You're a thief.'* On it went, the great wheel turning through the rushing stream, pulling at my mind, turning it inside out. From the office window I saw faces staring down. Was that Don Diego? Should I go up and tell him it wasn't me? That I was no thief? But there was nothing I could do. Fine particles of wheat flour floated down and landed in my hair and a mist passed across my eyes as if I was about to faint. Was I going crazy? I could bear it no longer so I turned and faced the sun, plodding away from the factory and down the road towards Gibraltar. Would they let me cross the border? Would someone give me food?' The rock was looming over the rooftops now and I could see the dents and furrows of its rocky surface. It was so close I could almost touch it and this gave me hope. It was the end of the land and the start of the sea. Everything finished at that rock; that magnified pebble planted on the edge of the world like a giant full stop. I trudged on, keeping it in my vision and when it disappeared behind a building, I moved a little left or right until it came back into view. As I got closer, I could see houses clustered against its sides and the funnels of ships standing to attention in the harbour. I could even see soldiers moving on the ramparts of the castle. Now though, there was a pounding in my head and a pain in my eyes. I could hear my breathing, and feel a heaviness in my legs as if I was about to collapse. I approached a corner. There were voices chanting and when I turned into the next street I found myself at the back of a demonstration. It stretched far ahead, men and women in ragged formation, marching forwards into the bright sun. I put my arm over my eyes to shield them and saw hoes, hammers, and saws, carried aloft by the protesters and I envied their bravado and their passion. Mine was all spent.

'Workers, we must unite,' someone shouted.

I wondered if they'd just left the flour mill and imagined Don Diego, angry at this new demonstration, pacing the room with his gun. I took a deep breath to give myself strength then ran forward, in and out of the marchers, realising that my dear Pablo must be up at the front with his father. Perhaps I could stop him, ask him to listen, explain how foolish I'd been and suggest we start again. Oh, Pablo. How wonderful that would be. Then I recognised his voice shouting over the crowd.

'We must free ourselves from the shackles of capitalism,'

I waved my arms and bellowed as loud as I could.

'Stop, Pablo. Please.'

He stopped dead and turned to look over his shoulder, turning to face me, watching me come towards him. I could see that his jaw was taut and his lips were white. I reached him and stopped to catch my breath. He stood still, staring at me as I tried to control my breathing. Marchers passed us by, observing the two of us standing together on the narrow pavement. We looked like lovers who'd had a tiff. He watched me with narrowed eyes as I readied myself to speak.

'Pablo, please, let me explain,' I pleaded, but he shook his head.

'They sacked me, Tia. Because of you I lost my job.' I looked at him puzzled. 'They didn't like it one bit, you coming to find me at my work. It's no place for a woman, they said.' His eyes filled with tears and I remembered how, despite me going off with Alfonso, he'd left that rose in the hallway as a token of his love, but then how badly I had reacted in the slaughterhouse. Poor Pablo, his pride had been ruptured and I could see how much he was struggling with the humiliation of my actions. His heart was broken but he couldn't tell me these things. I reached out to touch him but he pushed my hand away.

'They say you're a thief,' he said.

'No, Pablo, no,'

'And a flirt, going off with that man at the fiesta.'

'I...'

'He's told the whole village you started that fire.'

His words punched me in the stomach. I crumpled. There was no fight left. The world moved under my feet. I closed my eyes to get control but a wave of nausea struck me and when I opened them, Pablo was running to catch up with the others. He didn't look back, and for the last time I watched his silhouette diminish, blurred now, until it merged into the impenetrable rock. I put my hands to my ears to stop the jangling and then to my mouth to prevent the vomit from rising in my throat. The world was moving and I was standing still. Gibraltar slid out of view as I fell unconscious to the ground.

47. Mariangeles

After a surprisingly comfortable sleep Mariangeles woke alone. She peered out of the tarpaulin and saw that the sun was already high in the sky and Pepe was outside feeding Jefe.

'I've been thinking,' she said. 'Remember what the slaughter men told you about Tia's boy Pablo. Something about a demonstration down near the harbour? Perhaps he knows where she is, or better still, perhaps she's with him.'

Pepe nodded. 'I've been thinkin' that as well.' But there was resignation in his voice as though he was having second thoughts.

'What's the matter, Pepe? Don't you want to go down there?'

'I'd do anything for you, Mariangeles. You knows that,' he answered, but she could see that something was bothering him.

'What is it, Pepe?' she asked.

Pepe shook his head. 'Nothing Mariangeles.' But he was lying; she knew it.

'We're running out of options, Pepe. This is our last chance.'

After a moment's thought, Pepe nodded. 'Come on then. Let's go,' he said.

They set off until they reached a crossroads where they stopped. A mother and daughter were sitting on a wall.

'Have you seen a young girl pass this way?' Mariangeles called out, and to her surprise the woman nodded.

'She went that way,' she said, pointing towards Gibraltar. Mariangeles gasped with delight at the thought of being so close. Pepe flicked the reins and Jefe changed to a trot.

48. Tia

The world was black. I felt arms around my waist – someone was lifting me off the ground. There was a cacophony of sounds, of voices speaking quickly and the thud of a huge doorway being shut. A bowl of warm stew was pushed across a table. I remember stuffing my mouth with bread and chunks of delicious vegetables and succulent meat and someone was saying, 'Here drink this.' Then the world went black again as I surrendered to sleep.

49. Mariangeles

Pepe fixed his eyes on the road ahead, hardly speaking.

'What's the matter?' Mariangeles asked again.

'It's nothing. Let's get to the harbour and find your girl.'

They travelled on in silence. What was the matter with Pepe? Was he fed up with all this chasing about? Or perhaps he was annoyed at losing money being with her, rather than working? Or was he tired of her company? From the way he had held her last night she didn't think so. All these possibilities ran through her mind but she didn't ask again. It was obvious he didn't want to talk. Reaching a river, they stopped to let Jefe drink. 'We'll take it easy today, my friend,' Pepe said to his horse. 'You had a long day travelling yesterday.' Then he pointed downstream to a large building with a water turbine that drove the machinery. 'Looks like the local flour mill,' he said, observing the white dust that had settled on everything. 'Let's ask there.'

As they arrived, a siren sounded for the end of a shift and a few workers trudged into the yard. Other men were outside the gates holding placards with slogans such as *Workers Unite! Withdraw your Labour! Action Now!*

'Scabs!' they shouted at the men passing through, heads down, trying to ignore the insults. Mariangeles strode up to one of the pickets.

'Have you seen a girl walking this way?'

They shook their heads. 'Too busy, señora. These scabs need to be taught a lesson.

Mariangeles looked around. This didn't look like a major demonstration.

'Where are the rest of your group? she asked.

'They're down at the harbour picketing the stevedores and the deckhands and all them other dockers. They can't feed their families, señora. We have to fight.' Mariangeles smiled in sympathy, remembering the men in her old town queuing for scraps. She had called them down-and-outs as if they deserved to be there, but who was she to judge someone else's situation when hers was filled with such shame?

'Come on, Pepe, let's go,' she said. 'My Tia is close. I can feel it.' So they set off again and now the streets were narrower, with houses either side and cooking smells wafting out of open front doors. A little further in were single-storey shops, no more than shacks, some offering tattoos, others selling chandlery like boat hooks and hand pumps and hoses hanging on wires. Opposite a very noisy bar, was a two-storey building with marble pillars either side of a huge front door.

'That's odd,' Mariangeles said, 'Such an elegant building in a rough area like this,'

Pepe didn't respond. His mouth was pinched as if in pain. Stopping the cart, he turned to Mariangeles. 'I got something to tell you, Mariangeles, something important and please, for the sake of our friendship, don't say nothing. Just listen.'

They sat together on the roadside - carts passing, dogs barking, children playing - as Pepe explained. 'That building you just admired is where I work, where I does my second job. It belongs to a woman called Mary Palmer.' Mariangeles looked across at the marble columns of the portico entrance and the ornate wrought-iron balconies on the windows. At the side was a stable yard for several horses and space for deliveries too. 'She entertains wealthy businessmen so I fetch 'n' carry 'n' make sure she's stocked up with the finest food and wines from Gibraltar.' Pepe took a deep breath. 'But there's more, Mariangeles. Sometimes she gets me to take girls across the border and put them on them steamships – to Buenos Aires mostly. They seem to like Spanish girls over there.' Mariangeles frowned. What did Pepe mean? 'It's a brothel, Mariangeles, a high class one at that.' Mariangeles stared at the row of windows and counted six. Did that mean six girls were in there waiting for clients? Pepe continued. 'I don't like doin' it, Mariangeles, but when the factory burned down, I looked for other work. Alfonso don't pay much and Mary Palmer offered to top me up. So that's what I been doing. I works for the smartest madam in town. She's a bit of a tyrant but she pays well.'

'You take girls down to the ships?

'Yes, those what Mary doesn't want no more. Somehow she persuades the captains to pay her first, then I 'ave to deliver them next day or else there's trouble.

There was a moment of silence as Mariangeles took it all in. 'So you act like a pimp,' she said.

'I suppose so.'

Mariangeles could see he was dismayed at telling her, but she was thinking. Pepe was not the perfect gentleman she had thought he was, but she wasn't perfect either. Not so long ago she was going to release her daughter into the hands of The Fixer. Surely that was worse? She sat back and for the first time in this frantic search that had brought her across the country to search for her girl, she smiled. Pepe was just as flawed as the rest.

'It's all right, Pepe. I don't approve, but I understand. Now let's get back to finding my Tia.'

50. Tia

I blinked my eyes open. What a beautiful room with brocade curtains draped at every window, shielding me from the last rays of the sun! I saw my filthy clothing in the corner; discarded like a ghost and realised I was naked, immersed in a scented bath where my legs moved easily in the warm rush that passed between them. I raised my forearm and saw that the dirt had gone. My skin had been transformed from dirt-brown to virgin-pink, as if, after all that had occurred today - from morning till afternoon, from there to here, from sleeping under the pines to this sumptuous room - the grime of a lifetime had been washed away. I lay there soothed by the rich aroma of oil that was making me drowsy. Or was it that potion they gave me when I first arrived?

I looked up. There was a ceiling rose bordered with acanthus leaves and from the centre hung a chandelier. Beads of condensation were forming on the crystals and swelling into bulbous tears that could not contain their own weight. They dropped into the water, splashing my face like laughter. The whole room felt lovely, enveloped in mist and the oils were caressing my skin. I ran my hand over my body, discovering the curves that had been forming beneath my clothes. I saw the buds of my nipples peeping through the water and they were a revelation. I moved my legs, agitating the water, allowing it to swell and ripple across my breasts. The smell of lavender reminded me of summer and of wildflowers growing in fields like the hyssop collected by that girl today. They had sneered at me in my damp rags, that mother and daughter, so maybe they'd heard. Maybe the rumour that I was a thief had spread from the village. But somehow, I didn't seem to care because everything felt so light, so bright, so vacant.

Where was I? I listened for clues but the house was deadly silent. I thought of Ma, snuggled up at home with Pa and I wanted to speak to her, to tell her I was sorry for being so wilful. I opened my mouth and called out. 'Ma, Ma!' but my voice was a single thread, lost in the thick folds of damask at the windows. I called again, stronger this time, but there was no one else in that heavy, humid room. No one but me.

I dropped below the surface and the water muffled my ears. Why did you try to send me away, Ma? Why did I have to go? And what about Pablo? Why didn't you wait to hear what I had to say? Why wouldn't you let me defend my honour? The water smelt divine. My head was spinning. I remembered playing with the rich children, waving those canes and heading into that narrow sunlit gap by the harbour, screaming over the sound of the waves, fighting the sea dragon. Where had all that spirit gone? And why did I come east? Why did I come to this town so full of calamity and sin?

I raised my head and heard muttering downstairs. There was something in their talking, a questioning rise and fall as if they didn't know what to do with me, now that I was here. But no one came and soon the perplexing silence returned and I sighed. What had I done to deserve this? I had tried being a good girl, always doing whatever others asked of me, not answering back. At least not until yesterday with Agnes and that priest. And now it was too late. I couldn't go back, not now in this grown-up room.

The water in the bath was cooling. I should've got out, but I felt dazed and without the will to move. There was another noise below. Perhaps someone was preparing hot water to replenish my bath. I sat up and strained my ears in case someone was speaking, but I couldn't hear voices. Now I noticed a plaster frieze running around the top of the room and moulded into it were shells, painted white against a pale-yellow background - so pretty. They reminded me of my walks along the beach with Eva, and I remembered the pebble I had given her to keep her safe and wondered if she still had it.

I lay back into the cooling water and relaxed. Had they forgotten about me in the village? Had I escaped their accusations? Maybe I had nothing to fear. But that mother and child with her hyssop - had they report me to the authorities? I spoke to the air. 'I wish you were here, Ma. I wish you could protect me from their accusations.' I remembered yesterday as I strode away from the village, moving forwards, one foot in front of the other like a soldier marching, left right, left right, on and on as if a mysterious force was drawing me here to this destination. Was that you Ma? Did you mean to bring me here? Is it safe? Surely you wouldn't allow me to come here if it wasn't.' I shook my head. Ma wasn't here. And even if she was, would she care? I was getting confused. I shivered even though I was warm. It was silent yet I heard unvoiced demands inside my head. What was about to happen? Good or bad, I could not tell. I dropped beneath the surface again and heard the rhythm of my heart, pounding more than it should. If I was in danger, somehow I felt powerless to resist. But at least for now in this bath I was safe. My mind could float in suspension, looking neither back to the last few days nor forward to what might be. But the water was cold now so I raised myself again, blinking away the droplets from my eyes and telling myself these were not tears. Instead, I bit my lip and looked again around this beautiful room full of luxurious indulgence. How wonderful to be in a place where perfumed mists clung to ornate ceilings and where servants would probably appear, should I choose to call. How lucky I was, being rescued, then fed and now being treated to such pampering.

I heard voices, clear and robust this time. People were arguing, but I couldn't catch what they said. Should I be scared? Should I do something? Maybe I should go downstairs to ask them why I'm here. But I was too scared to do that, too scared to do anything. What should I do?

51. Mariangeles

Pepe and Mariangeles arrived in the town overlooking the bay. They found the main square where they joined the back of a demonstration. Hundreds of men and women had gathered around an ornate union banner, and a middle-aged man was speaking through a megaphone.

'Which one is Pablo?' Mariangeles whispered to someone.

'Senior or junior?'

'A young man,'

'He's over there, but don't bother him. It's his turn to speak, after his father.'

Mariangeles watched the older Pablo hand the megaphone to his son. What a handsome boy, she thought. They waited patiently as the younger Pablo spoke. His oratory was strong, his voice mature. One day he will make a fine statesman Mariangeles thought. When it was over Mariangeles pushed through the crowd desperately searching this way and that. Was Tia here? Was she by this boy's side? If they were together, she would be pleased. She studied every face but Tia was not there after all. She reached Pablo junior and pressed his arm. 'You know my daughter,' she said abruptly without introduction. She was too anxious for niceties.

'You mean Tia?' Pablo asked.

'Yes. Where is she?'

Pablo shook his head. 'I used to know her, but not now.'

Mariangeles frowned. 'What does that mean?

The young Pablo shook his head. 'I don't want to talk about.'

'Well at least tell me where she is,' she said, desperately.

'I left her up there,' he said pointing back the way they had come. 'Outside some fancy house.'

Mariangeles turned around and strode back to the cart, pulling Pepe with her.

'I know where she is, Pepe, come on quick, before it's too late.'

52. Tia

A door opened disturbing my sleep and a girl entered with an armful of logs. She had an apron wrapped loosely around her waist and her hair was neatly plaited into a white cap, making her look like a nun. She prodded the embers then added the extra wood. Sparks flew up, but her eyes were down and the only thing breaking our silence was the crackling in the grate.

'Where am I?' I asked but she looked away. Was she afraid? Surely not of me? When she left, I lay back into the cool water letting my thick hair float free. I closed my eyes and drifted off again into an opaque sleep wondering if I really had escaped my accusers in the village. I was woken again by the nun-girl and this time she was carrying a bowl of water. I waited as she drew up a chair behind me. She pulled my hair out of the bath. It felt stretched and heavy. She used a cup to scoop up the water, pouring it gently over my head, repeating the same motion over and over. I felt its warmth running down my neck and heard the droplets tip-tapping into the enamel bowl echoing around the room. My hair was filthy - she had to scrub my scalp with oil to loosen the dirt. I tried again.

'Thank you for making me so clean,' I said leaning back waiting for her response. But still she said nothing. Instead, she brushed the strands of my hair from crown to tip and I heard the squeak of cleanliness magnified in the silence. Ma never did this for me. I used to wash it myself. The nun-girl took a towel steeped in rosemary oil, wrapping it round my head until the fragrance burst into life with the heat. It felt nice but inside, I was fearful. Why wouldn't she talk? Had she heard about the accusation? Did she think I was a thief? If only I could explain. She had kind eyes and I was all alone. I needed someone to trust. But I'd been let down before. I opened my mouth to speak again but it was too late. She had gone. I felt a rush of cool air - the girl had left the door open. Now I heard more voices, deep and resonant coming from the floor below. I was sure I'd heard them before but where? I couldn't place them in my history. Maybe it was today or maybe last week, even last year. The air was thick; my mind was thin. Then the handle turned and the door was pulled shut. The girl must have come back to close it.

Look at me, so clean and fresh, my hair sparkling and my belly full of stew. My rescuers were very generous. I could hardly believe it. Everything was calm and light as if I was floating. Was it the oils in this bath making me feel like this or was their potion still working its magic? Whatever it was, I felt strangely content. It had been a terrible few days - everything so wrong and now everything so right. It is right isn't it, Ma? I asked the air. I am safe, aren't I? Or maybe not. It was hard to tell. Was I a swallow watching the world from the safety of the treetops or a deer quivering in the undergrowth as the stalker drew his gun? Whatever, somehow, I felt that I could not protest. Something was holding me back. Or was I too much of a coward to act? Because beneath it all I had another fear - one that I hardly dared express. Was there a click? Did I hear the nun-girl turn a key in that lock? Did she confine me here, and if she did, then why? Surely she wouldn't do that, would she? But I *had* heard something. Should I go and check? Should I get out of this bath and walk across the room, place my hand on the handle and see if it resists? Should I do that, Ma? Should I go and see? And what if she did lock me in? What would I do about it? I stared at the door, so wide, so dark. The handle was brass and the back plate engraved with flowers. It looked so pretty and yet so solid, set into the wood as if it had been there forever, as if it would never move and release the catch.

Perhaps I was wrong. Maybe I was only dreaming and I should relax and enjoy this bath while it lasts. Or should I go over there now to find out if I have lost my freedom? No I thought. Despite the chilling water, I could not lift myself out. I could not bear to discover I might be right.

53. Mariangeles

It was siesta time. No one was in the street - just dogs barking and chasing each other, whipping up the dust. Jefe came to a halt outside the fancy house that Mariangeles had seen earlier - the house where Pepe worked. The Madam house. Oh, Tia where are you? Mariangeles thought. She studied the entrance porch with its marble columns and huge wooden door. It looked more like a gentleman's residence than a brothel, but maybe that was the point. Mary Palmer must be a clever woman, she thought, momentarily impressed. But then she thought again. My poor girl, are you in there? If you are, surely it wasn't voluntarily? Even now her daughter's real character was unclear. Was she a good girl or bad? Then she thought about all the other people in her life - Pepe who had chosen to work for a madam, those drunks queueing for free food in the harbour, Incarna with her gossip, Garcia's fumbling assault, and her own complicit behaviour with The Fixer. None of us are blameless she thought. In this life no one escapes weakness and lack of judgement so why should she condemn her own child now? She sighed and in that moment a strange sensation came over her, as if a trapped bird had just been released from her heart. There was no need for recrimination. Tia was Tia, and whatever she had done didn't matter. She sighed, understanding, at last, the miracle of unconditional maternal love.

They went into the bar full of sailors and workmen shouting and laughing. Some were spitting onto a sawdust floor.

'Have you seen a young girl?' she asked over the din.

The barman scratched at his beard and leaned over, studying Mariangeles as if he was weighing up whether to trust her with his answer.

'Yeah, I did see a girl. She was with that union lot doing a protest. I noticed because she looked so different from the rest, like she didn't fit in.'

'So where is she now?' Mariangeles blurted out, exposing her fears.'

'She had an argument with a boy. She seemed desperate and he was just standing there with his arms across his chest. Then he walked off and left her there.' He pointed out onto the street. 'Poor girl, I thought she was going to cry but then she dropped like a stone, right there, on the pavement. Reckon she fainted.'

'So where is she now?' Mariangeles screeched. Her heart was racing and her words came out shrill.

'One of them tarts came out from that Madam house and took her in.'

54. Tia

'Ma, I've run away, away from them all, although it was never my intention to end up in this room. I was heading for Gibraltar when they brought me here. Is it a punishment, being in this house? Or are they taking care of me? People say I've done something bad, but it isn't true! Why would I steal? You always told me that was wrong. I'm not a thief. I'm a good girl and a good worker too. You should see the way I do the laundry, never any complaints except when I'm daydreaming. Am I daydreaming now? I suppose I must be, talking to you when you are not here. I feel strange, Ma, a little bit odd. Yet my mind is clearing - their potion is wearing off. I have to face it. This morning I thought I was free, but here I am, a stranger in a strange room with that door closed, or locked even! I heard a click, I'm sure of it, and now the sound repeats itself in my head, click, click, click, like drops of left-over rain after a storm. It's getting late, Ma, and soon they will come. 'They *will* come, Ma, won't they?'

The nun-girl entered again, carrying a large jug of water. Her muscles bulged with the weight and her face was flushed with the effort. I moved my feet aside as she lifted the jug and carefully tipped the water in. Heat rushed up, warming my body like a caress. I lay back watching. Her eyes were down but she knew I was studying her then she looked up and opened her mouth to speak. Her words were a surprise.

'You're that bitch who started the fire.'

The last drops trickled from the jug – drip, drip, drip. I heard them loudly as I adjusted to what she had said. The girl held the jug to her chest, studying my reaction. I couldn't speak. Steam rose from the surface of the water. The girl spoke again. 'But you got lucky, didn't you? Working for Don Diego, when the rest of us had nothing.' I heard the sarcasm and observed her face, all serious and stern. Were those tears in her eyes? She turned away.

'Wait!' I called

But she had left the room, leaving her words ricocheting in my skull like bullets.

Would I ever escape condemnation? Why hadn't I spoken out? Why hadn't I shouted to the girl that she'd got it wrong, that it was Alfonso's fault more than mine? Suddenly I felt exposed lying in this bath in the middle of the floor, as if centre stage in some important play. Steam was condensing onto the cool marble furniture, giving it a dull sheen as it settled around me, as pale as dew. There was a murmur now, of strangers somewhere in a room below and I imagined them hunched in deep debate like a jury considering their verdict. Or maybe they didn't care what happened to me. Maybe they didn't know about the fire or the shawl and they were about to leave the building and wouldn't come back and maybe my suspicion that the door over there was locked was all a misconception, and I could leave anytime I chose. But filth had begun to cling to the sides of the bath. The water had turned grey and the warmer water had created swirls of grease across its surface as if something was turning bad. I'd been here too long, wallowing in daydreams; remembering my past in order to forget the present. But now I had to face facts. I

266

was someone's prisoner and I had to act. Over there in the corner were my rags - perhaps I could put them back on. Perhaps I could escape. I raised myself from the grey sludge and placed a foot on the floor. Droplets of water ran down my calves towards my ankles and slithered onto the soft blue tiles. They sank into the surface, making the tiles a vivid blue. I placed my other foot down and took a step, then another and another, until, naked and wet, I reached my old skirts. I turned back towards the bath and saw that the wet footprints were pointing towards me, marking the tiles in a bright trail, reminding me of where I had travelled, where I had been. The prospect of dressing in my damp clothes seemed uninviting. Besides where would I go if I escaped? I looked towards the door wondering what to do. A dressing gown hung on the back of it and as I started to walk towards it, I saw a mirror and stopped; halted by my own nakedness. I studied the reflection. My face and neck were browned by the sun but my body was a pale yellowy pink. My ribs were bony and my breasts sat high on my chest as vulnerable as baby birds. There were hollows either side of my stomach and between my legs was a cluster of soft brown hair. I reached for the gown and trembled at its luxury, so soft and divine. I pulled it on, folding back the cuffs to fit my arms. Now I felt warm. I tied the sash around my scrawny bones and sat on the edge of a yellow couch, placing my bare feet neatly on the tiles. I brought my knees together as young girls should and sat there scrubbed clean, my hair smelling like heaven and wearing nothing but a robe of the softest cotton. I seemed to be waiting, neat and clean and ready for what might happen next. I strained, listening for a shoved chair or a saucepan placed on the stove; anything to indicate life. I waited a while longer but still there was nothing, so I went to the window and pulled back the heavy drapes, just a bit, in order to take a peep. There was a narrow street and through the silky rays of sunset I saw rubbish littering the gutters and posters peeling from the walls. The bar opposite was noisy with men arguing and glasses

267

banging on tables. On the pavements, people were emerging from their homes, walking this way and that, kicking the rubbish under their feet. Their motion agitated the gas flames of the street lights causing a discord between light and shade. A boy was leaning on a lamppost trying to smoke a cigarette and in the distance I saw a small group of mourners holding torches. They were going to the cemetery and I remembered that today was the Day of the Dead. I recalled the dream I'd had last night when a lady came to me and said *keep yourself steady*. Was this my grandmother? Did she know what was to come?

55. Mariangeles

Mariangeles slumped in a seat by the window.

'I have to get into that house,' she said but Pepe shook his head.

'Not yet, Mariangeles. The girls don't start for an hour or two. We got time to work this out.'

Mariangeles nodded. Everything told her to listen to her heart and rush right in through the front door, but Pepe was probably right. They needed a plan. She looked out of the window. An old woman passed by with a long taper, having just lit the gas lamps down the street, and their flames were flickering making everything dance. A few soldiers were walking by, shoulder to shoulder, carrying bottles of whisky as if they were off to a party. On the other side of the street, two girls sauntered boldly arm in arm towards the ships. Hiding under the clouds was the hazy circle of a full moon casting a dim light onto a boy trying to light a cigarette. A carriage was coming. She could see the rapid run of its wheels on the cobbles and steam rising from the horse's flanks, as if it had galloped here at pace. It came to a halt at the porch and the carriage tipped forward slightly. Mariangeles imagined the sound of creaking leather as a young woman got out, so very thin. She banged on the huge door. It opened and she rushed inside.

Then another carriage arrived, slower than the first. It slid to a halt outside the entrance and lurched sideways as its occupant stepped off, then sprung upright released from its burden. The driver flicked the reins and left, and now Mariangeles could see a woman wobbling on the pavement, gathering up her vast skirts. She waddled up the steps, unsteady on her feet and fiddled with a chatelaine around her waist. Pulling out a vast key, she inserted it into the lock. Pepe leaned over and looked across the street.

'That's Mary. Drunk as usual,' he said and Mariangeles felt a pinch in her stomach.

'We have to do something Pepe. And soon.

56. Tia

The door below banged as if someone had just walked in, and a few minutes later it banged again. A woman's voice all gravelly and slurred, bellowed up from below

'Eva, get down here now!'

Eva? Why was she here? Why had she come? Was it to fetch me? But then I realised and took a deep and desperate breath. Of course Eva was here because this was the house she had shown me from the parapet of Don Diego's house. This was the house where she worked. So the woman shouting must be Mary Palmer. I was in her house. I was in the house of a Madam. Oh god, I was in the bathrobe of a whore.

Mary Palmer shouted something and Eva shouted back.

'I went there to hide from Manolo.'

'To a client's house? You silly bitch.'

There was a pause and some muttering. Then I heard Eva speak.

'But she's only fifteen, Mary.'

'So what?'

'But Mary…'

'Shut up you bitch.'

There was a thud and no more talk. What had happened? Was Eva all right? I was still at the window. As I looked down, I saw a man approaching, walking oddly on legs as thin as sticks. He was wearing a long black cloak. It was The Fixer. I snapped the curtain closed to shut him out. 'No' I cried into the air. Please not him. The Fixer had already entered my dreams and sucked at my soul and now he was downstairs and coming in. I rushed to the door and turned the handle but it would not yield. I pulled, I pushed but the door was firm. Of course it was. I should have known. I sank to the floor, collapsed, degraded, undone.

57. Mariangeles

Mariangeles looked across the street and saw lights being lit in the bedrooms on the first floor, casting five regular blocks of brightness across the dark grey pavement. Only one room remained dark, but as she looked at it she saw movement as the curtains opened then closed again quickly. Who was that?

Just then a man came striding up the street and stopped at the portico. His shape was black like a silhouette and his movements were jerky and sharp. Mariangeles froze. The Fixer was placing a key into the lock. The door was opening. He went inside. No, she thought. Of all the men, please, not him.

'We've got to do something,' she shrieked.

Pepe leapt up. 'I'll take Jefe into the stable yard. They know me there so I won't be questioned. Wait here, Mariangeles and I'll find out what's goin on.' Mariangeles watched Pepe guide Jefe and the cart into the yard and to her relief she could still see him from the bar as he waved across to her before disappearing into what Mariangeles imagined was a kitchen. Once again Mariangeles was waiting whilst Pepe took action. This wasn't right. She had to do something herself, but what? She ordered a brandy to calm her nerves.

58. Tia

I was trembling when the nun-girl returned.

'Who is the man that just arrived? Is it Manolo Jimenez Torres?

'I'm not supposed to tell.'

'Please. I have to know.'

The girl sighed, giving in. 'Yes, it's him but we call him Manolo.'

My heart sank. So it was true. The Fixer *was* here. The man, who was going to take me away to Seville, the man who had haunted my dreams, the man to whom my parent owed an enormous debt, the man who had frightened Eva, was downstairs with Mary and I was upstairs, alone in this room. Did he know I was here? Had someone told him of my presence? If he knew he would surely try to get his revenge. I felt my knees starting to shake and my teeth begin to chatter. I couldn't control my fear. 'Been told to give you this,' the nun-girl said handing me a small glass and a decanter of what looked like water. I took a sip. It was delicious. 'It's anise,' she said. I took a huge gulp that ran down my throat with ease. She turned to leave.

'Don't go,' I said. 'Tell me what's going on.'

She hesitated then turned back and sat down. Perhaps she felt sorry for me. I must have looked a desperate wretch.

'You and Eva have upset a lot of people,' she said.

'What do you mean?'

'I shouldn't say.'

'Please.'

She sighed again as if she had given up on her silence. 'One of our best clients came here yesterday shouting about Eva being in his house, dressed like a whore. We didn't know what he was on about until he told us she'd stayed in his house all night, presumably with you.'

'But that wasn't my fault. Why was he upset with me?'

'Don Diego said he'd seen his servant girl watching from the rooftop, and that you'd been cavorting with some upstart socialist boy.' I took another gulp. The anise was nice. 'Then he pulled out a gun - and it was all fancy - and he came right up to Mary and shoved it in her face, demanding compensation. They spoke for ages and when he left, he shouted something about whores and socialists being bad for business. And it's true because there's been trouble at his factory all day today - some sort of demonstration.' The nun-girl let out a sigh as if she was sorry she'd told me all that. I thought of Pablo and those workers marching along the road to Gibraltar. Why didn't he listen? Why didn't he wait?

'And now what's happened? I heard a thud.'

'Mary hit Eva across the jaw, so hard she fell down.'

'So where is she now?'

'Smashed to pieces in her room. Mary won't let her out.' I imagined Eva, bruised and broken somewhere close by. We were both prisoners now. The nun-girl seemed more willing to speak. 'When you fainted outside our door, Mary thought you were one of Alfonso's girls, come looking for work, you being so filthy and poor, just like Eva when she first came. So she asked Eva to tell us all about you and at first she said no, but Mary threatened her

276

with more violence and Eva gave in. Told us how you'd escaped from Manolo years ago and how you'd come east and got together with Alfonso. Course the penny dropped then, that you were the one that started the fire. Mary was fuming, saying it must be fate, you turning up at her house like that. She was so angry I thought she'd explode and when she calmed down, she went all quiet and I knew that she was scheming. My ma's clever like that.' The nun-girl stopped abruptly and put her hand over her lips as if to hold back the secret that had already passed through them.

'Your ma? Mary is your ma?' The girl didn't answer. I repeated my question. 'Is Mary your mother?'

'What else were we supposed to do? Pa worked at that factory, same as you. We were respectable then. But after the fire he was nothing but ash. So it was go on the streets or starve. She started in Gibraltar, made a packet and came back with enough cash to persuade Manolo to go fifty-fifty. We've been doing all right 'til now.' I held my breath trying to take it all in. What a fool I had been fainting right outside this place, presenting myself to Mary Palmer like a worm to a bird. Of course she'd been keeping me locked in this room because I was the wretch of a person who started the fire that killed her husband and ruined her life. Of course she hated me and nothing I said or did would make her treat me with compassion. The girl was sobbing now. 'We have to keep my identity quiet, or the clients will want me as the speciality. Why do you think I wear these dowdy old clothes?' Her arms were folded against her chest and I pressed her arm to calm her. But inside, it was me who was jittery with fear. I wasn't dressed like the nun-girl. I didn't look dowdy or unattractive like her. My hair had been washed and prepared. I was wearing a luxurious bathrobe, and underneath it I was naked. 'I mustn't tell you anymore,' the nun-girl said getting up to leave. When she had passed through the door I heard the faint sound of the key clicking inside the lock but it echoed in my ears like the toll of a loud and insistent church bell. She had locked me in again, this time without pretence. Too much had passed between us for her to trust me now.

Below I heard more arguing.

'Didn't I tell you not to damage the girls?'

'Well it's not my fault,' The Fixer said and I recognised his squeaky voice.

'Yes it is. That Eva's in no fit state to fuck anyone tonight.'

I felt sick thinking of Eva, all bruised and broken, in a room along the corridor. How happy we had been in that factory, buying nice clothes and giggling at the silliest of things. Where was your rebellion now, Eva? All gone, disappeared. And it was my fault. She wouldn't have needed to choose this path if I hadn't caused that fire. Oh Eva! I cried aloud. 'I am so sorry.' I reached for the decanter, filled the glass to the top and gulped down the anise. It left a coating of sweetness that felt like my only friend. Poor Eva, they had stolen her soul. And surely they would steal mine too?

The nun-girl came back and unfolded a small table in front of the mirror where she laid out tins of makeup. I shivered as she pulled the bathrobe away to expose my shoulders and picked up a brush.

'What are you doing?' I asked.

'Making you pretty,' she said.

'Why do I have to be pretty? I asked, but again she ignored my question. The anise was kicking in. The sensation in my head felt nice so I took another swig. She painted a light dusting of colour into the open space between my breasts and got a smaller brush full of black powder that she swept across my eyelids. Then she rubbed a layer of rouge on my cheeks and smeared red grease across my lips. It tasted so foul that I swilled it down with more anise. She scooped my hair into a clip, draping it softly around the crown, and letting a few strands fall down over my forehead.

278

She held a mirror up for me to see and I stared horrified at the reflection. Here was a gaudy stranger and next to me was Mary's nun-girl daughter. My hair was gleaming with life whilst hers was sticking out of her cap like straw. I was bright and she was dull. I was painted in the colours of badness, like a harlot in waiting.

'I've laid a dress out in the room next door,' the nun-girl said, then handed me a towel. I felt my hands trembling as I took it from her. 'Put it under you before he arrives,' she added.

59. Mariangeles

The bar was full. A drunk came over and tried to embrace Mariangeles but she pushed him away. 'Leave her be,' the barman shouted. He seemed to understand her distress. Mariangeles rubbed at the window, misty with condensation and peered through the gap. The boy with a cigarette was leading two men down an alleyway. Did he have girls down there waiting to service them? If so, he was starting young. Along the upstairs windows, a girl was closing the rest of the curtains. Their evening was about to begin. Mariangeles looked down the street into the blue-black night stretching backwards into the woods. A shape she could not decipher was advancing along the street, first under the lamps then into the darkness, bright then dull then bright again until it came into focus and she saw that it was a rider on a white horse. Dressed in tweeds with a swagger stick stuffed in his belt, she recognised Alfonso immediately. He turned his horse into the stable, led the animal into a stall next to Jefe, and removed its bridle and saddle. Then he came out onto the street and went to the front door where he pulled on the bell. Someone let him in. Mariangeles frowned. Both The Fixer and Alfonso were in the brothel now and both men were known to Tia. Surely this was no coincidence. Mary Palmer was up to something and it involved her girl. Mariangeles could stand it no longer. Pepe shouldn't be doing this on his own. She had to do something too. Gathering her things, she rushed out of the bar, crossed the road and dashed into the yard. She found a door and opened it quickly. Pepe was in the kitchen peering through a keyhole. She ran to him and held her breath. On the other side of the door she heard loud, demanding voices.

60. Tia

Downstairs I could hear shouting. A man's voice, then another and a woman's gravelly voice too. She seemed to be laughing and the men protesting. What was going on? Then without warning the door opened and Eva lurched in. Her face was black presumably where Mary Palmer had whacked her and she was bleeding from her nose. I went to hug her but she paced the room and wouldn't look me in the eye.

'Tia, I'm so sorry, but just do it, please, I beg you.' She could hardly speak.

'Do what?'

'Go with a man, Tia. It's nothing, really.' I shook my head. How could I do such a thing? ' Eva gripped my arm. She was so close I could smell the blood that had dried on her upper lip, and see the panic in her bloodshot eyes. Her voice was shrill. 'Mary says she's bought us tickets for Buenos Aires. Says she wants to get rid of us because I'm too much trouble and you remind her of her past. So come on, Tia, for both our sakes.' My poor Eva dropped to the ground, bruised and broken. Another beating would kill her. I imagined Buenos Aires far away across the ocean. A new start, a new life, just as I had imagined up on that hill overlooking my village all that time ago. I took a gulp of anise. Eva frowned.

'Be careful with that, Tia. You know it's Chinchón?'

'The girl said it was anise.'

'Yes, and the strongest version you can get.' I shook my head. No wonder things were starting to spin. Eva reached into her pocket. 'Look, Tia. I still have it,' she said, pulling out the pebble I had given her when walking in the bay. 'Do you remember what you told me back then?' I shook my head. The drink was making it roll. '*It might bring you luck*, you said and I've kept it all this time just in case.' I grimaced. They were fine words but seemed so misguided now. 'Don't you see?' Eva continued. 'Do this one thing and then we will get our luck back.' The decanter was nearly empty so I filled my glass again, allowing the last drops to slide down the neck of the vessel and into my glass. Maybe I *could* do what they asked. Maybe I could endure it just this once. But would it hurt? Would he be cruel? Perhaps not. Perhaps it would be all right. Perhaps I could do it after all. Besides, the Chinchón was making me feel reckless. And what choice did I have anyway? There was no escape. We were locked in with no way out. I tipped the remains of the glass into my mouth and nodded. Immediately Eva jumped to her feet. 'In here, Tia, through this door.' I took a deep breath. All I had to do was walk through and everything would be different. I turned the handle and this time it yielded to my touch.

The new room was more beautiful than the first, with painted yellow panels and a dado rail of the palest green. There was a four-poster bed draped in gold jacquard cloth and on it laid a dress of iridescent blue, smoothed and flattened against the counterpane. I stared at it, so lifeless, so ugly, so flat and thought of those hides in the tannery lying lifeless on my bench. Like them I didn't stand a chance.

'Come on, Tia. Let's get you dressed,' Eva said. I felt no desire to inhabit the horrible garment but when she opened up the dress

284

and offered it to me, I didn't resist. Instead I dropped my bathing robe to the floor, wobbled slightly then stepped naked into the skirt and pulled the bodice into position over my breasts. My heart was fluttering. I felt faint. Eva stood in front of me and pushed my breasts upwards into the cups then pulled the two sides of the bodice together. 'We lace them from the front, here,' she said then folded the laces, to make each side equal to the other and threaded them through the eyelets, leaving the loops dangling 'So he can pull them away easily.' Then I slipped my legs into pale silk stockings and tightened them with fancy garters. Eva handed me some embroidered shoes. I slipped my feet in and they seemed to fit.

'There, you're ready,' Eva said turning me towards a mirror. I gasped. The scraggy little child had gone. A woman was standing in her place, a woman with a slim waist and rounded hips and the mounds of my breasts bulging above the bodice of a dress that had previously lain flat and lifeless on the bed. Tears appeared unbidden. Eva put her hands on my shoulders. 'I'm so sorry, Tia,' she said removing the little studs from my ears and inserting long, ruby-red earrings that dangled to my shoulders and stretched my earlobes until they hurt. I recalled the day I had endured Eva's piercing and later when she'd given me her extra pair of gold studs. I had loved her for that, and despite everything that was happening here in this room, I still loved her now. I put her studs in a pocket of the dress. 'I'm so sorry,' she repeated.

'It's all right Eva,' I muttered, but my stomach was churning. My head was spinning and last night's dream whirled into my head. *'Keep steady,'* my grandmother had said and I could see it all now. I would endure whatever was expected without complaint, and when it was over, Eva and I would both be free to travel across the ocean to Argentina where we would start a new life. My heart was like steel. Eva slipped her pebble into my pocket. 'There,' she said. 'All done.' Then she placed the towel onto the centre of the bed. 'To catch your blood,' she said.

We heard a bang as the door burst open. A woman as wide as she was tall entered the room panting heavily from climbing the stairs. She looked me up and down and I saw hate in her eyes. This must be Mary Palmer.

'What an odd little thing you are,' she said, wavering in the doorway. Even from across the room I could smell the alcohol rising from her gut. 'But I suppose you'll do.' I shook my head in fear and she smiled exposing blackened teeth. 'But, my dear, hasn't Eva told you? In exchange for your services, I have very generously bought you both tickets to Buenos Aires. They are here in my purse.' She tapped the pouch hanging from the chatelaine around her waist. 'In fact, Pepe is down in the yard right now, preparing that nag of his to take you to the harbour.' Then she steered herself round, waddled out of the door and staggered down the staircase into the salon where I could hear several men's excited voices.

61. Mariangeles

The kitchen was in semi-darkness, the logs in the stove were no more than embers. A kettle simmered on a back plate. Mariangeles and Pepe stood silently behind the door that led to the salon. She peered through the gap and saw a sumptuous salon. Enormous bouquets of freshly cut flowers sat on a sideboard next to glass decanters filled with ruby-red liquids. Alfonso was sitting in a wingback chair looking neat and tidy with oiled-back hair. His tweed hat, leather gloves and silver-topped swaggers stick lay beside him on a couch. What a fraud of a man Mariangeles thought. The Fixer was leaning against a mantelshelf with one boot on the grate and his cape draped over one shoulder like a villain in a melodrama. Mary was waddling down the staircase. She reached the last step, stumbled over to the sideboard and poured herself a drink. Then she sat in a low chair with her legs set wide apart exposing enormous thighs. She laughed at both men and even from a distance Mariangeles could see the row of black teeth that bordered a cavernous mouth. Mariangeles listened as she addressed them one at a time.

'Well, gents, I've invited you here for a bit of healthy competition. Are you up for it? After all you both have an axe to grind and so do I.' She turned to Alfonso. 'From what I hear, the girl refused your advances, not once but twice! She smirked then added, 'Well frankly I don't blame her, you ponce.' Then she looked at The Fixer. 'And what about you, mummy's boy? Hear you've changed your name a few times, so should I call you Don Manuel or p'raps you'd prefer The Fixer? Didn't fix much when that girl escaped from your weedy little clutches and left you with an unpaid debt did you?' Mariangeles frowned. The woman was teasing them to get the best price and for a moment she saw how clever Mary was and how pathetic the men were too. Mary was laughing again but this wasn't a joke. This was serious. They were talking about her girl and she had to do something, yet she felt paralysed as if she was watching a scene from a macabre play. What *could* she do anyway? Mary was in control, not Mariangeles. Mary Palmer started again only this time her words were so slurred they were hard to understand. 'Relaaax boys. You can both have her but it'll be the highest bidderrr who gets to snap this twig of a girl out of her virginity. So let's hear your opening bid.' There was a muttering between the two men that Mariangeles couldn't hear then Mary interrupted. 'Break her as hard as you can, just for me, eh? Take your time. Do what you want with her. That way we'll all be satisfied.' She raised her glass. 'So who will make the next bid?' Mariangeles felt sick.

Alfonso protested. 'I got here first, so she's mine.'

'But I saw her first. I've got more right than you!' The Fixer replied

Mary Palmer laughed. 'Now, now, boys. Up your bids'

'One hundred and fifty pesetas' the Fixer shouted.

'What? For that scraggy little virgin!' Alfonso replied.

Mariangeles felt the rise of bile in her stomach. My daughter, my poor lovely Tia being auctioned off to the highest bidder! She grabbed Pepe's arm and he held her close. Mary stood up, clutching the side of the chair for balance.

'Scraggy little virgin eh? I think you'll find her a little more alluring now that we've worked our magic.' She shouted up to the gallery. 'Eva! Get the girl down here now.' Eva and Tia appeared at the top of the stairs. Mariangeles gasped. There she was, her Tia, dressed in some foul creation and made up so garishly that she hardly recognised her. She shrieked and Pepe held her back.

'Sh, Mariangeles. They will hear you. Let's wait until we can take our chance.'

62. Tia

I walked into the corridor. The dress was heavy and it scratched my legs. Over the balustrade in the salon below, Mary looked up and waved her arm as if inviting them to regard me.

'So what do you think of our little virgin now?' she asked, and Alfonso raised his glass to me 'Not bad, Mary.' I watched him gulp the contents in one go then dab his mouth like a gentleman, and remembered his bleating after the fire, and the way he'd blamed me for everything. For all his fancy clothing and bravado he was nothing but a coward. The Fixer looked up and grinned; that same grin I had seen so many times in my dreams, and I thought I could see his mouth slowly widen into a smear of red. Mary beckoned.

'Come, my dear. They want to see you.' I placed my slippered foot on the stair and descended. The corset was tight; the slippers pinched. I grasped the balustrade to keep myself from fainting and when I reached the middle landing I held myself rigid, not daring to move. Alfonso stared up and laughed.

'Huh! What do I want with this frigid girl?' he said, but Mary interrupted.

'Don't come all coy with me, Alfonso. You want her as much as

Manolo does,' she said, sneering.

'I'll give you two hundred,' Alfonso said.

'Three hundred,' The Fixer snapped

'Five hundred and that's my lot,' Alfonso said and I felt my shoulders drop. I was being auctioned like a carcass in a market. Mary shouted at me.

'Come on girl. Look as though you mean it!'

I shook my head, and Mary bellowed.

'Eva, get your arse out here.'

Eva appeared behind me. I could feel her breath on my shoulder and sense her fear. Mary tried to stand, then gave up, falling back into the armchair and pointing up towards us. 'Remember, Eva, you owe me big time! So take the girl back upstairs and put some life into her while we get down to business.'

I turned to go but my feet wouldn't move. It was safer here on the landing; neither down there with those horrible men, nor up there waiting for them to abuse me. Mary shouted. 'What's wrong with you, girl? Get up them stairs, now!' I jumped at her sharp tone and when I reached the room Eva put her arm around me.

'Come on, Tia. All you have to do is smile. Men love a smiling girl. It makes them feel important, so remember not to frown, and everything will be all right.' I remembered the first time she had told me not to frown, back in the hostel with that cool sheet thrown over my head. What a world away we were now. I sat on the bed waiting. Eva was listening by the door. Alfonso was shouting. I could hear the bidding. It was crazy. Pa would never have earned that in a year! Why would they pay so much for me? Then there was silence. They had finished their negotiations. A man's footsteps were on the stairs. Eva closed her eyes and put her hands together as if in prayer. 'Please let it be Alfonso. At least he won't be cruel.'

The door opened. It wasn't Alfonso. The Fixer walked in. He shouted at Eva. 'Get out!' I watched her dash away on his command. Don't leave me, Eva. He turned his back and I heard the click of a key in the lock. He pulled it out and waved it in the air. 'Just a precaution, dear girl, in case you feel like running away…again! He moved towards me, coming up close, inspecting me. 'Hmm, not a bit like your mother, that dull old housewife,' he said, smirking. My heart fluttered, remembering Ma. If only she could save me. Downstairs I heard a bang as if someone had entered the house. The Fixer put his hand on my waist and, with the other, began to untie the cords on my bodice, pulling each loop slowly out of its eyelet. He was breathing heavily as he bent his head to meet my breasts. My stomach churned. What will he do? Downstairs a voice vibrated throughout the house. 'Where is the little thief?' It was Don Diego. I listened for Mary's reply; anything to distract myself from what was happening up here in this room. But nothing came. The Fixer raised his face to mine and transfixed me with his stare. He put a finger on my cheek and prodded it. 'Smile girl' he said. But I couldn't. I was paralysed. Downstairs Don Diego shouted, 'Have you forgotten, you old soak? You promised me the servant girl as compensation.' Still nothing from Mary. The Fixer was squeezing my throat. I shut my eyes. 'Aren't you pleased to see me?' he said pushing against me. My feet lost ground as I fell on the bed and the skirt of the dress billowed around me. Below in the hall I imagined Don Diego waving his gun. But now The Fixer had wrapped his cloak over us shutting out my thoughts and I smelt something putrid as if he was decaying from the inside out. His legs were astride me, hunched over, pulling at my unlaced bodice, exposing my breasts. He leaned over, taking one in his mouth. The whole thing fitted inside. He sucked it up until it hurt and I felt his saliva running down my ribs. Now it was my nipple. He sucked on it like a baby until I was sure it would bleed, but then he pulled back staring with wild eyes and gripping my throat. 'Smile, damn it, smile!' he screeched.

There were footsteps on the stairs. The Fixer raised his fist. I saw it coming but couldn't move. He smacked me in the jaw. I was silenced. He lifted my skirt and, with his knee, shoved my legs open. I remembered Eva's words. *'Plunge into darkness. Rise into light.'* Someone was charging along the corridor, banging on each door. The Fixer was fumbling inside me. I braced myself. 'Relax girl,' he urged. There was a loud bang. Someone shouted 'Open up!' The Fixer panted like a goat. He was pulling down his breeches, showing white flesh. I felt his hardness against my thigh. A boot struck the door. It burst open; splintered. Don Diego was in the doorway. 'She's mine damn it,' he shouted. A shot hit the air. The Fixer jerked forward and grabbed his buttock. There was blood. A second shot hit the ceiling. I leapt off the bed. Don Diego threw himself at The Fixer and they rolled on the floor just as Ma appeared in the doorway. Ma? What was she doing here? 'Help me.' I cried. She rushed across the room and grabbed my arm.

'Tia, my love. Come.'

We ran along the corridor and down the stairs, one, two, three, four. Mary Palmer was halfway up. We were halfway down. Eva screamed from below. 'Run, Tia. Run!' Mary blocked the way, but Ma raised her fist. She whacked Mary Palmer across the cheek and the woman fell. We stepped over her as Eva rushed up. 'Let's get out of here,' she shouted, ripping the purse from the chatelaine around Mary's waist. The three of us flew down the stairs. We headed for the door. Alfonso was blocking the way. We had to get passed. He raised his hand. I grabbed it and pulled it towards me, sinking my teeth into the paper-thin skin. He squealed like a baby and fell to the ground. The nun-girl opened the outer door. We flew through it just as Alfonso got to his feet. Surely he would stop us. But then he tumbled back on the floor. Did the nun-girl raise her leg?

We ran to the yard where Pepe was on his cart with Jefe harnessed ready to go. I was shaking. Eva helped me on, Ma climbed up, and Pepe shouted, 'Go, Jefe, go!' Pepe flicked the reins. Eva and I hid under the tarpaulin as the cart rolled out into the street, but so slowly, oh…so…very…slowly.

'Hurry,' Eva screeched and Jefe jerked into a trot. I put my hands together as if in prayer. Don't be cautious, Jefe. Don't hold back. Make a charge as fast as you can.

Jefe cantered towards Gibraltar. How strong he was, pulling four humans and a wooden cart into this cool darkness. Under the tarpaulin I thought I could see Eva smiling so I pulled the tarpaulin back and took a deep breath of midnight air. Clouds were obscuring the October moon but I could see the Rock of Gibraltar, standing out black as coal against an indigo sky. We passed the ruins of the old cork factory still imprisoned in a veil of soot and lit with an eerie light as if ghosts lurked within.

A wind stirred and clouds scudded across the sky, revealing the bright full moon. Now we could clearly see the flat plains of no-man's-land stretching towards the border. I looked behind. There was no sign of Alfonso – not yet. But we were not free. Revenge was deep in his heart and soon he would follow. Even after re-saddling, his beautiful white horse would still catch us before we reached the border. Pepe was slashing at the reins. He must know it too.

We reached the race track and I saw its white railed fence illuminated in the moonlight. Jefe had seen it too and maybe he sensed all those horses that had raced here before, because he whinnied into the wind and changed to a full gallop. Did it feel good Jefe? Could you smell freedom surging through your nostrils? We braced ourselves, holding tightly to the sides of the cart. In the moonlight, Ma's silhouette looked magnificent sitting up there beside Pepe. How did you get here, Ma? How did you know where I was? And how brave you were, whacking Mary Palmer with your fist and sending her crashing onto those stairs. And me too, biting Alfonso on his scarred hand, so hard that he screamed like a scalded cat. We were both warriors now, Ma and me. She must have sensed what I was thinking because she turned around to grin at me and I grinned back. The cart was bumping over the race track where deep ruts and grooves, caused by racing hooves, buoyed us up, then dropped us down with such a jolt that I lost my grip. I giggled, feeling out of control, and just a bit crazy. The anise was still racing round my veins and I was wild with it - charging through the night with my hair unpinned, wearing an outrageous dress. Eva must have felt it too because she was waving her arms like a mad thing and I saw, at last, the girl she used to be. Now she was howling like a wolf and it must have been catching because I was laughing too. The wind grabbed my voice and threw it back at me like a cackling witch. Eva yelled into the night, 'The end of days, Tia. It's like the end of days!' And we both squealed. There was innovation in the air and it took my breath away.

Suddenly, Pepe shouted 'Get down!' I looked behind. The moonlight was strong. A white horse and rider was emerging from the darkness, coming up fast. Pepe snatched at the reins, urging Jefe on. Alfonso was whipping his poor animal with a stick. I could hear him screaming into the wind, calling us bitches, getting closer; becoming real. Eva and I dived into the base of the cart, closed our eyes and held each other tight. It couldn't end like this. It mustn't. Alfonso was gaining. Jefe was slowing. Hooves thundered up behind us – their rhythm was fast and lively, Jefe's were not. Pepe snatched and flicked and slashed at the reins, trying to get away, but Alfonso came alongside and for a moment the two horses moved together, their heads bobbing up and down like a pair of playful dolphins. Then Alfonso pulled his horse right across our path, forcing Jefe to swerve.

'Bloody bitches, you'll never get away,' he shouted.

But Pepe jerked us back into line.

'Go straight, my brave one,' he shouted. Jefe whinnied and charged like a bull. Alfonso raised his stick, screaming.

'You bastard,' he shouted and his mouth was set firm and his chin was jutting out with fury. He raised his swagger stick above his head. He was going to strike, and if Pepe fell, we would all fall too. I had to do something. But what? Alfonso was standing now, leaning on his stirrups, raising his stick higher to get a clear hit. I took a deep breath, stood up with my feet wide apart, and gripped Ma's shoulder for balance. The cart was slowing. Alfonso leaned over. The stick was coming down. I reached up and grabbed it, yanking it from his hand. Jefe tossed his head as I fell back into the cart. I looked up. Alfonso's arm was still raised, but he had leant too far. His weight was uneven and he tipped over. His horse reared up and suddenly its rider was falling, descending, cascading, grasping at nothing, arcing through the air. There was a thud.

'He's down!' Eva shouted as Alfonso bounced along the earth, tumbling over and over; receding, withdrawing, losing ground, lost.

The rider-less horse came up to join Jefe as we moved along the race track, slower now, catching our collective breath until we passed the finishing line, hot with sighs, and our breathing now relaxed. Alfonso's horse trotted away – its whiteness turning to grey as it disappeared into the corners of the night. In the distance we saw the border.

63. Mariangeles

It was five o'clock in the morning when Jefe passed into Gibraltar and dropped his passengers at the harbour. Mariangeles saw Tia touch her jaw which was beginning to swell. She dipped her handkerchief into the cold ocean and offered it to Tia.

Then she opened her arms and Tia fell into them. This was a new sensation and it felt good. Seconds seemed like minutes as she held her daughter against her chest, their bodies inseparable just as they should have been when Tia was a child.

Eventually they drew apart.

'I'm sorry, Ma,' Tia said. 'Sorry for being such a flirt; sorry for everything.'

'I am sorry too, Tia. I was a fool to make you feel the way you did. Please forgive me.'

They held hands and smiled together, mother and daughter in a new and delicate bond that only the two of them truly understood. They looked around the harbour at people striding about with purpose - some loading cargo, others releasing ropes from capstans - and Mariangeles stared in wonder, remembering the harbour back home and rejoicing at the sound of so many languages drifting across the crisp air. Tia must have noticed too.

'Look, Ma, it's like our old town,' she said and Mariangeles smiled, remembering the girl's delight, watching the boats sailing in and out of the harbour and how, wrapped up in her own anxieties, she had ignored her daughter's childish joy.

'It's all so wonderful,' she agreed.

Pepe stepped forward. 'See that chap over there,' he said pointing. 'He's a stevedore come to load the ships, and behind 'im some deck hands. Over there two captains are comparin' notes before sailin', and see that liner on the north Mole, Tia?' He pointed to a huge ship with three red and black funnels sitting tight against the harbour wall. Its engines were running, great plumes of steam were dissolving into the dawn air and the portholes were bright with artificial light.

'Agnes told me about liners,' Tia said. 'Is it going to Buenos Aires?'

Pepe shook his head. 'There aint no ship goin' to Buenos Aires today.'

'But Mary said there was.'

Eva laughed. 'There are no tickets to Argentina, Tia. Mary tricked us.'

Pepe nodded in confirmation and pulled a paper from his pocket.

'Look, these was the instructions Mary gev me when she found me in the yard. Eva snatched it from him and they all looked over her shoulder as she read out the schedule Mary had arranged.

'First to the victualler's yard in Rosia Bay. Hand Eva over to the Captain of the Albania. He's expecting her.' Eva scoffed. 'So, the bitch was going to turn me into a *gaviota* to service the sailors on the supply ships. Mary has sold me to the ocean.'

'And what had she planned for me?' Tia asked.

Eva read, 'Put the girl on the transatlantic steamer, the Taurus, headed for New York. And take care of her. They've paid top dollar for that girl.' Eva looked sad. 'Oh Tia, you've already been sold to a pimp who'll be waiting on the New York quayside the moment you step off that ship. Pepe shook his head as Eva read out an extra line. 'Do this, Pepe, or else you're out of a job.' Pepe sighed and turned to Eva.

'We should never've worked for that terrible woman.'

Eva slipped her arm in his, and said, 'It's all right Pepe, I was scared too.'

Tia still sounded upset. 'Here we are with nothing but these horrible clothes on our backs. What are we going to do?'

'Wait a minute,' Eva said looking in the purse that she had ripped from Mary Palmer's chatelaine. Her mouth gaped open like a baby bird.

'Tia, look at this.' She thrust the purse towards her friend. It was stuffed with so much money it was falling out onto the quayside. They counted it and counted it again in case they'd made a mistake. Eva grinned. 'This must be the money from the two captains as well as from Tia's auction.' They both laughed and she squeezed Tia's arm. 'Let's get out of this place. Let's leave Andalucía altogether.'

Tia nodded her agreement and Mariangeles frowned. Was she going to lose her daughter the moment she'd found her?

'I have to go, Ma,' Tia said. 'I'm not running away this time. It's just that I cannot live with your mantra about waves and sorrows. I have to find another way.'

Mariangeles nodded too, knowing that this was right and understanding that she'd found the real Tia, so she was quite content. The girl should make her own life now. She looked at her daughter still trembling in those terrible clothes. She had to say something to help her.

'I understand, Tia. I know you have to go, so here is a better refrain to guide you. *No mires atrás a la estela del barco. Mira adelante, hacia las olas que se acercan a la proa. - Don't look back at the wake of the boat. Look ahead to the waves that approach the prow.* Don't worry about the past, Tia. It is not who we used to be that matters, it's who we will become.'

Tia grinned. 'Thanks, Ma,' she said. 'But before I go, please tell me about Pa. Where is he? Is he all right?

'I've left him, Tia,' she said, looking towards Pepe with a gentleness that exposed her affection. Pepe smiled back and Mariangeles knew right then that despite being married to Bartolome, she and Pepe would start a new life together. It didn't matter about the gossips in her village or the disapproval of the church. None of those things were going to matter because, for the first time in her life, she was truly happy. And before they left, she and Pepe would retrace their steps back to that village and tell anyone who would listen, the truth about Alfonso and Don Diego and that dreadful Fixer. She might even go back to the drunkard Mary Palmer and force her to understand who really started that fire. She didn't care if they attacked her back. She would do all she could to restore her daughter's name.

The first rays of morning hovered at the horizon, spreading pale yellow beams across the harbour. A cool breeze wafted overhead. Eva kissed Pepe on the cheek and gave him a wad of notes.

He grinned and said 'Thank you. This will help me start my new business.' Then he helped Mariangeles onto his cart, mounted beside her, and together they headed back to the border. Behind them, two girls were waiting to start their adventure, and in front of them, under the first rays of a new day, Mariangeles and Pepe were about to start theirs too.

64. Tia

Ma looked so happy as they remounted the cart. Jefe turned it around and I watched their silhouettes diminish across the race track, imagining Ma and Pepe travelling back west, retracing their steps to that other glittering city by the sea, the place where Ma and I first began.

'I will write.' I shouted into the air, even though I didn't know how. I would pay my first wages to a letter writer and he or she would seal my words of love on an ink-laden page, and Ma would read them and know that I cared. And in the future, when we met again, things would be different. Next time our love would endure.

I watched the silver froth of a tide rolling in and thought of Ma's refrain; *'waves and sorrows never arrive alone'*, and decided that this wasn't really true. Waves came and went as naturally as the sun made its daily dance with the moon. It was simply nature performing as it should, and not some tangled up family curse. And in that salty morning breeze, fresh with possibility, I felt a glorious defiance run through my veins. Ma and I had broken our family spell and I no longer felt bound to accept my lot. I would be strong. I would defend myself and whenever I heard gossip turn someone else's world upside down, I would defend them too. I would speak up and put speculation down. I would tell my daughters not to keep secrets hidden like Ma and my grandmother did. And whenever men were aggressive and violent, I would speak up and tell my daughters and their daughters to do the same, because we owe a debt to one another and together we are strong.

I took Eva's arm. There was no discussion. We knew what we were going to do. We walked over to the natural harbour in Rosia Bay where, alongside the supply ship Albania, waiting in vain for Eva to embark, sat a small ferry boat that would carry us the seven miles across the Straits to Tangiers. We gave our details to the ticket clerk then stood on the jetty waiting; Eva covered in bruises and me in a ripped blue dress. In a few hours we would be docking in Tangiers and seeing, first-hand, the dreams that had been whispered to me by the sea. I called out Ma's new mantra *Look ahead to the waves that approach the prow*, knowing that I would no longer look back, nor judge myself too harshly for what had happened in my past. Then I felt in the pocket of my dress and pulled out Eva's pebble.

'Look,' I said. 'Maybe it did bring us luck after all.'

Then we both smiled.

The ocean was waiting.

About the author

Patricia Román was born and raised in Oxford, England and lives in rural Spain, drawing on her Spanish heritage to create timeless stories about ordinary people in extraordinary times.

Also by Patricia Román

Letters from the Mountains

Mafia murder, espionage, a troubled boy and a self-loathing man.

Letters from the Mountains was shortlisted for the Flash 500 international Novel competition 2022.

Praise for Letters from the Mountains.

"This is a valuable book, with characters that are familiar, three-dimensional and authentic" (Katie Isbester, Claret Press).

"An interesting, evocative novel with some lovely descriptive passages."

(Eleni Kyriacou, author of The Unspeakable Acts of Zina Pavlou)

The Cuckoo and the Cuckquean

Spanish suffragettes, feminine subjugation, sadness and joy.

Work in progress due out autumn 2024.